I0743876

Life
SUPPORT

A *Crush* NOVEL

ELOUISE EAST

Copyright © 2021 Elouise East

LIFE SUPPORT, CRUSH SERIES, BOOK 6

ALL RIGHTS RESERVED

No part of this book may be reproduced or transmitted in any form or by any means, electronic or mechanical including photocopying, recording, or by any information storage or retrieval system, without permission in writing from the publisher, Elouise East. No part of this book may be scanned, uploaded or distributed via the internet or by any other means, electronic or print, without premising from Elouise East.

The unauthorised reproduction or distribution of this copyrighted work is illegal. Please purchase only authorised electronic or print editions and do not participate in or encourage the electronic piracy of copyrighted material. Your support of the author's rights and livelihood is appreciated.

This is a work of fiction. Names, characters, places and incidents are either the product of the author's imagination or are used fictitiously and any resemblance to any actual persons, living or dead, events, or locales is entirely coincidental.

All products and/or brand names mentioned are registered trademarks of their respective holders/companies.

Publisher: Elouise East
Cover Design: Maria Vickers
Editor: Maria Vickers
Beta Readers: Emma Brown, Mike Van Eimeren, Lisa Kemp

*This book may contain scenes that are triggering for some people

CONTENTS

LIFE SUPPORT

DEDICATION

To those who are suffering in silence:
you are worthy
you are enough
you are important
Have the courage to speak out

CHAPTER ONE

CASEY

"How are things going with Marcus?" Chloe asked as they packed up the equipment, ready to drive back to the hospital. "Still in the lovey-dovey stage?" She grinned, nudging his shoulder.

He shoved her back, good-naturedly. "Yes, as a matter of fact. Everything is going great."

Casey had met Marcus four months ago and had persuaded him to bring a friend along for a double date with Casey's best friend, Alex. So far, as he'd told Chloe, everything was working out well despite his shift patterns. Or maybe *because* of his shift patterns. Twelve-hour stints, two days, two nights, four days on, four days off. The hours were crap, but it was part of his job, so he couldn't complain about it. He'd known the times before he agreed to the role.

They climbed into the ambulance, Chloe in the driver's seat. Casey didn't mind driving, but most of his colleagues preferred being in control of the ambulance, so he let them have it. He was happy to navigate instead. The engine's loud rumble reverberated beneath his feet and ass while he clicked his seat belt into place.

"Who was the guy I saw you with earlier today?" Chloe asked, pulling out onto the road.

Casey frowned, then smiled. "Oh, outside the deli? That was Craig." His heart felt heavy when he thought of the guy. "He's been through a lot, and I've spoken with him a few times at the hospital." He wasn't about to divulge Craig's personal details despite Chloe being bound by the same confidentiality rules. "He knows Alex, too. I was inviting him to meet some friends. I thought it might help him to socialise a bit more, rather than exist in his own little bubble."

"That's nice of you. Everyone needs friends. I'm not sure where I'd be without mine."

Chloe had also been through a difficult time. Eight months ago, her husband had left her with two young children. It had taken a lot of organising for her to be able to come back to work. Casey glanced at her, seeing her blonde hair tied back in a ponytail; pale, blemish-free skin; dainty nose and rosebud lips. Her blue eyes sparkled all the time—except for the first few months after her husband took off—and she thoroughly enjoyed her job. If Casey had been heterosexual, he would've flirted with her. He *did* flirt with her, but they both knew that was the extent of it.

"How are the munchkins?" Casey asked with a grin,

turning the subject to something he knew raised her spirits.

Chloe blew a hair out of her face. "Growing up too quickly. I know I have to give them time because of what's happened, but Gemma is a nightmare." Chloe shook her head and sighed. "She refuses to sleep in her own bed, which means I rarely get a good night's sleep —not that I'm complaining, I'd prefer her to be happy and settled. It's difficult. As for Jerome, he's carrying on as if nothing happened." A frown crossed her face.

"They'll process it in different ways, you know that. Just be there for them and ask for help when *you* need it. Don't do this alone, Chloe." He reached over and squeezed her leg gently, hoping to convey how much she meant to him.

"I know, and I do ask. I hate having to rely on so many people."

"I understand that. It's nice to be independent, but sometimes, it's just not possible." He looked at his watch. "Almost dinner time. I'm starving." As if his words reminded his body, his stomach growled.

Chloe snorted and flicked her gaze to him briefly. "You're always starving. If I remember right, you were starving half an hour after the deli."

"What can I say? I have a fast metabolism."

They both laughed, the sound echoing around the small cab. Their Terrafix Responder chimed with a new incident, and Casey checked the details, relaying the information to Chloe, who sped up as Casey flicked on the sirens and lights. He brought up the route they'd need and directed Chloe to the house.

Two hours later, at the end of their shift, they finally managed to grab some food from the hospital restaurant. It was one of the downsides to the job, but if he didn't eat while he had a spare minute, he might not get to eat for hours. A paramedic's schedule is based around people's bumps and bruises, not around when it's lunchtime or dinnertime.

Slumping at the table, his body and mind felt drained, and they sat in silence. Once he'd devoured his shepherd's pie, he clapped Chloe on the shoulder and said goodnight, heading straight for the staff locker room. He'd checked his phone as he was eating and had seen a message from Marcus, asking if Casey could visit him that night. Normally, Casey would have agreed, but he was exhausted. He hadn't replied yet because he'd wanted to see whether he felt better after eating. He didn't.

The staff locker room was a large space with individual lockers for each member of staff. They weren't particularly big lockers, but with the amount of staff at the hospital, they'd need a whole floor just for them if they made them any larger. The room also housed several showers, toilets and a couple of changing rooms. As it was a gender-neutral zone, all people used it.

Casey moved to his locker, quickly opening it and grabbing his bag, the need for sleep dragging at his movements. Usually, he'd have a shower, but tonight he wanted to get home.

"Have you had a good shift, Casey?" Dr Simon Acker's voice made him flinch, and goosebumps rose on his arms as his muscles tensed.

Casey glanced out of the corner of his eye and hurried his movements, his heart rate increasing. "Yes, thanks."

"Word on the grapevine is you've managed to keep hold of your *boy toy*." Acker's voice practically growled the last two words despite the smile on his face that didn't seem to reach his eyes.

"Yep, still with him." His voice was strained, each word pushing out with the effort and the hope of dispelling any other comments but to no avail. His whole body stiffened when Acker stepped closer.

"Looking good, Casey," the doctor whispered, and he squeezed Casey's shoulder, sliding his hand across his upper back too slowly for Casey's liking. Acker left the locker room, and Casey leaned against the metal boxes, blowing out a breath, his muscles relaxing enough to send him to the floor if he allowed it.

"That guy gives me the creeps. If he hadn't got a wife, I'd say he was gay."

Casey spun around, piercing the other paramedic with his gaze, annoyance flowing out of him. "Really, Kinton? And there's no way he could be bisexual, is there?" Casey glared at him and slammed his locker shut, the sound loud in the narrow space.

"I didn't mean... He could... Shit. I didn't think,

Casey," Kinton stammered, his face flushing, and his eyes widening.

Casey deflated, sighing and shaking his head. "Nah, it's okay. I'm feeling shitty. Sorry, man." Casey gave a half-hearted smile and exited, keeping his eyes peeled for the doctor who gave him some seriously weird vibes. Acker had made similar comments to Casey since Acker had started working there about a year ago. To begin with, it had been nothing more than nice words about how well he did his job, which Casey had appreciated, but they had become steadily more personal as time went on. There was nothing he could do about it, so he carried on with his job and tried to avoid the man where possible.

After that meeting, Casey decided to head to Marcus's place, after all. He thumbed out a quick confirmation message and headed to his car.

Marcus opened his front door with a smile. "Hey, you." He moved towards Casey, taking his bag from his hand and encircling him with one arm, guided him into his apartment. The door slammed behind them, making Casey flinch, though Marcus didn't seem to notice. "You look shattered, sweetheart. Do you want a shower before bed?"

Casey's eyes drooped, and resting his head against Marcus's shoulder, allowed himself to be directed to the bedroom. He wasn't sure he could keep his eyes open much longer.

Marcus chuckled. "I'll take that as a no." Tingles flowed across his skin as Marcus stripped him down to his boxers. "Come on, sleepyhead. Let's get your teeth brushed, and I'll tuck you in with a bedtime story," Marcus joked.

"Shut up," Casey retorted weakly as he did as he was told. He wasn't usually so easily led, but he *was* tired, and this had only been his first shift of the week. When Casey slid underneath the covers, he sighed and relaxed into the soft fabric. He heard Marcus pottering around, though it was more a distant noise than anything distinct.

His eyes blinked blearily, refusing to open completely when he felt hands roaming across his skin. Warmth spread along his back, the feel of wiry hair tickling along his shoulder blades. He rubbed his face against the pillow, trying to wake himself further and feeling like he'd hardly slept at all.

"Hmm, you feel amazing," Marcus whispered from behind him, pressing kisses along his neck and shoulders.

Casey could feel Marcus's hard cock thrusting against his ass, and he cleared his throat to speak, "What time is it?"

"You have plenty of time, baby. Rest, let me take care of you."

He wasn't sure how much he could rest, especially when Marcus pressed slick fingers against his entrance, pushing inside him with determined interest. Involuntarily, he clenched against the intrusion before breathing out and bearing down, allowing Marcus's digits to glide forward.

"Fuck, Casey. I can't wait to get my dick inside you."

Marcus thrust and withdrew his fingers until Casey was taking three, although not as easily as Casey would've liked. His boyfriend replaced his fingers with his cock and gripped Casey's hips as he rutted into his body.

"Shit, Marcus! Slow down!" he hissed as burning flared all around and inside him.

Marcus paused, although he moved position, making Casey's ass scream its discomfort. A hand rested against the back of Casey's neck, holding him against the pillow, and another hand lifted Casey's thigh higher, giving Marcus more space.

"You look fucking amazing, spread out on the bed like this," Marcus growled.

Casey didn't think he was spread as much as held but didn't comment. He was too busy trying to breathe through the rough entry.

"I'm going to move now," Marcus grated, his hand tightening against the back of Casey's neck.

Marcus thrust forward until he bottomed, causing Casey to cry out. Thankfully, Marcus stopped moving and braced his hands beside Casey's chest instead of holding him down. Tears leaked from the edge of Casey's closed eyes, and he swallowed hard, breathing through the pain. It wasn't usually like this, so he had no idea why it was so painful that time.

The sting receded, and Casey acknowledged that Marcus could move, although every move he made felt branded in heat and irritation.

"Oh, fuck, yeah. Take my cock!" Marcus slammed into him repeatedly, and Casey pressed a hand against the headboard to stop him from moving far enough to get knocked out.

"Fuck, yeah. Fuck, fuck! I'm coming, Casey!" Marcus drove forward a final time before pinning Casey beneath him as his release claimed him.

When Marcus pulled out, Casey winced and breathed out slowly, even as more tears escaped him. He flinched after Marcus slapped his ass hard.

"Fucking amazing, as always, Casey." Marcus grinned and strode to the bathroom, removing the condom as he went.

Casey stayed where he was for a moment, then moved, gritting his teeth as his ass smarted. Glancing at the clock, Casey cursed. "Marcus! Couldn't you have waited until morning? I've only been asleep for an hour!"

"I told you that you had plenty of time. Go back to sleep. You'll be fine by morning," Marcus called back.

Casey stared at his own cock, which had neither become hard nor orgasmed with the sex. Marcus, as always, forgot there were two people in the act. Knowing his ass wouldn't feel any better without some cream, he entered the bathroom when Marcus left and tended to himself before returning to the bed and finding Marcus fast asleep.

He rolled his eyes, climbed into bed and turned to face Marcus, wrapping his arms around himself. There would be no more sex that night if Casey had anything to do about it.

He said goodbye to his family after their usual Sunday dinner and drove home, parking his car in the driveway of the house he'd owned for the last three years. With help from his parents, he'd been able to afford a deposit on it, and he had been able to afford the mortgage payments thanks to his paramedic job. Unlocking the front door always gave him a thrill of knowing the house was his and his alone—he had already paid back the money his parents had given him, to their annoyance. They had wanted him to keep it, but he'd refused.

His phone rang as he shut the door behind him, and he threw the keys on the table to fish the phone out of his pocket.

"Hey! How are you?" he asked.

"I'm all right, thanks. How was lunch?"

Drifting through the house towards the kitchen, Casey answered Marcus's question, "It was nice. Except for the request for grandchildren."

Marcus spluttered on the other end of the phone, making Casey smile. He loved riling Marcus up. "What?"

Casey explained his mother's need to spoil her grandchildren before she was too old, and Marcus laughed. Grabbing a beer from the fridge, he strode to the living room, flicking on his huge, wall-mounted TV. It was a recent splurge, but he loved it.

"How has your day been?"

Marcus was a swimming teacher and worked mainly in the early evenings during the week and all day at the weekends. It made their schedules clash on more than one occasion.

"Busy, as always. The kids are great. I'm having a break to eat before my next set of swimmers arrive."

"Luckily, you don't have to go into the pool with them."

"Not the older ones, no. My little ones' classes are in the week, thankfully. I get to stay dry for most of the weekend."

Casey snorted. "Why are you complaining? You're a swimming teacher who loves swimming. Getting wet is kind of the done thing for the job."

The deep-sounding grunt in his ear had Casey closing his eyes. It reminded him of their nights together. The kind of noise Marcus made when he was aroused. He knew Marcus wasn't, but his mind still went there.

"When can I next see you?" Marcus asked tentatively. It was always a sore point between them, one they never seem to get over and, ultimately, was one of the reasons Casey was so reticent about their relationship despite it having lasted this long.

"Do you want to come over tonight after you finish there? I'm off tomorrow but start work Tuesday."

"Perfect. I'll be there around eight?"

"Okay. I'll get the food ordered in."

"See you soon."

Casey stared at the TV, not seeing anything. He knew Marcus would come over; they'd eat, have sex, then go to sleep. Tomorrow, Marcus would go to the gym to work out for a few hours, then he'd come back. They'd eat, have sex and sleep. It was what they did. Casey dreamed of more, though, and he felt so selfish thinking that. Other people had it much worse than he did.

"I didn't know you were friends with Craig."

Casey closed his locker, inwardly rolling his eyes as he moved slowly to face Alex. He could tell by the way Alex had spoken that he was annoyed about the revelation.

"I offered to take him out. Get him out of the house. It seemed like he needed a friend." All of that was completely true. Unfortunately, he hadn't realised Alex was going to be there; otherwise, he would've changed plans. He loved Alex, but his obsession with Craig was ruining his relationship with Heath. When he'd seen Alex sitting with his boyfriend at Crush four days ago, he'd cursed up a storm in his head and apologised to Craig.

"I am so sorry, Craig. I honestly didn't know Alex was going to be here. It's normally just my brother and his friends."

Craig shook his head and smiled. "It's fine. I have to face him eventually."

"Are you sure? We can go somewhere else."

"No, it's fine."

He introduced Craig to everyone, "Everyone, this is Craig. Craig, this is Sean; Asher; Logan, you already know; Max; Trent; Zak; Heath; and Alex, you know."

Everyone greeted Craig and pulled more chairs around their already full set of three tables.

"What would you like to drink, Craig?" Casey asked.

"Um, beer would be good, thanks." Craig fidgeted in his seat, glancing at Casey and around the group, appearing a little overwhelmed.

"Okay, I'll be right back." Casey glared over at Alex and mouthed, "Be good." He had no idea if Alex would understand the message he was trying to give him, but he'd done all he could. As he walked to the bar, he cursed again. This was a bad idea.

Casey came back to the present when Alex spoke, "Yeah. He's never mentioned friends. In the present tense, anyway."

Casey leaned his shoulder against his locker, narrowing his eyes at Alex. "Don't get too close, Alex. Craig is healing. I doubt he's ready for a relationship of any kind." Casey paused, ready to drill home his point. "Remember, you're with Heath now."

Alex nodded, but Casey was sure he wouldn't listen. He was far too invested in Craig, and it didn't bode well for Heath—or Alex, or Craig. Alex would never cheat on anyone, but Casey could tell Alex's heart was with

Craig and not where it should be—with his boyfriend. Poor guy.

Alex bid goodbye and left the locker room. Casey headed for the shower, and as the water washed away the grime of his shift, Casey relaxed under the warmth of the spray. When he was suitable for company once more, he dried off the excess water and wrapped the towel around his waist.

Picking up his shampoo and shower gel, he turned and froze. Dr Acker leaned against the entrance to the showers with his arms crossed over his chest and a look in his eye that had Casey swallowing hard against the fear immobilising him. His legs trembled, and his breaths came in gasps as he stared at the man. The doctor didn't move any closer, but his gaze inspected every inch of Casey's exposed body, hesitating on his towel before rising to meet Casey's eyes.

"You're looking better every day, Casey." The hoarseness of the tone had a shiver running down Casey's spine, and he briefly wondered if the doctor would try what his voice hinted at.

Casey stayed quiet, sweat dripping down his back, muscles tensed. His hands gripped the bottles tightly as dizziness invaded his brain. Trying to take deep breaths to stop himself from collapsing and being even more vulnerable, he blinked and, concentrating on his heart rate, timed his inhales with several beats.

"Keep up the good work."

When Acker turned away, Casey remained frozen until he heard the locker room door open and close. He didn't have proof the doctor had left, but Casey couldn't stay in the showers all evening. As soon as his feet moved, Casey began to shake harder, and he had to lock his knees to keep himself walking. With jerky movements, he unlocked his locker and dressed as quickly as he could, scanning his surroundings repeatedly. Once he was dressed, he grabbed his bag, his phone and his keys and raced down the corridors to the exit.

He didn't stop when he got outside; he ran towards where he'd parked his car, locking himself inside as soon as he reached it. His hands complained about the white-knuckled grip he had on the steering wheel. His breathing became choppy and sweat poured from his forehead.

He had never felt fear like that before. Acker had stepped way over the line. Although who would believe Casey? No one.

He had a certain amount of strength due to the physical nature of his job, but he wasn't confident he would be able to get away from someone should they try and restrain him in some way. And fighting someone off? He doubted he'd do much damage.

Grabbing his phone, he dialled. "Hey, Craig. I remember you mentioning getting personal training sessions. I like the idea. Can I ask who you use?"

CHAPTER TWO

LUKE

"Congrats, Dad. You made it!" Luke hugged his dad as he entered the large house.

"And you're almost late," his dad teased.

"Sorry, lost track of time." He smoothed a hand down the front of his clothes and cleared his throat.

"No worries. It's not like I'm going anywhere now that I've retired."

With his dad's arm around his shoulder, directing him to the kitchen, Luke inhaled and closed his eyes. The aroma of curry invaded his nostrils, and he smiled —his favourite.

They entered the kitchen to a cheer. Luke was the last one to arrive, it seemed, which meant they could all now eat. His mother had made the rule that when everyone was expected, they could not eat until everyone had arrived. So far, no one had been late enough for them to reheat the food.

Luke moved around the huge table, which easily seated twelve people, to hug his mother. "Hi, Mama."

She kissed his cheek. "You look tired, Lulu. Are you getting enough rest?" Oh, how he hated the name, but his mother wouldn't call him anything else.

"Yes, thanks. I'm doing fine."

He surveyed the table, seeing everyone there for Dad's special celebration meal: Samuel; Trent and his boyfriend, Max; Carter and his wife, Lia; and Ava. Luke sat next to Samuel, squeezing his shoulder in greeting.

Once they were all seated, his dad stood. "Thank you all for taking the time to be here."

"Had no choice," Trent coughed into his hand, smirking.

Luke's mother narrowed her gaze at her second eldest son.

Dad chuckled. "Regardless of what got you here, thank you. It's not every day I get to say I never have to work again."

"That's so not fair, Dad. I have, like, thirty years left," Carter groused.

"Yeah, well, suck it up, son. I've been working for fifty years. When you have that amount of time left, then you can complain." Dad's mouth curled up at the groans from around the table. "Anyway, let us enjoy the no doubt amazing curry your mother has made for us. Tuck in."

"Congrats, Dad!" they chorused.

Everyone began dishing up, making conversation throughout. Luke stayed quiet as he placed some rice, curry and poppadoms on his plate. He had always observed rather than taken part ever since he was younger. His personality was a lot more subdued than theirs, and the usual feelings of inadequacy began to rise as he heard his siblings' conversations. His family was a lot more accomplished than him. He looked at each of his siblings in turn: Samuel and Carter were both highly sought-after lawyers, Trent was a teacher, and Ava was a police officer. Luke was just a personal trainer, and although he didn't plan on changing, it wasn't anywhere close to how important his siblings' jobs were.

Trent caught his eye and tilted his head in question. Luke nodded that he was okay and concentrated back on his food.

"What about you, Luke? Have you found anyone yet?" his mother asked.

Luke sighed and fidgeted in his seat, hating the focus being on him. "Not yet, Mama."

"Bet you have a revolving door, don't you? Working at the gym, there's likely to be loads of your type of guy around," Trent teased.

"Trent! Don't be so crude," his mother scolded. "What about work?" Everyone remained silent as they waited for his answer.

His stomach churned, and he stared at his plate. "Same old. People need training to get fit. Some people want safety training." Luke shrugged, filling his mouth with the spicy cuisine, hoping to derail the inquisition.

The conversation flowed around the table

throughout the rest of dinner, and once he'd done his dishwasher task, he went to find his parents. He gave them both a hug, citing he was tired and shouted a goodbye to his siblings.

"Enjoy your first night as a free man, Dad."

On the way home, he couldn't help the relaxing of his muscles now that he was away from his family. He felt awful about it because he didn't hate them; however, he felt so… inferior.

His house smelled a bit musty, so despite it being eight in the evening, he flung his living room windows open, allowing the soft breeze to flow through the rooms. His two-bedroom place looked like an autumn forest with all the different leaf colours. As he sat in his favourite armchair looking around, he felt small and lonely with a long weekend stretched before him. All he wanted was someone to share his life with.

Luke arrived at his gym, Distinction Fitness, for seven o'clock on Monday morning. Having checked his schedule before he'd left work on Friday, he knew he had a full day ahead of him, so he completed his personal workout before his first appointment.

By eleven o'clock, he was ready for the day to be done. The client who had just left could not understand Luke was gay regardless of the fact he had told her several times since she started with him six weeks ago. She was a twenty-something brunette who watched the mirrors as much for her appearance as to check her posture. She also constantly tried to get him into positions where she could rub up against him. He shook his head as he grabbed his water and swallowed a large gulp, the cool liquid reducing his temperature slightly, more so when he rested the bottle against his forehead.

He had already trained with a guy who had been coming to him for around three years and started with a new sixteen-year-old for some safety manoeuvres. As sad a case as it was, the training was needed to make sure the teenager never felt so helpless again. Luke had seen it more than he wanted to in his line of work, but the expression on the kid's face when he mastered a move was priceless.

Checking his watch, he knew Theo would be there soon. Ever since his stalker had been arrested a few months ago, Theo had been coming to him for training. A lot of what Luke did was make his clients feel more confident in their abilities to get away from an attacker or to run the hell away. It was what Theo still needed, although he was improving with every session.

"Hey, Luke!"

Luke turned as the newcomer entered Luke's training room. "Hey, Matt. How're things?"

"Good, thanks. Did you hear about the guy who got arrested over at Triple-A Bootcamp?"

Luke knew exactly who he was talking about, but he wasn't a gossip and shook his head. "No."

"The guy has been accused of domestic abuse. He's in jail until the court case, so I heard."

Luke didn't change his expression. "I'm sure he's an asshole. No nice person can abuse someone."

"True."

Luke glanced over at the door when it clicked open. "That's my client. Talk later, Matt." He nodded at Matt when he exited the room and headed over to Theo, who believed no one took a second glance at him. He was average height with an athletic build, though he spent his time in a kitchen more than at a gym. His muscles were becoming more defined since he started working with Luke. It didn't change Theo's opinion that he was nothing special. Luke—and Theo's boyfriend—disagreed; Luke often saw the twinkle in Jasper's brown eyes.

"Hey! How are you doing?" He held out his hand to shake Theo's before bringing him in and slapping him gently on the back.

"I'm good, thanks."

"Is Jasper still away?"

Theo shook his head and grinned. "Nah, he came back yesterday, thank god. I think I've spent more time at the bakery in the last two weeks than I did before he came into my life." He chuckled, not the least bit bothered by it if Luke's understanding was right. Theo still struggled being alone in a house, but he was doing better. He had some great friends to help him, including Luke, who had gone from a regular at Sweet Tooth to Theo's personal trainer.

"Come on. Let's work up a sweat. I thought we'd practise with the strong holds today. Are you feeling up to it?" Luke always checked the mental and emotional strength of a client before agreeing to their session plan. If a client was feeling edgy or unsettled, different tactics could be used where they didn't need to be too close to each other or even touching.

"Yes, I'm all right today. Must have something to do with Jasper being back." Luke could hear and see the sincerity in his voice, which settled him enough to stick with his session plan.

They warmed up, and Luke put Theo through the motions for an hour before calling it quits.

"Good job. You're getting quick on your feet. I like it." Luke grinned and held out his hand for a fist bump. "See you in a few days. Say hi to Jasper for me."

Theo waved and headed off for the showers. Luke cleaned the mats they'd used, making sure to use antibacterial spray. Once everything was set to rights, he headed for the locker room to clean up before it was time for lunch.

After one more training session, a dual trainer class session and a two-hour weight room supervision session, Luke knew if he sat down, he wouldn't get back up. He had one more appointment, and he was done for the day. This client was new, so he had no idea what to expect. He didn't book the clients in, that was the receptionist's job, but each new client received a meeting to discuss what they needed before they were assigned a trainer. Luke was the only trainer who did safety manoeuvre instruction, so it was his speciality and always had him busy.

He jogged to the staff room to grab a couple of bottles of water from the fridge, then wandered back to wait, leaning on the window to watch the world go by.

When a guy walked in, looking around, Luke furrowed his brow and tried to figure out where he'd seen him before. He had a short, styled head of dark hair, and though he wasn't beefed up, he had a good amount of muscle on him. He also had a clenched jaw and a frown on his face.

"Hey, are you Luke?"

Luke nodded. "And you're Casey. I'm not saying this as a come-on or anything, but you look familiar."

Casey tilted his head. "You do, too."

Luke rubbed at his chin but couldn't figure it out. "Never mind. Maybe it will come to one of us later." He held out a bottle of water, which Casey took with a small smile. "So, I know you would like to learn some evasive manoeuvres. Is there anything I need to be aware of that may trigger you into panicking before we get started?"

"None I'm aware of."

Luke's mind raced as he interpreted Casey's 'back off' signals. "Okay, one last question for now. Have you been attacked, or is this a preventative measure?"

"What do you mean by preventative measure?" Casey narrowed his eyes at Luke, the crease between his eyebrows becoming more pronounced.

"I mean, are you here to make sure something *doesn't* happen to you or are you here because something *has* happened to you and you don't want it to happen again?" Luke watched Casey's movements and expressions carefully. He had learned about body language in his training, and throughout the years, he had honed his skills so he could identify his client's emotional states within their sessions.

"Nothing has happened."

Luke was sure he heard a quiet "yet," but he wasn't sure. "All right. Because this is your first session, we will go through some basic steps first. This is the most important place to start because you need to think about where your feet and hands are before you can do anything with them."

Casey nodded, his jaw ticking, and his Adam's apple bobbing.

Luke took him through some steps, explaining everything as he went. When the session was finally over, they were both sweaty, and Casey's lips were pursed, and his nostrils were flaring.

"That's it? Am I not doing any actual movements today? What was the point of this?" Casey lashed out, throwing his arms wide, and Luke waited until he finished his tirade.

"I told you at the beginning, this was the basic steps training today. You need to learn those before you can do all the fancy footwork you'll need for the evasive manoeuvres. You can't run before you can walk, Casey."

"Don't patronise me. I need to learn how to defend myself, not how to step around someone." Casey stormed off, throwing his empty bottle in the bin by the door before he left, the door slamming back against the wall before slowly closing.

Luke shook his head; he was used to this kind of behaviour, but it usually happened after the third or fourth session. Something must have set Casey off, other than what they'd gone over. He had no idea whether Casey was likely to return, so he passed by reception to tell them what happened. Casey hadn't booked a second appointment yet, but they would try and catch him before he left to get his feedback. Luke had done everything he could; therefore, he went for a shower, the water helping to cool his overheated body. He usually worked out himself again after his sessions had finished, but he'd been slammed. He didn't need any more exercise than what he'd already done.

After he clocked out of work, he wandered to his car, the heat of the summer making his shower pointless. He was not looking forward to going home to an empty house. He decided to go out. There wouldn't be many places he could visit on a Monday evening, but he was sure he could find somewhere he could just relax for a bit.

Wearing jeans and a shirt, he entered a gay bar near the city centre and immediately knew he'd made a mistake. He sighed. The need to hide away from prying eyes prickled down his spine, and he wished to be at home despite the hollowness. He didn't know why he bothered. One drink and he'd head home again.

"Rum and Coke, please," he said when the bartender met his gaze. The guy nodded and went about making his drink, and Luke listened to the clink of the ice cubes hitting the glass and the fizz of the Coke. When his drink was placed in front of him, Luke passed over the money, thanking the guy. "Keep the change."

Luke held the drink, the condensation cold against his fingers. He shook the glass gently, focusing on the sway of the ice within the dark brown liquid.

"Can I buy your next drink?" a voice asked.

Luke cut his gaze to the left, seeing a tall, slim guy with short blond hair and the palest blue eyes Luke ever remembered seeing. A delicious scent wafted his way, and Luke was tempted to lean forward and see if it was coming from this guy. He'd not come here with any conscious expectations of finding someone, although maybe subconscious ones. The hollowness he felt needed filling with something. Or *someone*.

"Sure." Luke's stomach fluttered at the possibilities before him.

The guy held his hand out. "I'm Dev."

"Luke." They shook, Dev's hand smooth and dry.

Dev leaned his elbow on the bar, getting into Luke's space. "So, are you here for a pickup?" he murmured.

"I hadn't been." He kept eye contact with the man.

Dev smirked. "Did I change your mind?"

Luke inwardly rolled his eyes. "I might be reconsidering."

"Me? Or the not picking up?"

"The second."

"Oh, it's my lucky day," Dev replied, licking his lips.

The guy was certainly not lacking confidence, that was for sure.

"Do you fancy getting out of here?"

"What about the drink?" Luke asked.

"Do you really want another drink when you've hardly touched the one you have?"

Luke glanced down and saw Dev was correct. He couldn't even remember taking a sip from it. His eyes flicked back to Dev as he raised the glass and took a large gulp, staring into the blue orbs as he swallowed. When he replaced the glass on the counter, he stood, causing Dev to step back. "Let's go."

They drove separately to Luke's house. Apparently, the guy had a roommate. Luke didn't care either way.

As soon as the door was closed, the guy practically jumped Luke. He wasn't opposed to being manhandled, but a little warning would have been nice. Luke kissed him back, surprisingly tasting mint while trying to gentle the movements and slow things down, but Dev was not interested.

"You can pull my hair and hold me down if you like. I love that," Dev whispered in his ear.

Luke kissed along Dev's jaw. "I don't do that."

Dev sighed, and he sagged against Luke. "All right."

Walking back towards his bedroom, their footsteps loud as he dragged Dev with him, Luke continued their kisses, tangling their tongues when Dev opened for him. He cupped the back of Dev's head, deepening the kiss and being rewarded with a groan.

Dev pulled away. "God, you're an amazing kisser. Do it harder." He nipped at Luke's bottom lip.

Luke's gut instinct kicked in, and he knew they wouldn't be continuing. He pulled away. "I'm sorry. This isn't going to work."

Dev paused. "What?"

"I'm not going to be able to give you what you want, Dev."

"What do you mean?"

"You seem to want things rough. I don't work like that." Luke stepped further back, running his hands through his hair.

"We don't have to be rough." The hopeful note reached across the space between them.

Luke raised his eyebrows at him. "It seems like it's what you need."

Dev's shoulders sagged as he sighed. "Yeah. Kind of."

"I'm sorry, Dev. I should've realised it's what you needed."

Dev waved his hand. "Nah, don't worry." He thumbed over his shoulder. "I'm gonna go."

"Okay."

Luke saw him to the door, feeling bad even though it was the right decision. "Sorry again."

"Don't be sorry." Dev wrapped his arms around Luke, and he reciprocated. "I think I knew, too. I didn't want to admit it. I was feeling…" He paused, searching for the right word.

"Lonely?" When Dev nodded, Luke continued, "I

know the feeling. Hookups for comfort." Luke forced a smile. "Take care of yourself, Dev."

"You, too."

He closed the door and rested back against it, banging his head back several times. "You're such an idiot, Luke Walker," he muttered.

Luke entered Sweet Tooth, inhaling deeply of the sweet scents as he waved at Theo, who was behind the counter, and headed to the table where Trent was sitting. Seeing a second cup of coffee opposite Trent, he assumed it was his and sat, wrapping his hands around it. The warm temperature outside did nothing to mitigate his need for caffeine.

"God, I need this today," he mumbled before taking a sip and groaning as the hot liquid warmed his stomach. He couldn't wait for the much-needed kick of energy.

"Good morning to you, too, brother," Trent said with a chuckle. "How're things? You were quiet on Sunday." Trent focused on him with a tilted head, what Luke called his teacher stance.

"I'm always quiet. The rest of you make up for me." Luke laughed.

"That we do." Trent grinned.

Luke sat back in his chair and regarded Trent. "I'm okay. I..." He gazed around the bakery and exhaled heavily. "I want what you and Max have," he finally admitted, though refused to directly look at Trent.

Trent leaned forward. "You'll find him when you're not expecting it. He'll be the last person you expect, too." Trent waggled his eyebrows and smirked.

"As long as it's not the guy from the other night, I'm good." Luke went on to explain about his failed hookup, the feelings of inadequacy rearing up.

"Concentrate on you, Luke. You do so much for others; there is no way you haven't got someone amazing on their way to you soon," Trent said.

Luke raised his eyebrows. He hadn't had a comment like that before from *any* of his family. "Thanks." He frowned. "I've just realised. Why aren't you at school? Haven't they started back now?"

Trent shook his head. "Nah, I have a reprieve for a few more days. They return on Tuesday, so I'm back on Monday. Four more days of freedom before I get back to teaching cranky kids who want the school holidays to last forever." Trent pumped a fist in the air in mock celebration.

Luke laughed.

"Are you working tomorrow?" Trent asked.

He nodded. "Yeah, not too many sessions. I'll finish at two."

"At least you get a bit of a break for your birthday, and then we're out celebrating!"

Shaking his head, Luke snorted at Trent's exuberance. Anyone would think Trent never went out, when in fact, he went out every week. It might be nice to meet up with some friends for a change, although he wasn't looking forward to being the centre of attention —it sent a flutter of nausea through him.

They ordered their breakfast from Cara, another staff member Luke knew. He'd been coming here regularly for years and knew all four members of staff and the owner. Usually, he dropped in for some takeaway items; he rarely ate in the bakery.

When they parted ways an hour later, Luke was feeling better about his life.

CHAPTER THREE

CASEY

Casey was still vibrating and heated several days after his session with the so-called specialist trainer. If Casey had wanted to work on basic moves, he would've asked Marcus to teach him, but he hadn't wanted that. Before the session, he had already been in a mood because he'd argued with Marcus about his reasoning for going to Distinction Fitness instead of Marcus's gym. When Casey had tried to offer his opinion of mixing pleasure and business, so to speak, Marcus had flown off the handle, saying Casey was acting immature. Casey had stormed out of there, ready to prove him wrong.

He was second-guessing now. Luke hadn't given him any feasible manoeuvres he could use in case of getting caught somewhere he didn't want to be. Luckily, he hadn't needed them; he grimaced with the thought.

Casey made sure to stay with others and shower at home since the incident the previous week.

The thought had crossed his mind to speak to his boss, but he knew Acker's position was more highly thought of than a lowly paramedic. Casey didn't want to chance losing his job over it. He sighed heavily and rubbed at his head; his headache hadn't abated no matter how many paracetamol he threw at it.

"Have you calmed down yet?" Chloe asked.

Casey huffed a laugh and crossed his arms over his chest. "I'm trying, girl. I'm trying," he muttered, shaking his head.

"What's got your panties in a twist this week? You've been in a foul mood for the past two days. I love you, but I'm glad I'm not with you for the next two." Chloe drove along the city streets back to the hospital for the end of their shift. "You need to go and find Marcus to help you release all that tension."

"That's it!" He sat upright, dropping his hands to his lap.

"Well, it's not long until we get back, and you'll be free to find him."

Casey shook his head. "No, I need to go out and have a drink. I wonder if Fridays are busy at Crush?" He rolled his eyes. "Stupid idiot. Things are always busy at Crush now. Plus, Friday is almost a weekend."

"Why is it always busy? I've never been there." Chloe glanced across at him, a small frown on her face.

"The owner has thrown some serious money into redeveloping the outside area and is bringing in new food options soon. It has made it the place to be in Cambridge." Casey grinned, feeling some of the tension release. "You should come and check it out." He rolled his neck, trying to ease the stiffness from holding himself so rigid for so long. He didn't know why he hadn't thought about going out before now.

"I'm working tomorrow, remember? There's only one person in this ambulance who has a two-day week this week. And it's not me." Chloe narrowed her gaze at him in jest.

Holding up his hands in surrender, Casey said, "Hey! I was owed a holiday! It was use it or lose it."

"Hmm. Next time we're free on a weekend together, yes, I'll come out with you and visit your favourite bar."

Casey walked with Chloe to the locker room, making sure to grab his things quickly and headed out. He hated being scared to be alone in an environment he loved. A search for another place that provided training was in order. One that wasn't Marcus's gym. He was adamant he wouldn't go there. The tension crawled back into his body as he thought about his boyfriend. He was such an asshole sometimes.

His phone rang, and he quickly answered when he saw Craig's name.

"Hey, everything okay?" His heart rate increased whenever his new friend called him, fear that something had happened racing through him.

"Yes. I'm all good. I wanted to see how your session went with Luke. You went on Monday, didn't you?" Craig was unsure about their friendship and was tentative with reaching out usually, so to have him do so today was a step in the right direction.

"Yes. I did. I was not pleased with the result, I must admit."

"Why not? Luke is amazing. He's taught me so many things." Surprise radiated through the phone in Craig's voice.

Casey sighed. He didn't want to deflate Craig's bubble, so he tried to cushion his words. "Luke was okay, maybe a bit arrogant. I wanted more than what he taught me. We were doing lots of steps, basic footwork. I want to learn more."

"And you will, but you can't learn until you know those steps. Those steps are the ones stopping you from tripping over your own feet when you're in a rush."

Craig was so enthusiastic about it, but Casey was still unsure. "But don't I need to know how to do the manoeuvres before I know what I need to avoid? Did that sentence even make sense?" Casey laughed, avoiding an ambulance as he exited the hospital.

Craig chuckled in his ear. "Yes, it did make sense. Only Luke can tell you that, to be honest. He explains things well when I ask questions. Don't give up on him. He is really good."

Casey inhaled and exhaled heavily, the noise of engines drowning it out. "All right. I'll give him another chance." He wasn't sure where the words came from.

"Good. You won't regret it."

"How are things with you?"

"Yeah, good. I'm taking each day as it comes." The strain was noticeable in his tone.

"It's all that can be expected of you, Craig. You've been through a lot."

Craig had been the victim of domestic abuse that had spanned several years, and Casey had been one of the paramedics to patch him up when the emergency call came through. It hadn't been a pleasant experience for Casey, but even more so for Craig.

They spoke for a few more minutes, then said goodbye after Casey invited Craig out the following night, to which he declined. After what happened the other week, Casey was not at all surprised with his answer. Resting against his car, he dialled the gym and booked another session with Luke.

Casey took a deep breath, trying to loosen his tight muscles as he walked through the door to Crush. He hated crowds, but he knew as soon as he found his friends—who he would guarantee were here on a Friday night—he'd be fine. He elbowed his way through the masses, telling himself it would be over soon and searching for familiar faces until he saw Max's head and pushed in that direction.

"Hey! I didn't realise you were going to be here," Max said, wrapping his arm around Casey's shoulder and bringing him closer. If he noticed the tension in Casey's body, he didn't mention it.

"I hadn't planned on it. But I had an unexpected couple of nights off, so thought I'd make an appearance." Casey glanced around the four tables which had been placed together. Only four seats were occupied. He waved at Sean, Asher, Zak and Ethan, then raised a questioning eyebrow at Max. "Expecting more people?"

Max nodded. "Yep, there's a birthday celebration afoot tonight."

"Oh, I wish I knew. I would've brought something. Oh, well, I'll buy them a drink."

"I'm sure it will be appreciated." Max glanced over his shoulder, let go of Casey and whirled around, arms wide. "And here's the birthday boy!"

Casey twisted around with a smile, then frowned and diverted his gaze to find a seat. He dropped himself next to Zak as Max threw his arms around Luke and shouted, "Happy Birthday!" loud enough to be heard above the roar of conversation around them.

Of all the people in all the world, it had to be him. At least he might be able to figure out where he'd seen him before now.

"What's that look for?" Zak whispered in his ear.

"What look?"

"The confused, 'I don't know what to make of it' look."

Casey shrugged. "I met Luke last week at a gym, and we couldn't figure out where we knew each other from. Looks like we have the same circle of friends, but I can't figure it out."

Zak grinned. "He's Trent's brother."

Casey glanced at Trent, who had entered with Luke, and he could now see the resemblance. "That was probably why. They look alike."

"They do."

"Hey, Casey? Have you met Luke yet? He doesn't come out with us often enough. Like you, I suppose." Max smirked, his eyes narrowed in playful banter.

"I'll have you know, Mr Hughes, I am a busy man. I don't have time for frivolities," Casey replied in a posh tone. "And, yes, I know Luke. Happy birthday, Luke."

"Thanks. At least, I've figured out where I know you from." Luke smiled tentatively.

"Same here. Now that I've seen you side by side, I can tell you're Trent's brother."

Luke grinned widely, showing his white, slightly crooked teeth. "Yeah, there's no getting away from this doofus." He shoved his shoulder into Trent's, who smiled and shoved back.

"Just because you're another year older does not mean you can take what I dish out. You're still my younger brother," Trent growled.

"I know. It's my birthday, though. You'd be a mean big brother if you were horrible to me on my birthday." Luke pouted and blinked rapidly.

Trent laughed. "Shut up."

Enjoying the banter between the two, Casey had to admit this Luke appeared different from what he'd seen at the gym, more relaxed. Which reminded him, he needed to apologise. He'd wait until Luke was in less demand, then say sorry for being an asshole. He tightened his lips and fists as the thought reminded him that Marcus hadn't cooled down after their argument, which was why he was out alone, and in all honesty, he was glad to be solo that night. The uncertainty of their future was rolling through his mind.

There were several people he knew, and several more coming, by the looks of things; therefore, he wouldn't be alone in so many words.

As the table filled up, Casey found himself next to Luke, which would make things easier when he apologised, but first, he needed a drink.

Leaning forward to gain Luke's attention, he asked, "Can I buy you a birthday drink?"

Luke smiled. "If you don't mind. A beer would be great."

Casey stood, sliding his way between people until he reached the bar. Charlie immediately saw him and came over, leaning forward to talk, "Hey, Casey. Not seen you here in a while."

"Yeah, I know. My shifts aren't the best to be able to get here when the others are here. I keep trying, though." He'd much prefer to come on days when it wasn't as busy.

"Well, just remember, you're welcome here anytime. Even when those idiots aren't here." Charlie nodded in the direction of their table and chuckled. "What can I get you?"

"A couple of beers, please. One for the birthday boy."

"Coming right up." Charlie bussed away to grab the

bottles, opening them and placing them in front of him. "Do you want to open a tab?"

"He will not," said a familiar voice in his ear. Casey flinched and turned to see his brother Logan stood to his side. "It's my treat." Logan passed his card over to Charlie. "Open a tab for us all, please."

Calming his breathing, he said, "I'm supposed to be buying it for Luke. I didn't realise I was crashing his birthday party; otherwise, I wouldn't have come. I haven't brought anything for him."

"He's not to know you didn't buy it," Logan argued. "And anyway, we can say this is from both of us." He held up a small, wrapped gift, complete with bow.

"Aww, you're getting so good at wrapping presents," Casey cooed.

Charlie came back with Logan's card and another beer, and they headed back to their group. Casey reclaimed his chair, passing a beer to Luke, while Logan stood behind them and thrust the present in Luke's face. Casey chuckled when Luke leaned back to avoid being hit.

"Thanks," Luke said, sliding a glance at Casey. "Do you want me to open it now, or does it need to be done in private?"

Casey raised his eyebrows, focusing solely on Luke. "Why would you even need to ask that question?"

Luke returned his gaze with a sympathetic look. "Oh, dear. What fun your siblings will have with you in your naivety." At Casey's blank expression, Luke chuckled. "Trust me when I say opening a dildo in front of your parents is not fun."

Casey's mouth dropped open. "Seriously? They did that to you?"

Nodding, Luke continued, "And it's not the only thing either. One year was lingerie—which I don't wear, by the way—another year, it was nipple clamps. I've learned to ask if a private opening would be better. It's not always foolproof because my family tends to bend the truth."

Snickering, Logan said, "You are welcome to open it now, but it's your choice. I promise it's nothing that will get you into trouble."

Luke thumbed over his shoulder and stared at Casey in faux seriousness. "See what I mean. They appear so innocent." He turned to Logan and smiled. "Thank you. I think I may leave the surprise for later."

A thought entered Casey's head, and he turned to Logan, pointing a finger at him. "Do NOT get any ideas! Otherwise, I will refuse to open any presents for my birthday or Christmas."

Logan grinned. "No promises."

Casey groaned, knowing he would get some random gifts now, and he narrowed his gaze on Luke. "This is your fault."

Luke held up his hands and chuckled. "I'm staying out of it."

Seeing how different Luke was there in relation to the gym, Casey was glad he had booked another session. Checking the people around them were otherwise occupied, he leaned closer and said, "I wanted to apologise for what happened on Monday."

Shaking his head, Luke said, "Don't worry about it."

"No, it's not fair. I'd had an argument with my boyfriend, and I took it out on you. I shouldn't have, and I'm sorry."

"Thank you. Are you coming back?" Luke tilted his head.

"Yes. With a brand-new attitude."

"Glad to hear it." He paused and chuckled. "The coming back bit, I meant."

"YO, CASEY!" Casey glanced over at Trent. "Does this reprobate belong to you?"

Marcus stood by Trent's side, and Casey had the overwhelming urge to deny knowing him. Especially as he couldn't tell Marcus to piss off like he genuinely wanted to in front of all these people.

"You can say no, you know," Luke whispered, the heat of his words caressing his ear.

Casey felt his lips twitch, but he nodded at Trent. "Yes, I know him." He could see Marcus visibly relax at his words, but the man would not be off the hook. They would be having words shortly.

"Hey, guys! Thanks for coming." He took his gaze off Marcus when he heard Luke's words as he rose to greet the newcomers. "Casey, this is Theo and Jasper. Theo works at the bakery Sweet Tooth and Jasper is his boyfriend."

Casey narrowed his gaze at Jasper, the feeling of knowing him prominent, just like it had been with

Luke, but he shook it off when Jasper began to fidget. "Sorry. Where are my manners? Nice to meet you. My boyfriend is over there." He pointed to where Marcus was currently in a conversation with Logan, poor guy. "Currently being grilled by my brother, who he's never met before."

"Ouch!" Luke laughed.

"Yep, but he was an asshole, so I'm not rescuing him."

"Fair play."

Casey returned his gaze to Luke. "You've had a good turnout tonight."

"To be honest, most of these are Trent's friends. I tag along sometimes." Luke shrugged and focused on the table and his beer bottle, suddenly appearing less sure of himself.

"I don't know many of them. It's only recently I've started mixing with them, and that was because of Logan." Casey studied the men around the table and those who stood nearby. "Is there anyone you don't know?"

"Most of them?" Luke snorted.

"All right, a quick name drop of each of them, which you can forget as soon as I've said it. How about that?"

Luke nodded. "Theo, Jasper, you listen, too. You're better at names than I am."

"So, starting here. We have Zak, Ethan, Sean, Asher, Max, Trent, Logan, Marcus, and I don't know who that is." Casey said, scrunching up his nose.

The unidentified man came closer. "I hear we have a

birthday in the house." The guy produced a bottle of champagne from behind his back and presented it to Luke. "Happy birthday from everyone at Crush."

Luke's eyes lit up. "Thanks."

"In case you don't know me. I am Tom, the manager of Crush. Charlie mentioned your happy day. I thought you deserved to be pampered."

"Thank you so much, Tom. I appreciate it."

Casey noticed a glistening in Luke's eyes and him swallow hard before Casey returned his gaze to Tom. Tom nodded and left.

"That was nice of him."

Luke stared at the bottle. "Yeah, it was," he whispered.

There appeared to be a well of emotion right at the forefront of Luke's demeanour, and although he didn't know Luke well, Casey thought he wouldn't be the type of guy who wanted to lose himself to tears in front of friends. So, Casey began describing his shitty callouts at work to make them all laugh.

As the night wore on, Casey decided he was glad he'd ventured out. He hadn't planned on being out all night, but when Marcus had said he was heading home, Casey told him he was staying. Yes, he might have been purposefully adolescent about it, but until Marcus apologised for being an asshole, he wasn't getting anything from Casey.

When the bell rang for last orders, Casey could hardly keep his eyes open, so he bid goodnight to everyone, wished Luke another happy birthday, even though, technically it was the next day by then, and weaved his way through the still surprising number of people to the exit.

A hand grabbed his arm, dragging him to the edge of the room and Casey twisted his head to see who it was. He was pressed against the wall before he knew what had hit him.

"Have you had an enjoyable night, Casey?" Acker asked, crowding closer against Casey's front and sliding a hand to the base of his neck.

A chill ran down Casey's spine, and his whole body shook, but he didn't say anything. He couldn't. Dizziness whirled in his head and from more than the alcohol, though he kept himself focused on Acker, the sounds around them disappearing.

"There is a lot more to you than meets the eye, isn't there?" he whispered, stepping closer and nuzzling beneath Casey's ear.

Casey heard him inhaling and sighing against his skin, and he swallowed hard, his legs barely keeping him upright. He flinched when Acker's teeth scraped the skin under his jaw and his hand tightened against his neck.

"You smell amazing, Casey. Always so tantalising and tempting. You don't know what you do to me!"

Casey exhaled shakily when he felt Acker press his hard cock against his stomach. Acker was several inches taller than he was, and Casey was blocked from the people around him. His heart rate increased with the thought that something could happen in plain sight of the crowds, and no one would be any the wiser.

"CASEY! You forgot your jacket!" Max's voice called to him over the noise of the remaining patrons.

Acker narrowed his gaze on Casey and removed his hand slowly before disappearing into the crowd. Casey had never been more thankful for forgetting something in his entire life.

"Here… hey, what's wrong?" Max encircled Casey's shoulder, bringing him into Max's body. Casey only just stopped himself from gripping onto him and never letting go.

"I'm fine," he muttered, swallowing hard against the fear still working its way through him. "I need some water, I think. I'm a bit warm."

Max didn't look convinced, but he didn't say anything when he guided Casey back to the table. A bottle of water appeared in front of him as he sat, and he gratefully took a large drink, the cool liquid doing nothing to settle him.

Why was Acker there? He hadn't realised the doctor was a patron of Crush. If he was, Casey might need to avoid the place from now on. The appearance of the asshole who was making Casey uncomfortable in his own shoes confirmed Casey's need to get Luke to train him. Casey glanced over at him. If Luke was the best, he needed Luke to train him as fast as possible.

It also meant he needed to be honest with the guy.

CHAPTER FOUR

LUKE

Casey and Luke went through some basic manoeuvres at their next session. Casey had complained a bit about it, to begin with, but once Luke had explained where they were heading, Casey had acquiesced. Luke could tell he didn't like being told what to do. There was a tightening in his eyes every time Luke told him where to step or what to grab, but Casey was withholding his comments, which was more than Luke would've expected.

Luke could tell there was something else bothering Casey. Other than asking if he had a good weekend, they hadn't talked about anything outside of training. If he excluded the eye-tightening, Casey seemed jumpy and stressed. As the session came to an end, Luke stepped closer to Casey, keeping an eye on him for signs of Luke being too close.

"What's wrong?"

Casey raised his eyebrows. "What do you mean?"

Luke wasn't fooled by the relaxed response. Casey's body language screamed at Luke to back off the subject, though he didn't seem to mind his closeness. "Well, I know you don't like taking orders, and I thank you for keeping your complaining to yourself, but something is bothering you, and it's making you jittery."

"No, there's not."

The quick answer did nothing to assuage the instinct Luke had, and although he hesitated, he still asked, "Why are you so jumpy?"

"I don't know what you're talking about. Are we done?"

When Luke nodded slowly, Casey pivoted and stalked out of the room, calling his thanks over his shoulder. Sighing, Luke picked up his belongings and spotted Casey's watch, remembering he removed it when it kept getting caught. He wandered to the customer changing rooms and searched the room for Casey. Not spotting him, he stood by the showers and called his name.

"Shit!"

The expletive was followed by a thump, a shout and a "Fuck!"

Luke dropped his things to the floor, uncaring of what happened to them and raced into the showers, finding Casey lying on his side, facing away from Luke.

"Shit, Casey. Are you okay?" Casey jerked when Luke spoke, so he gentled his voice. "Let me help."

"No! I'm good. Um... can you pass my towel,

please?" Casey's breathing was loud and fast despite the sound of the shower.

Luke reached past Casey, unable to miss the recoiling of Casey's body away from him, to switch off the shower before turning his back to grab Casey's towel from over the divider. The towel covered Casey's front as he closed his eyes and reclined on his back with a wince and a groan.

"Can I check what damage I caused?" Luke asked into the silence, crouching low but not moving any closer.

Casey rolled his head towards Luke, eyes opening to stare. A minute nod was the only response Luke received, so he slowly stood and made a wide circle around Casey before lowering to his knees on his opposite side. The below-the-knee shorts he wore got wet, but he didn't care. He wanted to make sure he hadn't inadvertently caused Casey to break a bone or anything.

"I need to move the towel a little so I can see lower on your hip. Is that okay?" He waited until Casey nodded again before flicking the towel over Casey's hand, where he'd put it to secure the towel over his groin. Luke winced when he saw the darkening red mark already appearing on Casey's hip and thigh. "You are going to have one hell of a bruise. I'm so sorry, Casey."

"It's fine," he whispered hoarsely.

"It's not fine. You're hurt because I didn't think." Luke rubbed a hand across his mouth, frowning and chastising himself. He should've known better. He'd recognised that Casey was agitated and edgy, but he still startled him. He could've given the watch to reception for them to give to him when he signed out.

They were silent for a few moments before Luke said, "Do you want to try and get up?"

"Do I have to?" Casey grumbled. "I could live here in this position for the remainder of my life?"

Luke forced a chuckle, though he didn't feel like laughing. "Sorry. I wouldn't recommend it. The floor is not at all comfortable for long periods."

Sighing, Casey opened his eyes again and met Luke's gaze. "I best get up."

"You keep hold of the towel, and I will take your weight and help you upright." When Casey agreed, Luke moved to Casey's opposite side, away from the quickly forming bruise, slid an arm around Casey's back and moved him to a seated position, complete with pain-filled whimpers. Once Casey was sitting, Luke pulled Casey's arm over his shoulder, wrapped an arm around his waist and lifted him to his feet, being mindful of the towel.

"Fuck, it hurts," he hissed.

"We'll move you to the chair here for a moment, and I'll grab you some clothes. Did you put them in a locker?"

"Yeah. The key is on the hook by the shower." Casey grunted as he was lowered to the chair, his grip on the towel easing as he arranged it over his lap properly.

"Okay. Dry yourself off if you can, and I'll be right back."

Luke snatched the key, and with a glance at Casey's hunched position, he strode to the correct locker, cursing himself silently and bringing the whole contents back with him. Placing it on the dry part of the floor next to Casey's chair, Luke asked if Casey wanted some help.

The negative response was expected, and Luke moved to stand until Casey reached down for his bag and lifted back up with another curse, and without having grabbed anything.

Casey glanced over at him, then down to the floor. "Yes, please," he whispered.

Luke nodded, flicked open the bag and passed over the boxers to Casey. Movements slow, Casey managed to manoeuvre them over his feet to above his knees. Luke helped him to stand again, and Casey pulled them over the bruise before removing the towel.

"Why don't you stay standing, and I'll help put your trousers on, then you won't have to sit and stand again?" Luke asked.

Casey sighed but nodded.

There were several pairs of joggers in the bag, so Luke chose one and knelt at Casey's feet, pulling them up his legs once his feet were in them. Casey took over when he could reach, covering the soon-to-be black mass on his hip.

"I need to get going," Casey stated once he had a t-shirt on.

"I have to fill out an accident form before you go."

"No!" Casey shook his head vehemently. "You don't need to. I'm fine."

Raising his eyebrows, he tilted his head and pursed his lips. "You're not fine, Casey. You have a bruise the size of a football developing on your thigh and hip. I need to fill out a form for insurance purp—"

"I won't sue, Luke. I promise. But please. You don't need a form."

Luke frowned as he interpreted Casey's body language. Everything about him screamed fear: tense muscles, arms wrapped around his waist, darting gaze and the tremor in the voice. What was he frightened of?

As much as it went against his work ethic, he chose to trust his instincts. "Okay. I won't do a form, but," he continued before Casey got too excited, "only if you allow me to check up on you in a couple of days." He held up his hand. "That is the only way I will ignore what my contract explicitly tells me to do as part of my job, which, by the way, could get me fired." He wasn't above using his job prospects as a way to get Casey to agree.

Casey sighed and stared at the floor. "Okay. But you do realise I'm a paramedic, don't you?"

"Yes, but it doesn't reduce my fear that you have done more damage than I know about. If something happens to you because of this fall, it's my job on the line. No doubt, I will also have your brothers and sisters on my back, too."

Casey's face lightened, and he grinned. "Probably. I

wouldn't worry too much. I would never set them on anyone; I know how they get."

Luke laughed. "Uh-huh. Exactly my point."

Casey bent down and grabbed his bag, his movements slower than usual, but he appeared to be managing.

"Are you going to be able to drive?"

"Yeah. It might sting a bit, but I'll be fine. At least it's not the leg I'd need for an emergency brake." He chuckled.

Luke shook his head and leaned down to grab the items he'd dropped on the floor when Casey had first fallen. Seeing Casey's watch, he passed it over, explaining his reason for being in the changing room in the first place. In fact, he was surprised no one else had entered the changing rooms during the incident, especially as he knew how busy the place was. He had his answer when they exited.

"Ah, there you are. Is everything okay?" asked Pierce, one of the other trainers.

"Yeah, all good." Luke wasn't sure what else to say.

"Glad to hear it. I stopped customers from coming in while you got sorted." The muscular mountain of a man would certainly be a deterrent to anyone wanting to get in.

"What do you mean?"

"Someone asked to speak to you, and I came in to see if you were there because we couldn't find you in the staff locker room, and you hadn't clocked off. I saw you helping this gentleman, so blocked the room while you dealt with it."

Luke had no idea someone else had come into the room, but unless he could bend the truth, it was not good news for Casey. "Yeah, Casey has pulled a muscle in his thigh and was struggling. When I went to return the watch he'd left in the training room, I found him in pain." Luke watched Pierce's face to see if he bought Luke's reply.

"I thought it must be something like that. Showers are a bitch when pulled muscles are involved. People recommend cold water to soothe the muscles, but they make mine feel worse." There was no hesitation or false pity on his face, so Luke relaxed. "How are you feeling now?" Pierce asked Casey.

"I'm all right. It's going to sting for a while, but I'll be fine."

"Get some rest, and make sure you don't do any somersaults." Pierce cackled as he moved away.

"Do you need to do an accident form for a pulled muscle?" Casey whispered, darting a glance at Luke.

"Nope."

Casey visibly sagged and smiled. "Good."

"Which reminds me. I need your number, please."

Sighing, Casey recited his number as Luke entered it into his phone. "Thank you. I will check up on you tomorrow, and..." he sent a text with his name, "I've now sent you my number. I'll know if you ignore me, and I'll hunt you down and have you fill out a form." Luke glared at Casey, daring him to argue.

Casey held his hands up. "Okay! Okay!"

Luke watched as Casey signed out at reception and waved at Luke before exiting. Shaking his head, Luke asked at reception about the man who'd been looking for him. Once he'd finished with the enquiry, he strode to the staff locker room to sort himself out. Just before he locked his phone away while he had a shower, he received a text.

Asshole.

Casey's reply made him smile. He'd think of something witty to send him later.

It was only as he sat staring at the TV eating his mum-made dinner that night, he recalled Casey's body language when Luke had first entered the shower. Fear had been a predominant emotion. Luke believed that fear was what had brought Casey to his sessions in the first place, although Casey had told him differently during their first session. Luke sat back, resting his fork on his plate. If something had happened to Casey, Luke needed to know because how else would he know what Casey's triggers were?

What part of the incident had Casey trembling in fear? Was it the fact Luke had scared him when he'd called his name? Luke didn't think so. And why didn't Casey want the incident on file?

There were so many unanswered questions, and Luke needed to rectify the situation. He grabbed his phone from the coffee table. They'd sent a couple of messages back and forth earlier after Luke had sent a funny quote to Casey. This time, Luke wanted answers, and he hoped by not being face-to-face, Casey might give them.

What aren't you telling me? What's got you running scared? You know I will help you, but I may do more damage if I don't know what I'm working with.

He didn't add anything else; he wanted to see if Casey would respond. When he hadn't heard from him by the time Luke went to bed, he surmised Casey would ignore his message, but he was proven wrong when he woke to find several messages from him when his alarm blared him awake the next morning. He yawned and rubbed the sleep from his eyes as he sat against the headboard. Once he was coherent, he opened the messages.

I know you would help me.
I also know you won't leave it alone.
There is something, but I want to deal with my way.
If it gets to the point I can't, I will ask for help.
I promise.
The shower thing was... a shock. I didn't

realise it would happen. But there are no other triggers. You have my word.

Luke tried to decipher the meaning behind some of the words, but it was too early in the morning to figure it all out. As soon as he had a shower and some breakfast, he would think them over again. He would reply at the same time as checking up on him. Luke bet Casey was aching like crazy that morning.

After completing his dreary morning routine, he checked his watch and decided to jog to work. He had plenty of time and nothing better to do. He would also swing by Sweet Tooth too. Checking up on Theo was important to Luke, especially after what Theo had been through. He knew there were others who were fighting in his corner, but the more the merrier as far as Luke was concerned.

"Hey, long time, no see, Luke," Cara joked as Luke entered the bakery to the scent of coffee and all things sugary sweet. The best smells in the world.

"Hey, Cara. How're things?"

"Good, thanks."

Luke smiled and headed to the counter, where Audrey, the manager, was cleaning. "Hi, Audrey. Are things that quiet, you have to clean?"

"Luke! How are you?" She stopped cleaning and washed her hands before picking up a takeaway cup and setting it on the counter. She heated the milk, the noise stopping Luke from being able to answer her question.

When she finished frothing the milk and grinding the beans, she glanced at him with a smile.

"I'm doing good. How was your holiday?"

"It was fantastic. When I retire, I've told my hubby I'm retiring to Greece. With or without him." She laughed, pouring everything into the cup and held it out.

Luke swapped the proffered cup with some money while chuckling at her statement. "I don't blame you, although I'm not sure I could stand the heat over there. I'm happy being in England, as bleak as it can be some days."

"I love the heat. Always have."

"Best idea for you." He smiled. "Is Theo around?"

"Yeah, he's in the back. Do you want me to fetch him?"

"Is he busy?"

"I don't think so. I think he's getting a head start on tomorrow. Let me go check." Audrey popped her head around the door that separated the back kitchen from the front counter, swapping words with someone before returning. "He'll be out in a minute."

"Thanks. I'll go sit."

"See you later, Luke."

Luke stared out the window, his hands wrapping around the cup and warming them, and thought about Casey's messages. Luke still hadn't replied. He would, but he wanted to make sure he said the right thing. It was important to him that he help rather than hinder.

Resting his mouth against his palm, he tried out a few responses in his head, but nothing good materialised.

Theo slid into the seat opposite him, bringing him out from his musings. "You could've sat with Jasper, you know."

Luke glanced around the bakery, noticing Jasper sitting towards the back. He ran a hand through his hair. "I honestly didn't see him; otherwise, I would've said hi."

"What's got you thinking so hard?" Theo's forehead creased.

"A client isn't being completely truthful with me, and I'm struggling with how to deal with it," he admitted, being careful to keep confidentiality.

Theo frowned. "Shouldn't you tell them they have to be honest? That you won't work with them if they aren't?"

Luke nodded slowly, struggling to find the right words. "I should, but… it's difficult with him. I honestly think pushing him will make him back off rather than make him do as I've asked. I don't like the idea of him retreating. My instincts are telling me this is his only chance to get the skills he needs."

Theo was quiet while he appeared to digest what Luke had said. "Well, you're good with non-verbal tells, so I think you'll be fine with him. Do you have any idea what could've happened?"

"No, but there was an incident yesterday at the gym, which is why I thought something more was wrong."

"I don't know what to suggest."

Luke shook his head. "It's okay. I'm just… trying to figure it out. Sorry for interrupting your day."

"Don't be silly. I don't mind at all." He tilted his head and paused, his gaze going unfocused for a second. "Do you want me to ask Amanda?"

Luke frowned. "Your therapist?"

Theo nodded. "Yes, she might be able to give you an idea of how to play it. I know you have psychology… whatever you've got—sorry, can't remember the name —but she always tells me talking things out sometimes brings the answer right to the front of your head."

Luke thought about it. Theo was right. Even talking non-stop and letting whatever come out of your mouth helps the brain process things. "That's not a bad idea. Would you mind asking her? If she agrees, give her my number and tell her to call me. Don't worry if she says no. It's not a problem."

"Will do. I'm seeing her tomorrow, so I'll ask her."

"Thanks, Theo. How are you doing?"

"I'm good," he said with a huge grin on his face. "Things are going well."

Luke smiled. "I'm so glad. You deserve it." He took a sip of his coffee now he was feeling more settled.

"We both deserve it," Theo amended, glancing over his shoulder at his boyfriend.

"That you do."

CHAPTER FIVE

CASEY

The responder unit chimed in the early hours of the morning, and Chloe immediately started the engine of the ambulance and headed towards the city centre.

Casey recognised the address as being Romano's, the Italian restaurant next to Crush. He hadn't been there for a while, but he knew Logan and Alice went there often. It beeped again with more information. His heart sank. Old Joe was not doing so well. Old Joe had bought, renovated and opened the restaurant many, many years ago. His son was married and had two kids; his daughter worked at Romano's and lived above with her father. Casey hated the idea of getting old, but only because it meant you were living on borrowed time.

They pulled up outside the restaurant and jumped out, grabbing the monitor, oxygen and drugs bag before they entered the alley to where they'd been told to gain access to upstairs.

As they entered the house, Rosalia was there to lead them to Old Joe.

"Hey, Old Joe. I hear you're not feeling well." Casey could see by the look of him that he wasn't. He had his hand clutching at his opposite arm; he was short of breath, grey and sweaty. All the signs of a heart attack. They needed to work quickly.

"How bad is the pain on a scale of one to ten?" he asked Old Joe as he checked his pulse. At his whispered, "eight," Casey drew that to mean ten. "Where is the pain?" Old Joe indicated where he was holding his left upper arm and shoulder. "When did it start, Old Joe? Have you been out partying again?"

"He told me it started a few hours ago but wasn't too painful, just a niggle. Then he shouted right before I rang for you saying it was bad," Rosalia answered.

Chloe was busy getting the blood pressure cuff onto Old Joe's arm, so Casey clipped an oxygen saturation cap on his finger. As he waited for it to register, he pulled out the ECG. He began placing the stickers attached to cables on the relevant areas: wrists, ankles and chest before he entered Old Joe's age and gender.

"Old Joe? I need you to sit as still as you can for me now, all right?" Casey watched as the ECG was taken and began to print out. He exchanged a look with Chloe. They needed to get Old Joe to the hospital as soon as possible.

"Has he been given any aspirin?" Casey asked Rosalia.

"Yes, when the operator told me, I gave him four as they said." She was standing, wringing her hands together.

"Great." Chloe pulled out the spray to help with his chest pain and asked Old Joe to open his mouth so she could spray it under his tongue. While Chloe did that, Casey prepared some morphine. It would hopefully help with the journey to the hospital.

"Let's get him into the ambulance," Chloe stated. Casey agreed and headed down to the ambulance to get the carry chair and to phone ahead to the hospital to prepare them for their patient. Once he was back in the room, they began getting Old Joe ready to move.

"Rosa!"

"Up here, Raf!"

Old Joe's son burst through the door, face draining of colour when he saw his father. "Papa." Raffaele crossed to Rosalia and wrapped her in his arms, his gaze never leaving Old Joe as Casey and Chloe worked to get Old Joe ready for the journey.

Before they got the chance, Old Joe's heart gave out. Despite all the attempts at resuscitation, Giuseppe Romano, Old Joe to everyone who knew him, died. Right in front of his family.

By the time Casey and Chloe got back to the hospital for the end of their shift the next morning, they were still in shock. Old Joe had been such a part of the community, it was unbelievable to think he would never be there again.

This was the part of the job Casey hated. He knew, realistically, he couldn't save everybody, but it sucked when he lost someone. Even more so when it was someone he knew.

Knowing he wouldn't be able to sleep and with a heaviness to his movements, he messaged Luke. He should have gone through the gym itself, but he didn't know if Luke would have room.

Do you have space for a session today at any point?

Within seconds, Luke replied.

Yes. I have a free session at ten?

Perfect. I'll be there.

He needed to work himself to exhaustion so he'd be able to sleep before his shift that night. Grabbing his stuff from his locker, he avoided everyone and headed straight for the gym. He'd be over an hour early, but he couldn't go home. It would be too quiet.

When he arrived, he couldn't decide what to do. He had planned to get here but hadn't extended beyond that timescale. Casey climbed out of his car and paced up and down in front of the car, running his hands through his hair and trembling despite the warmth in the air as he listed, in minute detail, what items were needed in the back of the ambulance for their next shift. The monotony of the recital helped steady him.

He relaxed further when a furry bundle came bounding up to him and jumped at his legs. Casey grinned and crouched, giving the bundle of energy a scratch behind his ears.

"And who do you belong to, little fella?" Casey glanced around, seeing a woman running across the car park towards them.

"I'm so sorry! He slipped his collar," she panted.

"It's no problem. Cute dogs are more than welcome to greet me." He laughed when the dog jumped up and licked at his face.

Casey held the dog until the woman had reattached the collar, then waved goodbye, his mood lifted from the short interaction. At least, until a hand clamped on his shoulder and scared the shit out of him.

Casey spun and bent his knees, hands outstretched, automatically assuming one of the stances Luke had taught him. When he saw Luke standing there, he exhaled in a rush and stood, pulse beating erratically.

"Shit, sorry. I thought you'd heard me," Luke said, backing away hands raised. "Fuck! This is the second time I've don't that. I should know better."

Casey shook his head. "No. It's fine. I'm fine. I was lost in my head."

"Is everything okay?"

Resting his tongue against his upper lip, Casey

stared at his hands while he contemplated his answer. "Yes and no."

"My previous client hasn't turned up. Would you like to come in now?"

"Fuck, yes." Casey snatched his bag from the car and locked it, following Luke to the training room, grateful for the lack of questions coming his way. He didn't expect it to last, but at least he had a few minutes to try and clear his scratchy throat and runny nose. Diverting to the changing rooms and removing his uniform, he replaced it with joggers and a t-shirt, locked everything else up, except his bottle, and headed back to Luke.

"Okay. Would you like to tell me what's wrong?" Luke asked once Casey had stepped onto the mat, arms crossed over his chest.

Casey inhaled deeply, letting it all out slowly. "I've had a rough shift. I need to be tired before I try to sleep."

"There's more."

Nodding, Casey worked his jaw, his vision blurring slightly. "There is, but I can't do it now. Can we …" he trailed off and flicked a hand back and forth between them.

Luke tilted his head to the side, studying him, and nodded. "On one condition."

Casey raised his eyebrows. "I don't like your conditions."

The shrug Luke gave him said everything. "Once we are done, you tell me what's wrong and go home to bed."

Gaze scanning the room, Casey thought about Luke's request. He didn't know if Luke knew Old Joe, but pretty much everyone did. Casey wasn't supposed to give the information out, that was the family's job, but he trusted Luke. As for sleeping, he couldn't guarantee he'd fall asleep, but he'd try. "Agreed."

For the next hour, Luke worked him harder than previous sessions, which Casey was immensely grateful for. By the time they finished, they were both breathing heavily, and sweat clung to them. Luke traipsed over to their drinks, bringing them back and handing Casey his bottle before indicating they should sit.

The bottle was half-empty by the time Casey was ready to talk, and even then, he wasn't sure if he could find the words. "My job comes with a lot of..." He rubbed a hand over his mouth and tried again, hoping his voice would hold out. "There are downsides to my job. Being able to help people is amazing and so rewarding, but when things go wrong... it's heartbreaking." His voice caught on the last word, and he cleared his throat. Casey stared at the floor as he slowly spun the bottle in place. "You need to keep this to yourself, please." He glanced up at Luke to see him nod and returned his gaze to the bottle. "Do you know Old Joe?"

"Yes," Luke whispered.

"He passed away early this morning."

"Oh my god," Luke whispered. He scooted closer but not close enough to make contact. Casey didn't know if he could take being touched at that moment.

"And you responded to the call." It wasn't a question, though Casey nodded anyway.

"He was having a heart attack, and we tried to get him into a chair to take him to hospital, but it was too much for him." Casey's voice was quiet, and he pressed his lips together, swallowing hard against the emotion that wanted to be set free. As he rubbed his hand over his face again, he noticed his hands were shaking. Refusing to break down, he stood abruptly, snatching his bottle off the floor. Luke called his name as he reached the door. He stopped but didn't turn around.

"It wasn't your fault."

Casey's nostrils flared as he tried to contain his tears. He looked to the side to show he had heard but didn't say anything. Knowing how selfish he was being but also knowing his limitations, Casey didn't look to see if Luke needed comfort. He exited the room and hustled to get his things. Despite how sweaty he was, he needed to leave. Right away.

"Casey?"

Casey's blood froze at the voice of the one person he wanted to avoid... forever, if possible. Unfortunately, working at the same hospital, it was next to impossible. He looked over his shoulder to see Acker standing at the entrance to a room, holding a file.

"Can I borrow you for a moment? I need some help with a patient."

Not wanting to cause a scene, Casey nodded and held up a finger before slowly finishing the sentence he was writing on a patient's notes. They had brought the patient in, and Chloe had left to ring her kids while Casey filled out the paperwork. Closing the file, he handed it to the nurse on the desk and drifted towards the room. The door was ajar, and Casey entered with a light tap so as not to frighten the patient but made sure to leave the door slightly open. There was no way he was shutting himself inside with Acker, regardless of whether there was another person in there or not.

"Thank you, Casey," Acker said, voice pitched low.

"What do you need help with, Dr Acker?" Though his voice was strained, Casey refused to drop the niceties in front of a patient. He wandered over to the bed, then stepped back, frowning at Acker when he saw that the patient appeared to be asleep.

Acker appeared at his side, and Casey flinched and tried to step away, but the doctor grabbed his arm and dragged him behind the door, away from anyone who might look in. "Now, now."

"Let me go," Casey stammered, keeping his voice quiet.

Acker stepped forward, and Casey mitigated the move by backing up until he hit the wall, and his breath left him when he realised he'd put himself in the wrong position.

"I think I need to teach you some manners," Acker murmured, resting against Casey as he had done at

Crush and pressing a hand next to Casey's head. His other hand gripped Casey's hip.

Casey slipped to the side, but the other man was faster than he appeared and dragged Casey back against him—his back to Acker's chest with one of Acker's arms around his waist, and his hand cupping his throat. "Ah, ah, ah. No need to run. I'm here to give you as much pleasure as you give me." He thrust his hard dick against Casey's back, and Casey swallowed hard, feeling his Adam's apple move against Acker's palm.

Casey tried to pull away, but the movements only earned a sound of approval in the form of a growl. When Acker nuzzled his nose up the side of Casey's neck, Casey began to tremble and froze. Acker slid his hand down and covered Casey's cock, which was as flaccid as ever.

"I know a way to make you feel better," Acker whispered in his ear, licking his lobe. His hand went to Casey's belt, but Casey began to fight harder, adrenaline rushing through him. Acker held him tighter, groaning when Casey moved against his cock.

He suddenly remembered the moves Luke had taught him and, without further thought, went lax in the doctor's hold. As Acker wasn't expecting it, his grip loosened enough Casey could duck out of the man's grip and dart sidesways.

Breath heaving from fear but immensely proud of himself, Casey bit out, "Leave me alone." He glanced at the patient, who seemed to still be sleeping, and turned on his heel and left, closing the door behind him.

The thought of being seen as he was had him hustling down the corridors to the locker room even though he didn't need anything from there. He entered the room, grateful for the noise of other staff laughing and talking. He sat on a chair and pulled his phone from his pocket, his hands shaking. Knowing he would be all right in the locker while there were other people in there, he settled in to wait until his heart rate had calmed enough to get back out there. Chloe would message him if he was needed before then, and he would go regardless, but if he could take a couple of minutes…

He distracted himself by checking his social media until his breathing had returned to normal. He stood, clenching his jaw at the chill that was still permeating his body, and left the room, heading to where he knew Chloe would be. When he got there, Kinton was there instead.

"Where's Chloe?" Casey asked, frowning.

"She had to go home. I've been sent as a replacement."

Inwardly, Casey sighed. The two of them had never seen eye to eye about most things, but there was nothing wrong with Kinton. He was a bit of an ass sometimes and spoke before he thought, but he did his job well.

"Okay. Are you ready to head out?"

"Yep. All set."

As they hustled to their allocated ambulance, Casey typed a message to Chloe.

Hope everything is okay. Let me know if you need anything.

He placed the phone back in his pocket and hauled himself into the passenger seat. Kinton was a driver, so Casey didn't even have to ask.

The following six hours were excruciatingly slow. Not only because he was with Kinton, but because there were few callouts. While he was happy people weren't hurting themselves, it made for a night of retrospection, which Casey hated.

Once his thoughts went down that route, he struggled to make his way out of it. The events of the previous night rolled through his head like a movie, and he second-guessed every move he made with one of the community's patriarchs.

"I heard what happened with Old Joe," Kinton said into the silence, making Casey startle. It was as if he'd heard Casey's thoughts.

Casey glanced over at him briefly. He expected most of the town knew about it now.

"I honestly thought he'd outlive us all."

That made Casey's mouth twitch. Yeah, the old man was a legend among the population of Cambridge. "Goes to show how quickly life can change."

Kinton nodded. "That it does."

They lapsed into silence again, and Casey's thoughts turned to Acker. He felt his pulse rising as he remembered what had happened. There were no witnesses, especially with the patient being asleep, so Casey didn't have a leg to stand on. It was his word against the doctor's, and he knew which side the hospital would take. It was a lot easier to replace paramedics than it was to replace doctors.

Casey needed to make sure he never put himself in that situation again. If Acker called him again, he would make sure he took someone else with him to 'assist.'

His phone vibrated in his pocket, and he dug it out, seeing a reply from Chloe, but also one from Luke. He checked Chloe's first in case she needed him.

Thanks, Casey. Gemma got sick with a fever, and Mum was worried. She'll be fine. See you next shift.

After the relief hit, Casey sent a reply, telling her to stay well, then opened Luke's message. He looked at the timestamp and saw it had been sent an hour earlier, which meant Luke was awake at four in the morning for some reason.

How are you? I know you have a session booked for Wednesday, but if you need anything before, please, let me know.

I've been better.

He pressed send before he realised what he was doing, staring at the message as if it would delete itself. Casey had no idea why he'd said it. He scrambled to send another.

Ignore me. It's a slow night, although I shouldn't say that. Superstition and all. How are you?

He didn't expect a reply, so he was shocked when the bubble came up, indicating Luke was typing. The bubble appeared and disappeared several times before the words came through.

I've been better, too. My family knew Old Joe well. We often went to the restaurant for celebrations. We even went to his son's wedding. It's a lot to take in.

Casey rested his head in his hand, feeling like shit. He'd left the previous morning without checking to see if Luke was okay after dropping that bombshell on him. Threading his fingers through his hair and rubbing his hand across his mouth, he shook his head. How selfish could he get?

I am so sorry. I should've checked to see if you were all right. I had no right to drop that all on you then leave. I'm such an asshole.

Don't be stupid. You're fine. It was a shock. I didn't know him as well as everyone else did.

Doesn't matter. I should've made sure you were okay.

Look. You're beating yourself up enough about what happened with Old Joe. Don't start doing it about me, too. I'm fine. Which you will see on Wednesday.

Casey would've loved to tell Luke about how he had used his newly acquired skills to get himself away from Acker, but he refrained, knowing too many questions would ensue.

Well, I am sorry. And I will see you Wednesday. If this awful shift finishes.

Casey didn't get to message with Luke any longer because a call came through for them. Kinton knew the area, so Casey didn't need to direct, but he kept an eye on the map anyway because it would tell him if there were any road closures along their route.

After dealing with a child with suspected appendicitis and getting the patient and her mother to the hospital, Casey clocked out and went home. Lack of sleep from the previous night on top of a slow night had Casey feeling jet-lagged. Striding to the exit, he was glad to see the back of the hospital for a few days.

There was a text on his phone when he plugged it in on his bedside table, and he realised he'd forgotten to check it after sending his last message to Luke.

Don't be sorry, be safe. SYW.

Casey assumed the acronym meant 'see you

Wednesday,' but he'd have to ask Luke when he saw him.

He'd also received a message from Marcus, but he refused to look at it, not wanting to get drawn into yet another argument when their other one had yet to be cleared.

Now that he was sitting alone with nothing to distract him, everything flooded into him at once. He trembled, a feeling of cold invading his limbs as he tugged at his hair. He slumped onto his side, not removing any of his clothes as he pulled his legs up and wrapped his arms around himself. The tears fell, stinging his tired eyes. What had he done to deserve this? Why had Acker chosen him? Casey didn't flaunt himself. He didn't flirt. He kept everything professional at work.

Visions of what had happened between them had Casey crying out, the emotional pain ripping through his throat. He contemplated leaving his job, leaving the city, but hyperventilated at the thought of leaving his family.

He had no idea how long he lay there, but when his muscles were stiff from the position he was in, and he'd finally stopped shaking, Casey rose from the bed, shucked his clothes down to his boxers and climbed under the covers. He'd sleep and deal with the cleanup tomorrow—both types of cleanup: physical and emotional.

CHAPTER SIX

LUKE

Wednesday couldn't come fast enough as far as Luke was concerned. After Casey had dropped the bombshell about Old Joe on Monday, Luke had been dying to know how Casey was doing.

Luke hadn't been lying. He did know Old Joe, although not as well as his family did. They went to the restaurant more often than he did—he only went when there was a celebration. Unfortunately, due to Casey's confidentiality clause, Luke was unable to say a word to his parents until they had said something about it, which, admittedly, hadn't taken long. By Monday evening, he'd had texts from several of his siblings and his mother about it.

The memory of a dejected Casey kept flitting into Luke's head, and he admitted to himself he was worried about him. That level of misery seemed deeper than he would've expected from a seasoned paramedic. Not that he thought health professionals should not grieve—quite the opposite. But Luke would've expected a larger degree of separation from their grief and their work. Maybe he was wrong. They were human after all was said and done, and he had no idea how they worked through everything they saw.

He shook his head as he lay in bed, waiting for his alarm to go off. The past few days, he'd woken extremely early and hadn't been able to get back to sleep, allowing for plenty of time to think. Hence the reason he had been thinking about the grieving process of hospital workers.

A raging desire to help Casey through whatever was bothering him rose inside Luke, and he acknowledged his concern, though the reason behind it eluded him.

Sighing, he checked the clock, rubbing his face when he realised he had another two hours before he had to get up. He climbed out of bed anyway and dragged on some underwear, joggers, t-shirt and a hoodie. Tucking his phone and keys into his zip pocket, he exited the house to the usual five o'clock dew-laden air. Inhaling a lungful of crisp, fresh atmosphere, he warmed his muscles, using the brick wall as resistance. He set off in a direction and let the beat of his feet pounding on the pavement soothe him.

As he ran, he thought back to the sessions he'd had with Casey since he'd talked to Amanda. Theo's therapist had been a wealth of information for him. Even though Luke had been through a psychology course at college, his knowledge wasn't as in-depth as hers. Luckily, she had agreed to talk to him and gave him her thoughts on the way to handle it. Luke hadn't given any personal information about Casey, although Amanda knew it was someone who worked within a hospital environment.

Her first comment was that Luke couldn't treat every client the same, which he knew, but when she said it, she explained what she meant. There needed to be some bending of how the process continued. She understood the basics were needed, but she also said things could be unlearned and reworked later if needed. Luke had never thought of it that way before and had always been set in his ways of learning the basic steps before anything else.

After speaking to her the first time, Luke had decided to throw some manoeuvres at Casey and see how he managed. He'd been extremely surprised. Despite the footwork being clumsy, Casey had learned quickly. After the session, Luke had known he needed to change the way he ran his sessions.

Since the first new-style lesson, Casey had two more, including the impromptu one that Monday. Luke had seen Casey's body was exhausted, but his mind was spinning. At any other time, Luke would've cancelled and told the client to go home and rest, but knowing what Casey did for a living, he knew Casey needed some relief.

He waved through the window at the staff in Sweet Tooth but couldn't stop because he'd forgotten his money, then headed back towards his place. A shower, a change of clothes and a car journey had him back at what felt like his second home. He had never felt more settled than he did at the gym. When he'd first set foot in there, everything seemed to click into place, and he knew where he belonged.

His thoughts were on Casey throughout the whole day—typically, Casey's session was his final one for the day—and several times, Luke had to pull himself back to the present to figure out what he was doing. Thanks to Amanda's suggestions, his clients seem to appreciate the new content. He was due to speak to her again on Friday so Luke could update her. She was interested in how the sessions helped and whether it would be beneficial for her to recommend them to her clients. It was a good working relationship for them and a new contact for Luke.

Finally, Luke saw Casey walk past the room while he was finishing with his previous client. He knew he had around fifteen minutes before Casey's began, so once he was free, he wiped all the mats and went in search of a drink, grabbing an extra bottle for Casey in case he hadn't brought one.

The studio smelled of the spray he'd used to clean mixed with sweat, which wasn't pleasant. Unfortunately, although the room had windows, none could be opened to air the room out. He checked his phone, and a wry smile graced his face. He'd not heard from Otto in a while. They had grown up together, and Otto had moved down to London to go to college, and although they still kept in touch, it wasn't often.

Hey, man. How's life treating you? You know what a shit I am. I'm sorry, I forgot your birthday. What? I'm only three weeks late, this time! Happy birthday, Lulu.

Luke shook his head, chuckling. It was Otto's damn fault he had that name in the first place. When they were younger, Otto couldn't pronounce the k sound, so it translated to Lu, then when his brothers heard him say it… well, they thought of calling him Lulu, and it stuck. As much as he hated it, he also loved it, especially when his mum used it.

He heard the door open and glanced over, seeing Casey entering. Luke placed his phone on the table and called out, "Hey." He refused to ask how Casey was because he could see Casey wasn't great.

"Hi, Luke."

"Let's warm up, shall we?" It wasn't a question, and Casey knew it if the half-smile he gave was any indication.

Casey appeared a little sluggish at times during their session, but he followed directions and got the positioning correct every time Luke asked, so he didn't say anything until the end of the session.

"So, how are you coping?" He watched Casey closely.

Casey's gaze darted to Luke. "What do you mean?"

Luke watched as Casey's breathing accelerated the longer he stared at Luke. "I wondered if you were okay after what happened with Old Joe."

Exhaling, Casey clenched his jaw, briefly closing his

eyes and nodded when he reopened them. "I'm doing all right. It's part of the job, you know." He shrugged and bit his lip. "Some of us are going to Crush on Friday. It's Eric's birthday, and he's managed to get into town for once, but we're also going to celebrate Old Joe."

"Who's Eric?" He didn't miss the change of direction the conversation took.

"Ethan's brother? You know, the actor."

Luke nodded when he realised. "Yeah, I know who you mean now. I keep forgetting Ethan has a brother."

"He has a sister, too. Emily." Casey cleared his throat. "Would you like to join us? On Friday? You don't have to, but if you—"

"Yeah. That would be nice. Thanks."

The corner of Casey's mouth lifted. "We'll be there from around six, but others won't be coming until later. There's no set time for anything, so arrive whenever you want."

"Thanks, Casey."

They stared at each other until Luke's phone beeped, breaking the moment. Luke had no idea what the moment was, though his pulse was racing.

"Well, I better go. I'll see you on Friday. For the session and the party."

"See you then."

Luke watched as Casey exited after picking up his bottle. As soon as he was out of view, Luke sat on the chair, frowning. What had that been about? There had been a good five feet between them, but it had felt as if they were toe to toe. He cleaned the equipment they'd used, grabbed his phone and headed to the staff room, checking for messages as he went.

Oh, and I'm coming for a visit soon. It's okay if I stay at yours for a couple of days, isn't it? Good, thanks. Lol.

Otto never failed to amuse him. It would be nice to see him.

Luke had no idea what to get a guy who could afford to buy whatever he wanted, so he chose a photo frame his mother recommended. If he'd had more time to prepare, he might've contacted Ethan and asked for a copy of a photo to put inside, but it would have to do empty.

He wrapped it in gold paper and bought a humorous card, which joked: In this card, I'm going to share the secret to staying young... lie about your age. He hoped Eric's sense of humour was similar to his own.

He dressed in a black button-up shirt with his dark wash jeans and a leather jacket. The noise met him at the door as he walked into Crush at seven-thirty. Instead of trying to find the group, he headed to the bar first. Charlie saw him, and when Luke asked, pointed him towards the Garden Bar. Luke was glad for his leather jacket if they were outside. It wasn't cold per se, but there was a definite chill in the air. He supposed after a few drinks, no one would feel anything.

"Luke!" Trent shouted as he stumbled towards him. Luke barely caught him.

"I see someone started the party early." Luke laughed.

"Iss a sebration," Trent attempted to whisper, his words slurred.

Max strolled up. "Come on, big guy. Let's get you some water." Max rolled his eyes at Luke and manhandled Luke's brother away. Trent wasn't always drinking, but more so lately; maybe he needed to check in with Max at some point.

Luke shook his head and continued towards the large tables, which were better seats for their large group. Not counting properly, he guessed there were close to twenty people there. He saw Eric standing next to his brother, Ethan, and someone who must've been his sister, Emily. Luke surmised they didn't see Eric much with his work schedule being all over the world. He headed that way.

"Hey, Eric. Happy birthday." He held out the gift.

"Oh, man. You didn't have to." Eric stood, holding out a hand to shake. "Thanks. I appreciate it."

"You're welcome. I'll leave you to your family."

"Come join us."

Luke waved a hand. "No, it's okay. I'm going to say hi to Casey."

"All right. Drinks are free tonight. Just tell them you're with my party."

Luke smiled and nodded, having no intention of letting the birthday guy foot his drinking bill. He strode around the table and sat in the chair next to Casey, who was in a heated discussion with his boyfriend if Luke remembered the face correctly.

Luke ignored them, allowing them the illusion of being alone. He leaned onto the table and tilted his head when Sean, one of their group, asked him about his job. They chatted back and forth for a short time before Luke's attention was pulled away by a growl from his left and a chair being knocked over. The guy Casey had been talking to stalked off, but Luke's attention was on Casey, who sat, muscles tense, hands clenched tightly together, face pale. If Luke took everything into consideration about his body language, he would say Casey was scared. Very scared.

Leaning towards Casey but leaving enough room for him not to feel smothered, Luke said softly, "Let's go for a change of scenery, Casey."

Luke caught Sean's eye and indicated he was going to take Casey away from the group.

"Go to Tom's office. Head towards the bar, turn left down the corridor. It's the door straight ahead. He won't mind, even if he's in there," Sean stated.

Luke nodded and gently rested his hand on Casey's bicep, encouraging him to stand. Apart from the initial flinch away, Casey allowed Luke to guide him towards Sean's recommended destination. Knocking on the door of the office, he heard a man say, "Come in." He opened the door, keeping contact with Casey.

"Can I..." Tom started, then stopped when he saw Casey's state.

"Can we borrow the room for a short time, please?"

Tom rose slowly. "Of course, you can. I should be out there anyway." He made a wide circle around them, indicating he had experience with the fragile state Casey was in. "There's water in the fridge. Let me know if you need anything."

Luke nodded, and Tom left, closing the door quietly behind him, blocking the noise from the main area. The sofa was right in front of them, so he helped get Casey situated and went to the little fridge to get a bottle. When he reached Casey again, he crouched in front of him and rested a hand on his knee.

Casey flinched violently, and Luke cursed whatever had caused Casey to react this way.

"Sorry, Casey. It's me. It's Luke. There's no one else here. Just me and you." He spoke softly, not wanting to alarm him any more than he already had done, murmuring nonsense.

After a short time, Casey blinked rapidly and swallowed. Luke lifted the bottle, uncapping it before offering it to him. Casey drank half the bottle in one go before resting the bottle in his lap.

"Casey?"

Casey swung his gaze to Luke, eyes looking slightly glazed.

"Are you okay?" Luke knew he wasn't, but he needed to figure out what the hell was going on with him. There was something Casey had not told him, and maybe it had something to do with that guy. Casey seemed upset after the guy had left, although Luke hadn't seen him react that way when they were talking.

"There's…" Casey paused to clear his throat and take another swig of water. "There's a guy at work… a doctor… I don't like him." Casey's voice was so small and defeated, Luke resisted the urge to wrap his arms around Casey and never let him go. "He makes comments about… how I look… and… keeps trying to get me alone. I avoid him when I can. Sometimes…"

Luke waited. He didn't want to prompt Casey in case he locked up again. He stayed where he was, hoping his presence was a good thing.

"Sometimes, I see him when I'm out. But I think I'm seeing things. The showers at work…" Casey's hands began to tremble, and Luke reached out to remove the bottle and slowly rested his hand on top of Casey's, willing to pull away at the first sign of it being unwanted. When Casey grabbed hold of him, Luke sighed silently in relief. "He surprised me when I was in the shower. He didn't do anything but stare and talk… but it scared me. He caught me here too, pressing me against the wall." Casey was silent for a moment, and Luke thought that was the end. He was wrong. Casey's hands clasped Luke's tightly as his voice continued his story, "He requested my help with a patient in a room across from the nurses' station. I thought I'd be fine."

Luke's heart clenched in fear as thoughts of all the different scenarios of what happened to Casey ran through his head.

"He gripped me so hard, I couldn't get away. I froze. He grabbed my neck..." Casey's voice hitched, "I thought he was going to kiss me, but he nuzzled against me." Casey turned his gaze to Luke's. "Your voice commanded me to relax like you'd told me to. It shocked him, and I was able to get away."

Luke squeezed Casey's hand, pride and horror flowing through him in equal measures. No one should ever be put through that, but he was glad he'd helped Casey feel stronger about what he was capable of. "What are they doing about him?"

Casey blinked and frowned. "What do you mean?"

"Has he been fired?"

"No. Why would he?"

Luke had a sinking feeling he knew where Casey was going with this. "Did you report him?" he asked quietly.

Casey pulled his hands away and stood, pacing the room. "Of course, I didn't! They're not going to believe me. He's a fucking doctor, Luke!" Casey shook his head and licked his lips. "I need to ignore it. I'm sorry for spilling it all to you—"

"No! Don't you ever be sorry for talking to me, Casey. I'm here whenever you need me. It helps to know because I can teach you the right things now." He hesitated. "But you should report him. He could be doing this to other people."

Casey's brow furrowed, and he paused in his pacing. "Do you think he would?"

"If he can do it to you, he can do it to anyone."

Luke watched Casey as Casey stared back at him in silence.

"I don't know if I can tell them," Casey whispered.

Luke had a thought. "Why were you arguing with that guy tonight?"

CHAPTER SEVEN

CASEY

Casey blew out a breath. "That was Marcus. My boyfriend."

Luke didn't acknowledge he remembered who it was. "Okay. He didn't seem happy."

The need to escape the conversation warred with the need for someone to talk to. Casey knew he could talk to Alex, but he was going through his own issues. He didn't want to dump more problems on the guy.

He sat beside Luke again, grabbing and finishing off his water, though it didn't cure his dry throat. "He doesn't like the idea I went to another gym than the one he works at. When I tried to explain I didn't want him to see me as weak, he told me not to be stupid and refused to listen. Every conversation we have now ends with an argument about the same thing."

"Which gym does he work for?"

"Triple-A Bootcamp," Casey said. The same gym

Craig's ex had worked for, which was a second reason Casey didn't want to go there.

"At the end of the day, Casey, it's your choice where you go. You need to pick a place you feel comfortable."

"And I have. It's why I came to you. Craig recommended you. Marcus doesn't seem to care that I won't go to the gym because there were several people there who stuck by that piece of shit even when there was proof he was an abuser." Casey's gaze wandered to the far wall and the large glass French doors behind the desk. He could hear the merriment coming from outside. "I'm wondering whether Marcus was one of them," he mumbled.

It wasn't the first time the thought had crossed his mind, but it was the first time he acknowledged it. There was something about sharing his turmoil with Luke that helped him see he wasn't going to be with Marcus for much longer.

He turned his face to Luke, ready to tell him, but found the guy's gaze already on his. "What?" His heart rate increased while their eyes connected.

Luke wandered over to him. "You overwhelm me with how brave you are," Luke whispered.

Casey got lost in the expressive, deep blue pools. No one had ever said that to him before. They'd say he was strong because of his job, or he was clever, but no one had ever called him brave. His gaze flicked to Luke's mouth, seeing a sheen on them as if Luke had swiped his tongue across them. Casey did the same, swallowing hard. He could feel himself sway closer until Luke's breath was coasting across his skin. When Luke's hand rose and cupped his cheek, Casey closed his eyes.

Before their lips touched, Casey jerked back. "Marcus," he said, breathing heavily. "I can't do this to Marcus. No matter how much of an ass he is." His skin felt flushed, and his nerve endings were tingling with what could have been. At that moment, he wished he was single.

"I'm so sorry, Casey. I shouldn't have… I didn't… I'm sorry. You told me your story, and I tried to kiss you. I'm so sorry." Luke headed towards the door.

"Luke!" He waited until Luke turned back. "Don't go. I'm not ready to kiss you, especially as I'm with Marcus, but don't go." He sighed. "Tell me about you."

Luke hesitated. "Let's make a deal."

Casey's mouth twitched. "You and your deals."

Luke winked. "It gets things done. Anyway, people are going to be worried about you after what happened." He held up a hand to forestall Casey's questions. "Not everyone saw, but a couple did. How about we go back out, grab some drinks, pretend you're okay, and we will sit and talk. And you can ask about me."

Casey's gaze roamed the guy who stood by the door, one hand resting on the handle. His clothing was loose but accentuated his sizeable muscles; Casey didn't feel scared with him. Quite the opposite, in fact.

"Deal." He gave a slow smile.

Picking up his empty bottle, he diverted to the bin before moving to the door. The closer he got to Luke, the more his skin prickled with awareness. It had never happened in their previous interactions—at least, Casey didn't remember feeling it—and he wasn't sure how to react. If he hadn't been with Marcus, he might've started flirting, but that wasn't his style. The only reason he had met Marcus in the first place was that Liam had introduced them when Casey had gone to pick him up from the gym one day. Casey had been instantly smitten with Marcus's looks, which were complemented by his personality on their first date— the double date with Alex and Heath.

Casey had second-guessed their relationship when he'd found out that Craig's ex, Darren, was a trainer at the gym Marcus worked at and had spoken with Craig about it before feeling happy to try. He hadn't wanted Craig to feel scared or upset if Marcus was around. Why Casey had never acknowledged before the possibility that Marcus might take Darren's side of things, he didn't know.

"Penny for them."

Blinking, Casey saw they were still standing at the door to the office, and he felt his cheeks flush. "Sorry. I got lost in my head."

Luke grinned. "Don't worry. I do it all the time. My mother wanted to murder me as a child because I never heard her shout until she was right next to me. I was too distracted by what I was doing or thinking about."

The image of Luke with a woman standing over him, yelling at him, made Casey laugh. It was far too similar to what he'd experienced with his mother, which was why it was so easy to picture.

"Come on. Let's go get those drinks. I think we need them," Luke said.

The office was well sound-proofed, so the noise when Luke opened the door and waved Casey through was loud—not from music but conversation. Luke rested a hand on Casey's lower back and guided him towards the rest of their party.

"Hey! I wondered where you two had wandered off to. Are you enjoying yourself?" Logan said, wrapping an arm around Casey's neck and pulling him in roughly, as brothers do.

Casey pushed him off, his heart rate accelerating, even though he knew Logan wouldn't hurt him. "Get off me, asshole," Casey tried to joke. "Yes, the party's great."

"Are you not drinking?"

Casey shook his head. "I'm at work tomorrow."

Logan winced. "Damn."

Luke leaned forward and whispered in his ear, "I'm going to get us some drinks."

Casey nodded in his direction before refocusing on Logan. "When are you next working?" Logan was a Detective Sergeant and often worked worse shifts than Casey did.

"Sunday."

"Ah, missing Sunday dinner. Poor you," Casey teased.

"Yes, poor me! There better be leftovers," Logan groused.

"You know there will be. If Mum has her way, one of us will deliver it to your place before the day is done."

Logan fist-bumped the air, and it was then Casey realised how drunk Logan was. He chuckled, knowing his brother would be feeling the drink in the morning. An early morning wake-up call might be just the thing to piss his brother off.

When Luke returned with their drinks, they weaved their way inside but chose a table close to the doors, so they were able to keep an eye on what was going on out there.

"So, what did you want to ask?" Luke said before lifting the glass to his mouth.

Casey thought about the questions he wanted to ask, which could be summed up as everything. "Well, what do you like about your job?"

Luke stared around the busy bar, twirling the glass between his fingers. "I like the different people I meet. Everyone is so unique. Despite my job being the same all day every day, I have to be able to adapt things depending on who is there. I enjoy the challenge it presents."

The small smile playing around his lips had Casey staring for all the wrong reasons. He cleared his throat and asked, "What do your siblings do?"

The minute he said the words, he wished he could take them back. Immediately, Luke's demeanour shifted. His hands dropped to his lap, and his head bowed as his shoulders curled forward, hunched over.

"Um... Samuel is a lawyer, as is Carter. Trent is a

teacher, and Ava is a police officer. She works with Logan.”

“Ah, yes. I remember him talking about her.” Casey watched as one of Luke's thumbs rubbed against the palm of the opposite hand in a soothing gesture. He wasn't an expert or anything, but it appeared Luke was feeling uneasy about something. “Where are you in the birth order?”

“Second youngest.”

Casey grinned. “Me, too! Isn't it the worst being nearly the youngest?”

Nodding, a corner of Luke's mouth lifted. “Not as bad as being the youngest.”

“I can imagine that would be worse, but we have it bad enough, don't we?” They exchanged knowing looks that had Casey feeling lighter than he had for a long time.

“Yea—”

“There he is! How are you, baby brother?” Trent draped his arms around Luke's shoulders, listing over to the side and bumping into the table.

“Wow. Your head's going to hurt tomorrow.” Luke smirked as he studied his brother.

“Nah.” Trent smiled goofily and waved away the comment. “I'm good as gold, me.” He dropped into the chair next to Luke, propping his head on his hand after several attempts. “What are you doing?”

Luke's mouth twitched. “Talking.”

“'Bout what?”

“You. Or rather the lot of you.”

"Ooh, are you telling him about the time at the lake?" Trent attempted to whisper, but it ended up being his normal voice. Casey gawked, suddenly really interested in Trent's story.

"No!" Luke's eyes widened, and he flicked his gaze to Casey and back to Trent.

Intriguing. Casey made a note to ask Luke about the lake one day.

"Yeah. Don't do that. Story just for us." Trent waved a finger between him and Luke.

"God! I'm so sorry! I tried to keep him away. He slipped the leash when I went to the toilet." Max stood to Trent's side, sliding his hand around his shoulder. "Hey, sweetheart. The taxi's here. Time to go beddy-byes."

"Do I have to?" Trent pouted.

"Yes, darling. It's time for someone to sleep." Max winked at Luke and Casey, who withheld their grins until Max had Trent up and heading towards the exit after saying goodbye.

Luke cracked up, his hands covering his face as he laughed as hard as Casey was. He was glad the mood had lifted, but Casey would've loved to know what Luke's behaviour was about when on the subject of his siblings. It didn't seem to be *as* evident when his family was there in person, although Casey had noticed a definite tensing in Luke's muscles.

Casey and Luke moved back outside once Trent was safely in Max's care, and just in time.

"Everyone! Can I have your attention, please?"

Casey stretched up to see where Ethan was and saw him standing at the bottom of the Garden Bar, facing the guests. Casey stood so he could see better, Luke coming to stand by his side, shoulder brushing against his. Their gazes briefly met before flitting away, a small smile gracing Casey's lips.

"I would like to say happy birthday to my younger brother. Although he is away a lot, he is never far from our thoughts. And millions of other people's thoughts, too. Though, no doubt, in a different context." Ethan mock shuddered and wrapped his arm around Emily while everyone laughed. Casey conjured up the image of audiences around the world, worshipping posters of Eric pinned to their walls, and he snickered.

"What?"

Luke's breath whispered across Casey's skin at the softly spoken question. Casey closed his eyes and breathed deeply, opening them and explaining his vision, receiving a huff of laughter in return.

"While Eric is not always present in this city, he knows where his home is and where his friends are." Ethan grinned.

Emily nudged Ethan. "What he's trying to say in a very roundabout way is we love you, Eric. When you've had enough of the fame and glory, come back to us."

Eric smiled, although if Casey wasn't mistaken, it was a little forced. "I will be back before you know it." He strode over to his siblings. "I love you all, too," he called to the crowd before wrapping his arms around Ethan and Emily. "I would also like to send our thoughts to Old Joe's family at this heartbreaking time."

Casey sighed. Family was so important, and it always made him happy when other people had support. He knew Old Joe's family had a good network, which eased some of his worries, but he still hated being part of the reason Old Joe was no longer gracing the earth.

A hand touched his lower back, and he flinched, heart rate increasing.

"Fuck, sorry." Luke apologised and removed his hand, but Casey grabbed it and held it to his side, their fingers interlocking. He needed to get used to being touched and not jerking away every time. Casey's shoulders slumped and his head dropped into his hand as he got under control, gripping Luke's hand tightly. He never used to be jumpy, and he hated that he was now.

"I thought you realised I was still here."

"It's okay. I'd gone inside my head. Again." Casey forced a chuckle. "Why can't I do that but still be aware of the things around me?" He sighed.

"It would be nice, wouldn't it?"

Casey lifted his head and glanced over at Luke, seeing some of the tension had returned to his body. When their gazes locked, there was a subtle humming in the air. The knowledge something could happen between them was evident, but Casey knew he wouldn't cheat on Marcus. He was also strong enough to know if he was having these thoughts about someone else, Marcus was not the guy for him. As much as it would upset Casey, he would have to call things off before even potentially starting something with Luke. He didn't know if there was an ethical issue about relationships between personal trainer and client, but he hoped there wasn't.

That thought had him pulling his gaze away. There was no way he could start a relationship with someone, not when all this crap with Acker was going on. Casey refused to pull someone else into the crazy the doctor was throwing out. He had no idea what he was going to do about it, but he would not bring an almost stranger into his drama.

He let go of Luke's warm hand and stepped away. "I best get going," he said.

"Do you want some company?"

It was on the tip of his tongue to deny the need, but as he thought about seeing Acker at Crush previously, Casey changed his mind. "Only if you're leaving, too. Don't rush on my account."

"Nah. These things never hold my attention for long." Luke gave a lopsided grin.

Casey chuckled. "That would be great. Thanks."

Luke sobered and tilted his head as he regarded Casey. "I want you to feel comfortable, Casey. That asshole will not do anything on my watch."

Those words had a fluttery sensation start in Casey's stomach, and he had to clench his muscles to stop from throwing his arms around Luke and begging for him to never let him go. Those thoughts had nothing to do with what was happening with Acker.

Shaking his head, Casey ignored the thoughts of being held in those strong arms and turned to wade through the masses. He knew Luke was following. How he knew, he didn't understand.

When they exited into the cool night air, the noise receding and being replaced with traffic instead, they wandered along the street in silence until they reached the taxi area. Although Casey hadn't been drinking, he'd arrived in a taxi because parking was a bitch. Luke opened the passenger door and indicated for Casey to get in first, which he did, sliding over to the opposite side so Luke could get in after him. Casey gave his address first, and the taxi set off.

The streets flashed by in a pulse of alternating light and dark, and Casey gazed out of the window, his mind a jumble of thoughts.

"Casey?" Luke whispered.

He turned his head towards Luke, watching as the man reached out a hand, palm uppermost. Casey stared at it for a moment, then slid his hand into Luke's, closing his eyes at the warmth that seeped into his. Luke manoeuvred his hand and threaded their fingers together, resting their joined hands on the seat between them.

Neither said a word, the radio their only companion until they reached Casey's house.

Luke squeezed his hand and let go, and Casey immediately felt bereft, his chest constricting with the knowledge he'd be leaving Luke behind.

"Good night, Casey," Luke whispered.

Casey studied his face, nodded once and, with a small smile, exited the taxi. He reached through the passenger window to pass the driver some money, but the driver waved him away, saying it had already been taken care of.

Hunching to see into the taxi, Casey mouthed, "Thank you," receiving a smile in return before Casey turned and walked up his garden path. The taxi idled at the curb until Casey had locked the door behind him. He waved through the window, though he doubted Luke could see him, then rested his back against the door and slid down to sit.

Why did life throw so many curveballs all at once?

CHAPTER EIGHT

LUKE

Luke had no idea what he'd been thinking when he'd tried to kiss Casey, and again in the taxi when he held out his hand. He had no business doing it when Casey was spoken for. Even though Marcus didn't deserve Casey, it was Casey's choice. Blaming it on the alcohol would be nice, but he hadn't drunk that much, and anyway, Casey didn't deserve that.

As Luke worked through his weekend and Monday, he found his thoughts repeatedly moving to Casey. The animosity and anger that had fired up in their first session now made more sense. Harassment was a big deal, but Casey needed some proof before being able to go to his boss. As much as everyone would love to believe Casey's word would be taken as gospel, it wouldn't. It would turn into a head-to-head debate where no one would be able to find the truth unless there was evidence.

The thought that Casey had to deal with that every time he went to work had Luke's veins heating. It wasn't fair. He wished Casey would involve Logan, especially with him being Casey's brother as well as a detective, but he knew Casey wouldn't want that. Maybe Luke could get some advice from Samuel or Carter—not naming names or anything.

"Aren't you supposed to be leaving now?"

Mary's voice interrupted his musings, and he checked the clock.

"Shit!" Luke grabbed his bottle and towel and jogged to the door. "Thanks, Mary!"

"No problem."

He hurried through his shower and dressed in the clothes he'd brought, knowing he wouldn't have time to go home first. Teasing his hair into some semblance of style, he picked up what he needed and secured his locker.

Dialling his phone, he marched towards his car, the fine mist of rain ruining what little effort he put into his hair. "Hey, I'm getting in the car to come to the station. Is the train on time?"

"Yeah, for a change," Otto said, a grin obvious from his tone.

"Bloody hell! Why does that happen? When I'm running late, everything is on time; when I'm early, everything else is late!" Luke shook his head as he scrambled to get into the car and start the engine. "Hold on while I put you on speaker."

Fumbling with his phone holder, he finally managed

to situate it so it wouldn't fall off the dashboard. "Are you still there?"

"Yep."

"Good. You may have to wait a bit for me, sorry. I got side-tracked at work."

Otto chuckled. "You mean, you forgot."

"No! I didn't, you asshole. I genuinely got held up." There was no way Luke was telling him his thoughts were distracting him. It was a conversation for when they had some alcohol inside them.

"Okay."

Luke could tell from his voice Otto didn't believe him. "I could leave you in the rain, you know." Luke felt buoyed by knowing he would see his best friend within minutes. It had been way too long since they'd last had time to spend together.

Otto laughed. "Fine! All right. I believe you. You were busy."

"Are we going straight out?"

"God, yeah. I need a bloody drink."

"What's up?" He could hear what appeared to be frustration from the other end of the phone.

Otto sighed. "Nothing a few drinks won't solve."

"I'll get it out of you later, you know."

"I know you will. That's why I need drinks."

"All right. I'll be there asap."

Luke hung up. Otto was usually as upbeat as Luke was. Something must have happened for Otto to be, firstly, visiting Luke when he hadn't in several months, and secondly, wanting to get drunk before he could talk to Luke. Being best friends usually meant you could talk to each other without the drink. But, he supposed, he was in the same boat. A little liquid courage never harmed anyone, and possibly, the solutions to their problems would become clearer.

He pulled into the car park, seeing Otto standing under the overhang of the building and drove over to him. Jumping out, he hustled over to the guy and pulled him into a hug, slapping him on the back.

"Fuck, man. It's good to see you."

Otto squeezed tight before releasing him and tapping Luke's cheek. "You're a sight for sore eyes."

"Come on." Luke lifted Otto's bag and carried it to the car, opening the back-passenger seat because he knew the suitcase wouldn't fit in his boot, as large as the case was. "Anyone would think you were moving home with the size of this suitcase."

When Otto didn't reply, Luke glanced over at him, seeing a sombre and serious expression on his face. "I'm considering it."

Luke frowned but didn't reply. "Let's head to the bar." He knew Crush opened earlier now, so he decided to go there. With it being a Monday, hopefully, he'd avoid any of his family or friends.

Twenty minutes later, they entered Crush, which was quickly becoming Luke's favourite hangout—and a place for sharing your problems, it seemed. The noise level was almost non-existent, although music played in the background.

"I've never brought you here before, have I?" Luke

asked Otto as they stood at the bar to order some drinks. He could see Charlie working the bar, and as he craned his neck to see who was around, he saw Analise collecting glasses.

"No. Is it new?"

Luke shook his head. "No, it's been here…" He blew out a breath as he tried to remember.

"Seven years now, at least as Crush. It was The King's Head before," Charlie answered with a smile, coming to stand in front of them.

"Hey, Charlie." Luke held out his hand, and they shook. "This is Otto. He's from London, so ignore his manners."

Otto objected and nudged Luke's shoulder. "Hey, I'm a Cambridge man through and through."

"Yeah, until you deserted us for the dark side," Luke countered.

Charlie laughed. "Sounds like we need to persuade him to move home, Luke. Nothing beats being here."

"What's that?" Otto pointed to the wall at the end of the bar, circling Luke to move closer.

Charlie looked over his shoulder and smiled. "That's our hearts wall. We honestly believe people who… I don't know, meet, interact, whatever you want to call it… in Crush, fall in love and live happily ever after." Charlie pointed at the little red hearts embossed with names. "That one is mine and Josh's. This one is the manager's, Tom and his fiancée—my best friend—Ginny. We're waiting for the next couple to join them."

"Any bets on who will be next?" Luke asked as he reached for the beer Charlie placed on the counter.

Chuckling, Charlie nodded. "Yes. We have a bet going. Not sure what the odds are because Josh is keeping tabs on it, but in the running are Sean and Asher, and Max and Trent at the moment. At least, out of our friends, anyway."

"I'll put my money on Max and Trent."

"Do you have insider knowledge I don't about?" Charlie's eyebrows rose.

Luke snorted. "No. Trent doesn't tell me anything. I just know how impatient he is."

"I second that," Otto said.

"I'll put you down if you like?" Charlie said, flinging the towel over his shoulder.

Luke nodded. "Definitely." He paid for the beers and extra for the bet and headed for a booth at the back of the bar but with a view of the entrance. He wanted some warning if anyone he knew came in.

When they were settled, he started the interrogation, "So, what's been going on that you've not told me about?"

"I got fired."

"What? Why? You loved that job."

Otto's shoulders slumped, and he stared at his drink. "Yeah, I do. Did." He sighed, lifting the bottle. "Serves me right for breaking up with my boss." He took a healthy swallow.

Luke stared at Otto, his mind racing. He hadn't even known Otto had been in a relationship, let alone one with his boss. Sagging back in his chair, shaking his head, he asked, "How long were you with him?"

"Her. About a year."

Luke knew Otto was bisexual. It was something they had many discussions about over the years, but Otto had always leaned more towards guys, hence the reason Luke automatically said "him."

"Sorry." He apologised for the assumption, which Otto waved away. "A year! You never told—" He stopped, hurt that Otto hadn't felt like he could talk to Luke about his relationship, but redirected his words, "What happened with her?"

"When she first took over as manager of the advertising company around two years ago, it was great. We got on well and made a great team. We'd been working together for around eight months before anything happened, although we always flirted. Leandra wanted to keep it a secret from everyone, including family. At first, I was fine with it. I knew it would cause a problem with the company, and she hadn't been there that long." Otto paused to swallow some of his beer, his glazed eyes staring at a point across the room. "When I began making hints about telling people, she'd either ignore it, or we'd end up arguing about it. I'd always back down. I'd been with the company for years; I knew what they were like."

When Otto stayed silent, Luke asked, "What did she do?"

Otto's expression hardened. "When I finally told her that I couldn't keep us a secret any longer and wanted to end things, she didn't say a word. Within two months, every contact I'd made refused to deal with me; every job I sent work to, declined what I offered. When I finally confronted her, she smiled. Three weeks ago, I received an email from human resources saying they were giving me my months' notice due to declined workload." Otto huffed. "Within weeks, she single-handedly ruined the reputation I'd built over the last ten years. I have nothing to go back for."

"Jesus Christ, Otto. Can you not sue her? Or the company? It has to be unlawful dismissal, surely?" Luke rubbed a hand over his mouth, unable to believe what Otto had told him.

Otto shook his head. "I've looked into it and had a lawyer look. Her case is ironclad. There is no proof she had anything to do with anything. All the information came from businesses and companies who worked with us—them. I don't have a leg to stand on."

"Even admitting your relationship?"

"Yep. Even if I did, it wouldn't change what had happened. She made sure to keep her hands clean of everything and make it look like my work was not up to standard."

"Fucking hell. What a bitch."

Otto finished his beer and stood. "I'm going to grab another. You want one?"

"Yeah, go on then."

As Otto strode to the bar, Luke sat back, fuming at the woman who ruined the life Otto had made for himself. It wasn't fair. Luke would love to have Otto back here, but only if he wanted to be. He knew Otto would never be happy unless it was something he wanted, not something he was forced into. Having known him since they were kids, Luke knew Otto would push back hard if he was backed into a corner. Although Otto was rightly pissed about what happened, he didn't seem opposed to moving home. Luke grasped at that hope.

The beers were placed on the table, and Otto returned to his earlier position with a heavy exhale. "So, what's going on in your neck of the woods?"

Luke pursed his lips. "I might be interested in one of my clients."

Otto's eyebrows rose. "Might be?"

"All right, I am. But he's in a relationship and going through a tough time at the minute."

"Shit, man. You don't need that. Find someone straightforward."

Luke laughed. "You should talk! Good luck with finding that, though. No one in this world is straightforward. Everyone has quirks or issues. Doesn't make them any less worthy."

"You always want to help people. It would be nice for you if your relationship had less drama."

"You can't help who you click with." He rubbed his thumb against the palm of his opposite hand.

Otto nodded slowly.

"Nothing will happen anyway. As I said, he's in a relationship." He heard the strain in his words himself and knew Otto wouldn't miss it, but he didn't comment on it.

"What type of training are you giving him?"

"Evasive manoeuvres." Luke picked up his bottle, scraping at the label.

Raising his eyebrows again, Otto said, "Why does he need those?"

Luke's stomach churned, the heaviness making him feel nauseous. "He's being harassed at work and wants to make sure he's safe as can be."

"In other words, he's not safe; he's just acting like he is."

Luke shrugged, staring unfocused at his drink. These were not new ideas to him but having them said out loud made them more difficult to ignore.

"If anything is going to happen between you two, you need to get the harassment out of the way first." Otto moved forward, leaning his elbows on the table. "I know you don't want to hear this, but he could be feeling safe with you, Luke, and mixing it up with real emotions. I'm the worst person to give advice at the moment but be careful. I don't want you to get hurt because he thought he had feelings for you, but when it's all over, he realises he doesn't. You are worth so much to the right person."

Luke took a drink of his beer. He knew Otto meant well, but he wasn't sure this was something he could ignore. Well, he could, for now, because Casey was with someone else, but if he was ever free... Luke wouldn't be able to say no, even if Casey deserved so much more than what Luke could give him.

Luke wasn't sure whether Casey would even turn up for his scheduled appointment. After their almost kiss the previous weekend, Casey had been working, so this would be their first contact since Luke's inappropriate behaviour.

He finished tying his laces, grabbed his water and wandered towards his training room, the clink of the weights and the pounding of footsteps loud even though he was a floor above the weights room.

Casey was improving quicker than others who took his classes; he wondered if it had something to do with the guy who was making his life miserable. There had to be something that could be done. He made a second mental note to ask Samuel about it; he'd forgotten when he'd seen him on Sunday.

Turning the corner, Luke bumped into someone and immediately apologised. The man waved him off, and Luke watched as he hurried to the changing rooms. Luke frowned and shook his head before entering his space. Each of the trainers had a room they used solely for themselves. Most gyms didn't have to space to allow this, but because of where the gym was located, there was plenty of space to extend if needed. With Distinction Fitness being popular, too, there was enough profit to allow for the luxury of individual rooms, or so he'd been told by the owner, Drake.

"Hey," Casey's voice made Luke jump as close as it was behind him.

"Shit, Casey. Warn a man."

Casey laughed. "You would've clawed at the ceiling no matter how I approached. You were away with the fairies, as my mum would say."

"Hey! Less of the fairy remarks, please. You'll hurt my feelings." Luke pretended to pout as he turned his back, then grinned and headed towards the mats in the centre of the room. Truly, he was pleased they could continue building a good friendship despite what Luke had almost done. "Come on, buttercup. Let's get training."

"Oh, that's how it is, is it? I can't call you a fairy, but you can call me buttercup. How is that fair?" Casey stepped onto the mats, hands on his hips.

"Never said it was." Luke smirked and walked them through the warm-up before pouncing towards Casey, who reacted instinctively and blocked Luke's attack.

After several minutes of attacking and defending, Luke paused the session. They were both breathing hard. Over Casey's shoulder, Luke saw someone through the window of the door but couldn't see who it was. He ignored it, knowing if he was needed, the receptionist would come and get him.

"Very good, Casey. You're picking this up really quickly."

"Thanks." Casey wandered over for a drink.

Luke followed and asked, "Have you had any more interactions with the doctor?"

Casey shook his head. "No, luckily enough. I've been kept busy with next to no downtime in between. It means less time at the actual hospital."

"That's good." He tilted his head. "I mean that you've had less time at the hospital. Not that you've been busy. Being a paramedic, it doesn't bode well."

They headed back to the mats and resumed their positions. Luke explained what they were going to work on for the rest of the session. Before they started, Luke saw someone at the window again.

"I wish they'd go away," he muttered, refocusing on Casey once more.

"Who?"

"A guy is hanging around the doorway. It's distracting. Let me ask him to move away." Luke strode to the door.

"He's probably interested in what we're doing."

Luke opened the door and stuck his head out, seeing someone walking away. "Excuse me?" The guy turned around, and Luke recognised him as the man he bumped into earlier. "If you're interested in training, you need to go to reception, please. These sessions are private. You shouldn't be staring through the windows."

"Sorry. I'll go speak to someone now." The man's voice was deep, almost hoarse and made the hair stand on end on Luke's neck.

Luke frowned but nodded and closed the door,

walking back to Casey, shaking his head. "No idea what that was about." He ignored what he thought he'd felt, dismissing it as the chill from the hallway cooling his body.

"Who was it?"

"Don't know. I've never seen the guy before. Sounded like he was interested in training, though."

"Extra clients for you." Casey smiled, sending waves of warmth through Luke.

Luke shook his head in humour. "Hush! Don't send me any more clients. I have enough at the minute. I can barely fit in the ones I have."

Grinning, Casey braced, ready for Luke's attack. "You love it. Stop complaining."

Luke smiled at the lightness in Casey's expression, hoping he was the cause of such joy, or rather the training was. He loved that he was able to help Casey relax, even if it was only because he was teaching him ways to protect himself. To Luke, it was as important to know how to defend himself as it was to have fun.

They spent the next thirty minutes tussling around with Luke throwing in some comments to Casey about where to put his feet or hands or pausing their session to give Casey a different variation on what they'd tried. As their training came to an end, Luke suggested they finish with some light weight lifting, so they grabbed their drinks and towels and chatted through the hall-ways to the main gym area, which was the whole length of the building on the ground floor.

With only one weight station available, Luke indicated for Casey to sit and showed him how best to lift to increase his strength to be able to do the manoeuvres Luke had been teaching the past few weeks. It wasn't essential to have strength behind him, but it certainly helped.

"Hey, Luke."

Luke turned and saw James wiping his face with a towel as he drifted towards them. "Hi. What are you doing here?"

"No pleasantries? 'Hi, James. How are you? I'm good, thanks, Luke. How are you?'" James raised his eyebrows, and Luke's stomach roiled when he highlighted his lack of social skills.

"Not for you, no," Luke joked, slapping him on the back as he returned his attention to Casey. "Can you do five more?"

Casey glared at him but continued.

"Are you torturing the poor guy?" James said.

"Nope." Luke's gaze stayed on Casey. He had no idea why James was at the gym. He *never* went to the gym as far as Luke knew, especially this one. This was *his* domain. He didn't need his brother invading his space. "Well done." He took the weight from Casey. "I'll see you on Saturday, is that right?"

Casey nodded. "Yeah, I'll be here."

"Okay. See you then."

Luke wanted nothing more than to stay and talk to Casey some more, but with James there, it was more difficult. He knew he would never be able to hide his attraction to Casey, and he wouldn't hear the end of it if anyone from his family found out.

"What *are* you doing here, anyway? You never come here." Luke turned to face James and crossed his arms over his chest, glancing at him before looking at the floor.

CHAPTER NINE

CASEY

Casey didn't move far from Luke. He'd heard the question Luke had asked the guy, who undoubtedly was his brother with how alike they looked, but it was Luke's demeanour which had him hesitating to leave.

Luke had made himself appear smaller and had a more serious air about him. The same thing had happened the previous weekend when they had been out for Eric's birthday. Luke had been happy and funny until Trent had turned up, and then he'd become quieter and solemn, even though outwardly, he seemed the same, Casey had been able to see the difference. There was something about his family, which made Luke feel uncomfortable in their presence, and Casey would love to know what it was. In his eyes, there was no reason for him to be uneasy, but Casey didn't know the family that well. Only Trent, and now Luke.

Unable to stay eavesdropping for too long or he'd be seen as a weirdo, Casey headed to the exit, studying the different equipment as he went. Maybe he should start coming to the gym when he wasn't training with Luke. It might increase his strength at a quicker rate. As he turned away from the treadmills, his gaze caught on the reflection of one guy in the mirrors, and his heart stopped, though his feet kept moving.

Acker.

The man met his gaze and the corner of his mouth turned up, and he licked his lips. Casey's pulse tripped, and the sweat that had been dripping down his back froze on his skin. His breathing increased as he stumbled his way through the doors and into the hallway, trying to get as much distance between them as possible. Further down the corridor, he rested against the wall and slid to the floor, eyes staring at the opposite wall but seeing what could happen if he got caught in the changing rooms with Acker. There was no way he'd be able to go there while he knew the doctor was in the building.

Why was he there? Casey hadn't realised this was his gym. If he had, he would've thought twice before signing up with Luke.

"Casey?" As if his thoughts conjured up the man, he blinked at Luke while wrapping his arms around his chest. "Fuck. What happened, Casey?"

"He's here," Casey whispered, his voice trembling even in how quiet he spoke.

"The doctor?" Casey nodded. "Fuck. Let's get you to the changing ro—"

"No! I can't... He... No! I can't." Casey couldn't get his words out, but Luke seemed to understand.

"All right. Come with me."

Luke helped him to stand, and with his arm around Casey's shoulder, guided him to the changing rooms, explaining the plan when Casey tried to scramble away. When they arrived, Casey's heart was in his throat, and he gripped Luke's t-shirt when a wave of dizziness came over him. Still holding onto him, Luke took them through to the locker Casey had used, and Casey passed over the key. Luke let go of him to unlock it and took out all of Casey's belongings while Casey's focus was firmly on the door, panic racing through his veins.

"Right. I've got everything. Let's go." Luke wrapped his arm around Casey again and steered him to the door just as it opened, and Acker came through.

"Casey! I didn't know you came here." His voice was jovial and polite, though, for Casey, it gave him goose-bumps and not the good kind.

"We're heading out. Thanks," Luke said as the doctor widened the door for them to leave.

"See you at work, Casey," Acker called.

Casey sped up, not even knowing where they were going, but luckily, Luke corrected any of his wrong turns. When they came upon another changing room, Casey frowned. "What's this?"

"The staff changing rooms. You can change in here.

There's no way he'd get back here." Luke showed him in. "I'll wait here for you to finish."

When the door closed behind them, it muffled some of the sounds from the main area, settling Casey's pulse a little more. "Don't you have other clients?"

"Yeah, but they can wait. I'll send a message to reception, telling them I'm running behind."

Casey didn't say anything else. He took his bag from Luke's outstretched hand and turned to the showers. "Please, don't go," he whispered with his back towards Luke.

"I promise. I'll be here the whole time."

Casey rushed through his shower and drying off before rummaging through his bag for his clean clothes. When he was dressed, he shoved everything back into his bag, uncaring about the mess and drifted back to the main changing area. Luke sat on the bench, flicking through his phone, but looked up when he heard Casey coming.

"I bet you feel better after the shower," he commented with a grin. "I'm gross and will be for another two hours."

Casey gathered a smile for him and was mainly successful if Luke's expression was any indication.

"Let's get you to your car." Luke stood slowly.

Waving him away, he said, "No. It's all right. You've done enough already."

Luke shook his head. "Nope. I'm taking you there. No arguments."

Casey forced another smile, hating he was putting

Luke out and making him miss his other clients, but he didn't argue.

"If you need anything, Casey. No matter what time of day or night. Call me, okay. You have my number," Luke said as they reached Casey's car.

"Thanks. I appreciate it."

"Please come back on Saturday. If you want me to come out to the car to meet you or do anything else to make you more comfortable, let me know beforehand, and I will do everything I can. Just come back. I want to finish helping you trust that you can handle anything that's thrown at you." Casey nodded and studied the ground. Luke's hand came up and lifted his chin. "Don't let him win, Casey. You are an amazing person. He is nothing. Don't let him dim your shine." Luke leaned forward and pressed a kiss on Casey's forehead before stepping back and indicating for Casey to get into his car. As soon as he was in with the door locked behind him, Luke smiled, waved and strode back to the gym. Casey paused a beat before starting the car and leaving.

He pointed the car in the direction of home and took a deep breath, not knowing what to think about *him* being at the gym. If it was a regular occurrence, Casey would have to ensure he wasn't there at the same time or the same area. He might end up having to shower at home instead of at the gym, which was unpleasant, but he'd prefer it to the alternative.

His house had a car already on the drive, and though he recognised it as Marcus's, he was annoyed he'd taken Casey's space—and that he'd turned up unannounced.

He parked on the road and exited with his bag, locking the car behind him. As he walked up the garden path, Marcus climbed out of his car with a smile. Casey looked away, dragging his bottom lip through his teeth to refrain from saying anything. He was tempted to go inside the house and shut Marcus out, but that was petty.

It was an idea, though.

"Hey! What's got your knickers in a twist?" Marcus asked as he strode in behind Casey, shutting the door with a bang and chuckling at his attempt of a joke.

Casey withheld his flinch and closed his eyes, slipping off his shoes. He headed for the kitchen so he could throw his clothes in the wash before getting something in the oven for dinner. It was unlikely Marcus would be staying because he had work. Unfortunately, Casey wasn't bothered that he couldn't spend time with his boyfriend. It had alarm bells ringing in his head, once more.

Arms slid around Casey's waist, freaking him out due to the unexpectedness of it—Marcus could be stealthy when he wanted to be. He stepped forward, twisted and pushed Marcus away. Hard. It shocked them both.

"What the fuck was that for?" Marcus hissed.

"You scared the crap out of me, Marcus! Jesus." Casey shook his head and stormed to the freezer, opening the door and crouching to choose something less than healthy. Pizza would do the job. The drawer squeaked as he closed it, and he made a mental note to defrost the freezer soon. Spinning to the counter, he jumped again when he saw Marcus standing there, hands on hips. "What?" Sighing, he narrowed his eyes at his boyfriend.

"What is going on, Casey? You've hardly said two words to me since I got here. You're acting weird."

Casey nudged Marcus out of the way so he could reach the worktop and finally let it all out. "I've had a shit day, Marcus. Well, I've had a shit few weeks, all right." He slammed the box onto the counter and attacked it with some scissors when it wouldn't open quick enough. "I'm being harassed at work, so I went to a gym and a trainer who had been recommended by someone who had been to him, someone who had found themselves in a similar situation. Today, I find out the person who's harassing me goes to that gym too. My nerves are shot, Marcus. Give me a fucking break."

He was breathing heavily by the time he'd said it all, but he was glad he'd gotten it off his chest.

"See. I told you, you should've come to my gym."

Casey's mouth dropped open, and he whirled around to Marcus. Unbelievable. "That is, *seriously*, the first thing out of your mouth?"

"Well, it's true."

His blood began to boil, and he clenched his fists. "Get out."

"What?" Marcus moved away from the counter and frowned.

"Get out of my house." He pointed to the front of the house, his voice sharp.

"Why? What is your problem now?" Marcus threw his hands in the air.

Casey exploded. "My problem is I've just told you I'm being harassed at work, and the first words you say are about your fucking gym! I don't want to go to your fucking gym, Marcus. How many ways do I have to say it before you'll listen? I'm trying to make myself feel safer by getting some training, and all you're bothered about is keeping up appearances. Well, fuck you! Get out and don't come back!"

He pivoted away and rested his hands on the edge of the counter, head lowered.

"Look, Casey…"

"Fuck off, Marcus. I'm dead serious."

He heard Marcus sigh, footsteps heading down the hallway and the door opening and closing. Swallowing a few times against the thickness in his throat, Casey turned and slid down the cupboard to the floors, wrapping his arms around his knees and resting his chin on them. The tears were warm as they slid down his cheeks and onto the fabric of his trousers. The silence surrounded him, and he stared straight ahead, not seeing anything as he let himself feel—the panic, the helplessness, the fear. He had no idea how he would get through this but get through it he would. Even if Marcus wasn't there to help.

The sound of his phone slowly invaded his stupor, and he blinked repeatedly. Fumbling in his pocket, he managed to pull it out before it went to voicemail. He saw Luke's name on the screen, and he felt tears welling again. Sniffing hard, he swiped to answer and put it to his ear, but he found himself unable to speak.

"Casey? You there?" The warmth in Luke's voice relaxed his muscles, and everything unclenched.

"Yeah," or at least that was what he tried to say. His voice cracked, and he cleared it several times.

"What's wrong, Casey? The doctor didn't follow you home, did he?"

Casey pushed aside the thought for a later date because it was something he hadn't thought about. "No. I'm all right. I've… Marcus and I broke up." He hadn't planned on telling Luke, not wanting him to think he said it so they could hook up, but it seemed like he couldn't keep much from the man.

"Shit. I'm sorry, Casey." The genuine sorrow in his voice made Casey quirk a smile.

"Nah. It's okay. He showed his true colours, and I sent him packing. I've…" Casey didn't know how to end the sentence.

"Had enough?" Luke supplied.

"Fuck, yeah." Casey huffed a laugh. "More than enough."

"Tell you what, why don't I pick up a couple of pizzas and bring them over? I know you don't know me from Adam, and if you'd prefer not to be alone with an almost stranger, I won't be offended. I thought you might like the distraction."

Casey didn't answer straight away, and Luke didn't

push for an answer and didn't ramble a rebuttal either. He waited for Casey to make the decision himself. That in itself helped him to decide.

"Come on over." Casey gave him the address.

"All right. I'll be there in under an hour."

After he'd hung up, Casey continued to sit on the floor of the kitchen. He was bone-tired and unwilling to move until he had to. The tile floor was uncomfortable and chilly, but he didn't care. Focusing on the tick of the clock, he counted down the minutes, gratefully grabbing onto the normally annoying sound to stop his mind from wandering.

When the doorbell rang fifty-two minutes later, he uncurled stiffly and clung onto the cupboards to help him stand and stumbled down the hallway to the door. He checked the peephole, and seeing it was Luke, opened the door wide, a wealth of warmth flowing through him as he saw the man who was coming to mean so much to him.

"Hey." Luke held up the pizza boxes. "I come bearing gifts."

Casey indicated with his hand for Luke to enter. "Thanks." His voice was rough. A drink would be the first port of call when he returned to the kitchen. "What would you like to drink?"

"Water or milk would be good, thanks."

Luke pushed two table placemats together and placed the pizza boxes on top. Casey smiled at the thoughtfulness. Few people would have thought to protect the table. His phone buzzed as he filled the glasses with water, and after setting them on the table, he pulled it up.

When you've calmed down, ring me. You're overreacting.

Casey huffed and threw the phone on the table, startling Luke. "Sorry." He dropped into a chair, sighing, and scraped his fingers through his hair.

"Bad news?" Luke asked as he opened a box and twisted it for Casey to see the contents.

As soon as the smell hit him, Casey's stomach growled in response, and he chuckled, the humour easier to find than he expected. "I blame you."

Luke raised his eyebrows. "What did I do?"

"All this exercise you're making me do. I'm hungrier than ever at the minute." He reached for a slice of pizza and placed it on his plate.

"That's good. It means your body is working hard." Luke took a bite of the pizza, humming in delight as he chewed.

Casey watched him, transfixed, then diverted his gaze to his slice. His groan rivalled Luke's as the cheese, meat and vegetable concoction melted in his mouth. After he devoured several slices, he slowed down. "That's an amazing pizza." He wiped his mouth and leaned his elbows on the table, focusing on where his phone had finally settled. "The message was from Marcus. I'm overreacting, apparently."

"What? He's an asshole, obviously."

"I thought he was different." Casey smoothed a finger along the scalloped edge of his plate, needing the distraction.

"At least you found out now before you had kids."

Casey flicked his gaze to Luke, eyes wide. Realising he was joking, Casey laughed and shook his head. "Yeah, I suppose things would be more difficult with kids."

Luke's phone rang, and he fumbled to answer it after apologising for the interruption.

"Hey... Yeah... Give me half an hour... It's not a lifetime, Otto. It's half an hour." Luke rolled his eyes as he smiled. "You'll live... See ya." He pocketed his phone.

"If you have to go..." Casey said.

"No, I'm okay for a bit. Otto—a friend from London —came up on Monday for a few days. He went out with some old friends, but he got fed up. I said I'd pick him up in half an hour. It'll do him good to wait for someone for a change. Usually, I'm waiting for him." Luke grinned.

"Ahh, payback. I know it well."

"The joys of having siblings, eh?"

Casey's gaze locked with Luke's, and although they weren't moving closer, Casey certainly felt the need. Luke's features—short light-brown hair, chiselled jaw, smooth-shaven skin and ocean blue eyes—captivated him. Feeling himself staring, he flushed and studied his plate instead before standing and taking it to the sink. He rolled his shoulders and stretched out his neck, breathing easier than he had done in days or even weeks.

"Casey…" Luke hesitated, then continued, "I know you have family, but I'm assuming you haven't told them about your situation. Therefore, if you need anything, at any point, day or night, please ring me."

A warmth at Casey's back advertised where Luke was; it was different from how Marcus had been. Luke didn't touch him at all, just lent his strength by being there. Casey would not have been opposed to being touched, but it was for the best as Marcus hadn't been gone even three hours yet.

"Thank you. I will." He turned, leaning back against the sink and smiling at Luke. "It means a lot. Even if you are an almost stranger." Casey raised his eyebrow to show he remembered Luke's earlier words.

Luke beamed. "Glad I'm not a complete stranger."

"Nah, you've been upgraded."

Luke's hand lifted slowly enough to allow Casey time to pull away if he wanted to, which he didn't. The heat of Luke's palm cupping his jaw had Casey swallowing hard, his eyes closing briefly to withhold the tears that wanted to escape.

"You're strong, Casey. I'm here for whatever you need," he whispered.

The hand left his face, but Casey chased it, pulling Luke back. Uncaring of the repercussions despite his earlier thoughts, he wrapped a hand around the back of Luke's neck and pulled him close. Casey lifted his head and pressed his lips to Luke's. The kiss was gentle and chaste for a few moments until Luke groaned and slid his hands around Casey's back. Plastered against each other as they were, Casey could not miss the strength in Luke's body, but it didn't scare him. As the kiss deepened, Casey opening to Luke's questing tongue. Luke explored his mouth, and Casey sank into him, light-headed, his hands grasping at Luke's back.

Luke slid his hands down to the back of Casey's thighs, lifting him to rest on the counter. Unfortunately, he'd been right in front of the sink, so he nearly ended up falling in. Their teeth clashed as they laughed, and Luke moved him to the side, continuing to kiss him. Casey was able to run his fingers through Luke's hair, scraping his nails over Luke's scalp.

Luke pulled back, and they gasped for air, still wrapped around each other. Neither said anything, just stared as they shared their breaths. Leaning in, Luke pressed one more kiss to Casey's lips and stepped back, helping Casey down from the counter. A hand threaded through Luke's hair as he moved away.

"Call me if you need me, all right?" Luke's voice was hoarse, and when he looked at Casey, Casey nodded. Luke smiled. "See you Saturday." He whirled around and left.

When Casey heard the front door close, he lifted his fingers to his lips. "Fuck," he whispered as he smiled and closed his eyes, searing the kiss into his brain. He was under no illusion that it was meant as more than a kiss, but it was an amazing kiss, nonetheless.

CHPATER TEN

LUKE

"Where's the birthday girl?" Luke called from the front door.

"Zio Luke!" Harper came jogging down the hallway of his parents' house and threw her arms around his neck.

"Hey, nipote. How are you? Are you enjoying your birthday?" He hugged her and set her down, running a hand down her hair as she pulled away. He held out his gift. His niece looked a lot like Trent but with a Mediterranean look, and she had Trent wrapped around her little finger, especially since all the issues with his ex-wife. These past few weeks had been difficult for them all, so being able to celebrate Harper's seventeenth birthday was a joyous occasion.

"Grazie. Yes, it's been amazing! Papa and Max bought me a new laptop so I can do my work easier. It's got some fantastic things to help me learn Italian, too."

She spoke in a fast clip, explaining some of the things she had received as they walked towards the kitchen where the sound of conversation was coming from.

"Otto sends his love, too. He says there should be something in your bank account for your birthday." He smiled at her squeal.

"I'm glad you could make it," Trent said, clapping him on the back.

"Wouldn't miss it for the world." Luke smiled at Harper, who was busy stripping the carefully wrapped present he had given her.

"Oh my god! Zio Luke, really?" Harper's eyes widened when she saw the four plane tickets to Italy. It had been Harper's dream since she was little to travel and be a translator, but she never believed she would be able to do it. Italian was her favourite language, hence the reason for some of her words to be spoken in the other language. Luke had taken to calling her "nipote," which meant niece in Italian, to show his support.

"And now we can give you this," his mother said, holding out an envelope for Harper.

She opened it, barely keeping her tears in check. As she read it, the tears overflowed.

"What is it, Harper?" Trent asked, confusion on his face as he moved closer.

Harper held out the paper. The family had decided that Trent, Harper and Jocelyn had put up with so much over the last few months—and years, to be honest—and they deserved a break. Luke had come to them with the idea of paying for a holiday for them. As soon as the idea had been voiced, everyone wanted part of it. So, Luke had bought four plane tickets, to include Max; his parents had paid for a small house for them to stay in; and each of Luke's siblings had paid for a different excursion or something they could do while they stayed there. They had decided the family should go at Easter, and Harper would be able to view the university she wanted to study at.

Trent's voice broke as he thanked everyone, tears running down his face, too. He moved over to Max, who enfolded him in his arms while Trent pulled himself together.

"Grazie, everyone!" Harper said, holding onto her sister as she stared at the tickets.

"You're very welcome, sweetheart," his mother said. "Now, everyone, let's get some food inside us. Go on, out, all of you."

As they exited the house into the large back garden of his childhood, Luke took a breath, memories assailing him. His parents had been in the same house since before Samuel was born, extending the floor space as each child arrived. One day, he hoped he could have a house that was as deeply connected to family as this one was.

The weather had been predicted to be nice and warm that evening, even in late September as it was, so they had brought out the large garden tables they used for celebrations and set them up in a square so everyone could see everyone. The table had already been set with plenty of food beneath nets, so the flies stayed away.

Their family celebrations were events to be proud of, his mother always said. As they sat down, Luke glanced around at his family, a smile on his face. Despite his feelings of unworthiness, he loved them all. He wondered how well Casey would fit into the dynamic.

Studying his food as he picked at it, he thought back to Saturday.

Luke waited anxiously to see if Casey would show up to their session. He paced around the mats he'd already set up and cleaned, unable to keep still as he checked his watch once more. The door opened, and Casey walked through, a little pale, but he was there all the same. Luke could do nothing but step over to him.

"Are you all right?" He wanted to touch Casey, but the guy looked like he was ready to run.

Casey nodded and swallowed, giving Luke a small smile. "I'm good. At least as good as can be expected considering."

Deciding to distract Casey from his fears that the doctor would be there, Luke told him to get ready. Casey headed to the chairs, set his bottle down and changed direction to the mats.

"Today, we're going to dance," Luke said, smiling.

Casey raised his eyebrows. "What?"

Chuckling, Luke repeated his words.

"Dance? What does dancing have to do with this?" Casey frowned.

"Footwork. You need to know different types of footwork and be able to change steps at a moment's notice. By allowing

me to lead you in a dance, you won't have any idea what steps I'm going to get you to do."

"How do I know where to step?"

"That's the idea. You don't; therefore, you must adapt. There is no point in learning just steps because what if you are in a situation that doesn't give you enough room to move in a set way? If I teach you how to move in one way, you will not learn how to adapt to your surroundings, how to use your environment as a tool."

Casey looked thoughtful. "That makes sense. But why dancing? I can't dance," he whined.

"Yes, you can." Luke strode over to his phone on the windowsill and pressed a few buttons until a salsa beat came on. It was not a slow song, but it was slower than club music. "Come here." He held out his hand to Casey.

Hesitation was clear in Casey's body language, but he drifted over, placing his hand into Luke's. Luke drew him closer and began to move, using Casey's hand to steer him as Luke counted beats. Before long, they were moving across the floor with Casey stepping in time with the beat. Luke could see the happiness on Casey's face.

Once Luke had decided they'd done enough dancing—although he would've happily continued—they hit the mats. Luke taught Casey how to adapt on the mat, too, though it was more difficult. Light touches, eye contact, small smiles all made the session more torturous.

By the end of their session, they had both been visibly aroused, and Luke had wanted more, but he refused to push too hard. He'd wait for Casey to make the next move, especially due to his situation. Which reminded him…

"Samuel? Could I talk to you before you head out tonight, please?" Luckily, Samuel sat next to him.

Samuel furrowed his brow but nodded. "Sure thing."

The meal was spent catching up on each other's lives, and Harper talking about the things they'd be able to see when they visited Italy. Luke loved that some of her spark had returned since she had moved in with Trent. He hadn't realised how much she had withdrawn into herself until he saw her begin to emerge again.

Once everything was put back to rights after their food, Luke went searching for Samuel.

"Dad, is it okay to use your office for a bit?" Luke asked.

"Of course." Dad waved his hand from the sofa where he was engaged in a quiz show.

They headed to the opposite side of the house to where the office was located. When they were sitting, Luke began explaining.

"I can't give you a lot of information because I don't know everything, but I need your opinion."

"Okay. Go on," Samuel said, crossing his legs and resting an arm along the back of the sofa.

Luke leaned forward, his elbows on his knees. "A friend is being harassed at work. Due to their jobs, if my friend mentions it to anyone, it would be more likely for him to lose his job rather than the person doing it."

"What kind of harassment? Sexual? Verbal? Physical?"

"Sexual, I believe."

Samuel stood. "Hold on a sec." He left the room.

Luke blew out a breath and rubbed his face. He hoped there was something that could be done to help Casey. The door opened again, and Samuel returned with Carter in tow.

"Right. Carter is in criminal law, remember, so he will have more information than I will," Samuel said. "Explain as much as you can from the beginning."

Luke spent several minutes going through Casey's incidents, leaving out any identifying factors. After a round of questions, some of which Luke couldn't answer, Carter exhaled, steepling his fingers in front of his mouth.

"It's a tough one. I would like to say your friend would have all the backing possible to make sure this never happens again, but I live in the real world, and it probably won't happen. My advice would be for your friend to speak to someone within his workplace he trusts. Someone higher up the ladder than he is. He also needs to gather evidence where possible. Messages, photos—if he's being stalked—anything to prove this guy is an asshole."

Luke nodded but tightened his fists. "There's nothing else he can do?"

"There will be, but those are what I would do first. Depending on where he works, he may be able to have a video recorder going on his phone whenever there is a chance of him seeing the other guy. Evidence of every meeting, chance or otherwise."

"Okay. Thanks." He rubbed his hands over his face, wishing it was better advice, but he knew they would tell him if there was anything else Casey could do.

"You're welcome. If there's any other trouble, call me."

"Will do." Luke stood.

"What is he to you?" Samuel asked. Luke felt his face heat, and Samuel chuckled. "That answers that."

"No, it doesn't. I know what I want him to be, but until he's ready, he's a friend. Nothing more."

"You're a good man, Lulu," Carter said, squeezing his shoulder as he headed for the door.

Luke wished he *was* good enough for Casey.

By Casey's next session, Luke was impatient to see him, especially as it was the last session of the day. They had sent messages back and forth, not quite crossing the line in their content, but on the verge of something. He hadn't lied to his brothers. He would give Casey all the time he needed, but it didn't stop his right hand from getting a workout.

As the session ended, Luke found he didn't want Casey to leave. "Would you like to get some dinner? Together?"

Casey paused, gaze roaming Luke's face, making Luke want to fidget. "Yeah, okay."

Luke smiled, his heart pounding a frantic rhythm. "Great. I'll meet you at the exit when you're ready?"

"Sure."

Luke had a thought. "Oh. Do you need to use the staff changing rooms again? Because you can." He wasn't sure if Casey had been showering after their sessions or not, but he didn't want to cause any issues for him.

"It's fine. I'm all right with the member's ones. I need to face it at some point. Thanks, though."

In some ways, Luke was glad of it because if they were both showering at the same time, he wasn't sure he'd be able to keep his reactions to a wet and naked Casey to himself.

They parted ways, and Luke headed to get ready. Spending a little more time than usual on his hairstyle, he took a little longer than he wanted. He met Casey at reception, where he was talking to Portia, the receptionist, to whom Luke said his goodbyes and held the door for Casey, seeing Portia's smile from the corner of his eye. He chose to ignore it.

"I was thinking we could go to Pop's. Would that be good?" Luke said.

"Fine with me. I love Pop's." Casey grinned.

"All right. Do you want to meet me there, or do you want to come with me, and I'll drop you back here?"

Casey bit his lip and glanced in the direction of his car. "I'll meet you there if that's okay."

"Of course, it is."

Casey smiled and walked backwards. "I'll see you shortly."

Luke nodded, studying Casey's strong body as he turned and strode away. He waited until Casey was safely ensconced in his car before heading to his. By the time he was ready to leave the car park, Casey's car had already gone, but as he pulled into the car park of Pop's, he saw Casey waiting, and he sighed as his muscles unclenched.

They met at the halfway point, smiling at each other and quietly entered the small but amazing café. Pop's had been around for years, as long as Luke could remember. He loved the calm atmosphere, and when he wasn't at Sweet Tooth, or now Crush as he'd been going there more often, he was at Pop's. The gentle murmur of conversation surrounded them as they headed towards the server.

"Luke! Nice to see ya again. And Casey. We don't see ya in here as often as we should, my boy." Maria's Scottish accent made Luke smile, and he leaned in for a hug, pulling back and letting Casey receive one too.

"I know. Work keeps me far too busy nowadays, Maria," Casey replied.

"Go grab a seat, and I'll be with ya in a jiffy."

"Thanks." Luke rested a hand on Casey's lower back, without thinking, until Casey's gaze met his. "Sorry," he said, removing his hand.

"Don't be. I like it," Casey whispered.

Luke checked his expression, then returned his hand to its original place, feeling his cheeks heat. He couldn't feel any warmth through Casey's clothes, but he could feel the movement in his spine. When Casey stopped by a table, he raised his eyebrows to which Luke nodded in reply.

Just as they sat, a booming voice called to them from across the room. "Boys! Nice to see you."

Pop came across the room with a jug of water at a slower clip than he usually did but with the same amount of vigour. They both rose to embrace the older man, and Luke noticed his frailty. He glanced over at Casey, seeing his forehead creased and a glimmer in his eyes as he wrapped his arms around the older man. Luke wondered if his thoughts had gone to Old Joe as Luke's had.

"How have you been?"

"Good, thanks, Pop. Busy as always," Luke replied, sitting once more. "How's business?"

"Ah, same as always. I'm not getting any younger, though."

"All your customers keep you young, Pop," Casey remarked.

Pop chuckled, filling their glasses. "Well, don't be a stranger, you two. And tell your families, too. They need to come to visit more often."

Luke knew Pop's words weren't a sales pitch. Pop wouldn't care if they all came in to say hi and left again, but his slowed demeanour made Luke realise life was short. He would message his parents later, telling them to visit.

"We'll make sure we do," Casey agreed.

"That'll be grand. Well, enjoy your food, boys." Pop squeezed both their shoulders and retraced his steps through the kitchen door.

Luke looked to Casey, who's eyes were on the door Pop walked through. "Are you okay?"

Casey sighed and glanced at him. "Yeah. Reminders are hard. Life is so short, you know," he said, echoing Luke's earlier thoughts.

"They are."

"Anyhow… let's choose."

They both picked up the menu, though they probably knew it by heart; Luke knew *he* did.

"I love the smell of this place. It's not quite as compelling as Sweet Tooth, but you could almost figure out where you were just from scenting the place. Maybe we should do that as a game one night," Casey said with a grin. "Can you figure out where you are from the smell of the place?"

Luke chuckled. "I'd be happy to have a go, just don't give me the bowling alley."

Casey snorted his water and started coughing, patting his chest. "God! Don't do that!"

"Sorry." Luke rolled his lips inwards to stop himself from laughing.

Maria came to take their order, and they lapsed into silence. He couldn't bring himself to look at Casey in case his eyes professed everything he was feeling. Luke wasn't sure what to say that didn't revolve around how he felt or their sessions. He didn't want to cross any boundaries with Casey. The man had been through enough already without Luke adding to the burden. Casey deserved to be with someone amazing, someone worthy of him. The idea that Casey had agreed to have dinner with him both elated and confused him at the same time. Why Casey wanted to spend time with him, Luke had no idea, but he would not take back the invite because Luke wanted this. Even if this was all he could ever hope for.

"I won't bite, you know."

The humour in Casey's voice had Luke flicking his gaze to him and the heat seeping into his cheeks again. He cupped the back of his neck. "I know. Sorry."

"You're thinking too hard." Casey reached forward and rested his hand on the table, palm uppermost, waving his fingers in a 'come on' gesture.

Luke licked his lips and placed his hand in Casey's, who enclosed his fingers and rubbed his thumb over Luke's knuckles. A tingling followed the movement.

"Are you busy after dinner?" Luke shook his head. "Okay. You're coming to my house."

CHAPTER ELEVEN

CASEY

There was minimal talk during their dinner as if something unspoken had passed between them, and they didn't want to ruin the atmosphere. Nothing could spoil Casey's mood. He *needed* Luke. It had been building in him since they'd first met, and he'd had enough. When he had been with Marcus, it was easier to fight his emotions and push them away. Now, he didn't need to. He'd reached his limit and was pushing for what he wanted—what he knew they both wanted.

Luke paid for their meal despite Casey's argument. He acquiesced after a few minutes, determined to pay for the next one because he was certain there would be more.

As they stood beside Casey's car, Casey watched as Luke paused, rubbing his thumb into his opposite palm —a tell Casey recognised as Luke being uncomfortable.

"What's wrong?" Casey asked.

Luke shook his head. "Nothing. I..." He sighed and glanced away for a second. When their gazes met again, he continued, "I don't want to push you into something you're not ready for."

Smiling slowly, he took one step closer and lowered his voice, "Trust me, Luke."

Casey tried to convey with his expressions that he was more than ready for this next step. When he saw Luke's shoulders relax, he knew Luke understood. He climbed into his car, smiling as Luke waited until he was safely closed in before heading to his own car. He knew Luke would be mindful of Casey's situation at work, but he didn't want Luke to be careful. He wanted to forget his troubles. He wanted to be taken. Devoured. Owned.

Casey pulled out of the car park, checking to make sure Luke followed behind him, and directed the car towards home. He didn't have any reservations about what he knew was going to happen, what he'd instigated. In fact, he wanted it more than anything.

His driveway was blessedly empty this time, Marcus hopefully getting the picture Casey was no longer interested in what he had to say. Marcus didn't have a key, so there would be no interruptions to his and Luke's evening plans. He hoped.

As he stopped the car, he checked the time, realising it was just after eight. He didn't have to work for the next two days, which he was pleased about because it meant he could spend more time with Luke. Although he had no idea when Luke was next supposed to work.

When Luke pulled up to the kerb, Casey's heart began to race. He climbed out of the car and watched as Luke walked up the path towards him. The muscles Casey knew were there were hidden beneath the black jacket, although, as his eyes wandered down the perfect specimen in front of him, he could see Luke's thigh muscles were barely contained in the jeans.

Casey clenched his jaw against the heat suffusing his body, smiled and pivoted towards his front door without saying a word. The soft crunch of stones indicated Luke trailed behind him. The key opened the door without issue this time, for which Casey was immensely grateful. He needed to get it fixed, but that was a thought for another day.

Once they were inside, Luke hesitated, flicking his keys between his hands.

"Relax," Casey said, although it was the furthest thing from what *he* was at that moment. His hands trembled as he placed his keys on a hook in the hallway and removed his jacket. His heart raced as he watched Luke shrug off his own, then hang it in the same place as Casey had done. "Would you like a drink?"

Luke shook his head, and they stared at each other. Casey inhaled and grabbed Luke's hand, rubbing his knuckles again.

"Are you sure?" Luke asked, voice low.

The corner of Casey's mouth quirked up. "Hell, yeah."

Within seconds, he was yanked forward and pressed against Luke's chest, their mouths colliding. Casey distantly registered the sound of Luke's keys thunking to the floor when Luke's arms wrapped around him, crushing him against the solid mass of muscles. Marcus had muscles, but his were overworked; Luke's were the perfect size for Casey to feel safe and not overwhelmed.

Casey slid his arms around to Luke's back, one hand resting between his shoulder blades, the other gripping the material of Luke's t-shirt. His head was pushed back with the force of their kiss until Luke's hand came around and cupped the back, pulling them closer still. Luke's tongue licked inside Casey's mouth, drawing a moan from Casey, more so when Luke palmed his ass and rubbed their groins together.

Heat radiated through him, and Casey stumbled back a step, Luke following, their lips fused in an intense exchange that Casey felt all the way to his toes. A solid object stopped Casey's backwards momentum, and Luke used it to his advantage, gripping Casey's face and deepening their kiss, even though Casey was already running out of air.

When he became light-headed, he tore his lips away, gasping as air refilled his lungs. Luke didn't pause. Kisses rained down Casey's neck, sending shivers down his spine as Luke's hands smoothed along the fabric covering Casey. After reaching the hem of Casey's t-shirt, Luke slid his hands underneath, Casey's abdomen contracting with the arousal flowing through him at the feather-light touch.

Casey's hands repositioned themselves in Luke's hair, threading through the strands and gripping when

Luke lifted Casey's t-shirt to his underarms and proceeded to kiss down his chest.

"Jesus, Luke." Casey's head dropped back, knocking against the bannister as his eyes closed. Warm, wet lips enclosed one of his nubs, and Casey jerked, his hips thrusting against air but needing so much more. "Please."

Cool air flowed over his freed nipple, and Luke lifted his head, capturing Casey's mouth once more. Impatience increased the speed of his actions, and Casey reached for Luke's t-shirt, ripping it over his head once their lips parted. Luke was perfection personified. Casey watched the path of his fingertips following the muscles and valleys that formed Luke's body, goosebumps rising in his wake.

A groan sounded from Luke, and Casey lifted his gaze to him, seeing barely contained desire. "I need you, Casey." Luke's voice rumbled through his chest and onto Casey's palms.

Casey smiled slowly, replying, "Good job. I need you, too." It killed him to move, but Casey pushed against Luke, who immediately retreated. "Follow me."

The bannister creaked as Casey righted himself, and he turned, taking the stairs two at a time and stripping his t-shirt as he went. A chuckle floated up behind him. Casey glanced over his shoulder to check if Luke was following him and saw him removing his trainers before starting up the steps.

The fit of Casey's jeans felt tighter than usual, but it was no wonder with how hard he was. Turning to watch

Luke ascend, his fingers moved to his button and flicked it open, his eyes never leaving Luke's, though Luke's dipped to follow Casey's movements.

Ocean blue eyes darkened the closer Luke came to Casey's position. As Casey drew the zipper down, he began walking backwards, knowing the route to his bedroom by heart, but his knees trembling with every step. Luke palmed his own erection as he tilted his head, eyes fastened on Casey's groin.

"Show me." Luke's husky voice rolled over Casey, and he inhaled shakily as he parted his jeans. His cock sprang from the denim material, Casey having not put any boxers on after his shower. "Fuck."

The relief his shaft had gained from being free from confinement was reduced with one word. Casey's dick hardened, and it was all Casey could do to not orgasm there and then. He wrapped his hand around the base of his cock and squeezed enough to know he wasn't going to explode before continuing down his hallway and to his bedroom door. Luke stalked him. There was no other word for it. Despite having no shoes, Luke's footsteps were sure and solid, making his intentions clear.

Lifting his chin and biting his lip, Casey pivoted and pushed through his door, racing across the space to the end of his bed. As much as he wanted to be caught, he also wanted to make sure they were near enough to forgo needing to stop any time soon.

Luke entered the room, kicking the door shut behind him, and prowled towards Casey. Gone was the unsure guy. Gone was the shy guy. In its place was a man who knew what he wanted, and by the looks of him, Luke wanted Casey fiercely. The stalking didn't stop. Luke came closer until he crowded against Casey and took his lips in a hard, controlling kiss, bending Casey backwards but not letting him fall.

Unable to do anything but grip Luke's biceps and feel, Casey allowed his body to relax, knowing Luke would keep him safe. His cock was trapped between their bodies and was not-so-quietly demanding release. Casey moved his hips, his shaft rubbing against the warm denim of Luke's jeans.

Luke finally pulled away, breathing heavily as was Casey. Standing upright, Luke slid his hands into the back of Casey's jeans and pushed them down his legs. Luke went to his knees, leaving kisses along Casey's chest and stomach. Casey's fingers combed through Luke's light-brown hair, needing the tactile connection even when his brain was misfiring. Or maybe *especially* because his brain was misfiring.

Hardly any words were spoken between them. They were not needed. Every touch, every look, every sigh, every groan communicated how much they wanted— no, *needed*—this. Everything that happened outside of these four walls disappeared while they worshipped each other's bodies.

As Casey stepped out of his jeans, leaving him naked, Luke lifted his gaze to Casey's. Need blazed in the dilated pupils, and Luke's forehead creased, a grimace gracing his lips. Casey knew Luke craved this as much as he did.

Casey cupped Luke's jaw as they gazed at each other, his thumbs brushing against his cheeks. Luke's nostrils flared, and his gaze redirected to Casey's cock, standing proud between them. When Luke licked his lips, Casey groaned and closed his eyes against the picture it presented, but they flew open when the tip of his cock was encased in wet heat. Luke kept his mouth around the head of his dick, but his tongue was occupied, licking the sensitive underside, the slit and under the hood while Casey transferred his grip to Luke's shoulders, panting softly and trying not to come yet.

Luke dropped his mouth down, encasing Casey's dick fully before lifting. He licked his palm and wrapped his hand around Casey's cock. He slowly stroked, twisting with every lift and drop. Luke's gaze locked with Casey's as he dribbled saliva onto Casey's cock. Casey bit his lip against the impatience ramping up his need. Luke's hand continued its pumping as he rose to his feet, nibbling at each of Casey's nipples before claiming his mouth once more.

Casey wrapped his arms around Luke's neck, lifting onto his toes, and returned the kiss with more fervour than before. His blood was boiling with the need to come, but he wanted Luke resting over him, caging him in, coming with him.

With that thought, Casey pulled back, panting, and ripped open Luke's jeans, pushing them down forcefully and leaving Luke in his briefs. Luke used his feet to remove his jeans completely, and Casey's hands slid into Luke's underwear, cupping his ass. Casey sat on the edge of the bed as he hooked the waistband with his fingers and pulled them over the impressive bulge. When Luke's uncut cock was released, Casey murmured in anticipation of having it in his mouth. He quickly forgot about his plan to get Luke naked and wrapped his hand around the heated shaft. Eyes glued to the sight of the foreskin covering and revealing the cock, Casey saw when a drop of precome escaped.

Casey leaned forward, extending his tongue to lick the precome, whimpering at the taste of Luke. He pulled the foreskin back enough for the head to peek through and proceeded to lick the slit, head and foreskin as Luke moaned incoherently above him. His tongue ventured under the foreskin a little to see if it was something Luke enjoyed, and when he received a choked cry, he continued. He knew not everyone liked the feeling but was glad Luke seemed to.

After several minutes of worshipping Luke's cock, Luke pulled away and pressed Casey onto his back. "Move up," Luke growled.

Casey pushed himself up the bed until his head was on a pillow and spread his trembling legs, watching as Luke crawled over him. Smoothing his hands up Luke's arms, Casey smiled, his legs cradling the firm body. "Luke?" He waited until Luke's gaze was on him. "Fuck me, please."

Luke's gaze darkened, and his jaw clenched. "Supplies?"

Casey indicated the bedside table with his head, and Luke stretched out to open the top drawer, removing a condom and lube. Dropping them beside Casey, Luke leaned down and took his mouth in a soft, gentle kiss, sipping from his lips, his tongue lazily tangling with Casey's. Closing his eyes, Casey allowed the play as he melted into the bed. Luke's hips lowered, and they both groaned when their cocks came into contact.

"Now, Luke," he whined.

Luke lifted his head and smirked. "So demanding." He reached for the lube and lifted onto his knees, Casey losing the heat of Luke's body and wishing he could take back his words. At least until Luke slicked his fingers and reached for Casey's hole. When Luke's finger pressed against him, Casey pressed his head back into the pillow. "You okay?"

"Fuck, yes. Hurry." His patience was wearing thin.

Luke chuckled but pressed forward, breaching Casey's entrance past the ring quickly. He pumped his finger in and out a few times before continuing with two fingers, then three before he appeared satisfied. Casey was moaning and writhing on the bed by that time and repeatedly asked Luke to hurry the fuck up.

When Luke reached for the condom, Casey blew out a breath, trying to get his hyper-sensitive body under control. He wanted to feel every inch of Luke entering him and didn't want his orgasm to come so soon that he missed it.

Having donned the protection and slicked up, Luke placed one hand next to Casey's head and leaned down to join their mouths as he pressed his cock into Casey's channel. Casey widened his legs and bore down as the pressure became intense. His mouth grew lax under Luke's lips and tongue as he allowed Luke to possess his body. Luke entered and withdrew in small thrusts until he was fully seated and held himself above Casey, balancing on both hands.

Seeing the trembling in his arms, Casey pulled Luke down on top of him, wrapping his legs around Luke's back and his arms around his neck. "You're perfect, Luke." He pressed a kiss to his mouth. "I've been very patient. Now, please, fuck me!"

Shaking his head and smiling, Luke pulled back and thrust forward in one go, over and over, bringing them closer to their release. Casey's cock received friction from their movements, and he knew he could blow any time. Luke's hips increased as their lips joined in a passionate kiss until Luke rose to his knees. The change in position had Casey arching his back and gripping at the sheets beneath him because Luke hit his prostate with every drive.

"I'm close, Luke."

"Fuck, yes." Luke grabbed Casey's legs, resting his feet against Luke's shoulders as he powered into him while holding Casey's thighs.

"Oh, shit."

Luke's hips kept up their punishing rhythm as he leaned forward onto his hands, opening Casey further, and hammered into him.

"Fuck, fuck, fuck!" Casey reached above him to grab

hold of the headboard as his orgasm tunnelled down his spine.

"Casey!" Luke's rhythm faltered as his climax overcame him, and Casey watched through half-lidded eyes as Luke threw his head back and growled, his expression pained, as Casey's orgasm hit. His release painted his chest and neck, curled up as he was, but he didn't care as the ecstasy flowed through him. His muscles clenched and released rhythmically until he was left boneless.

Luke allowed his legs to drop to the bed and lowered himself to his elbows, resting his forehead against Casey's shoulder as he breathed heavily. "Fuck, Casey. I think you killed me."

Casey snickered but said nothing. All he did was wrap his arms around Luke and hold him tight, not wanting him to leave any time soon.

CHAPTER TWELVE

LUKE

"Let me get rid of the condom, and I'll be back." He pressed a kiss to Casey's sweaty shoulder and pulled back even though he didn't want to. Casey's arms dropped to the bed as if he had no energy left. Luke knew the feeling; he didn't think he had come that hard in a long time, if ever. "Where's the bathroom?"

"Door next to mine," Casey mumbled.

Luke stood, removing the condom as he opened the bedroom door and headed to the next room, glad that Casey lived alone. He cleaned himself up, disposed of the condom and wet a cloth. Returning to the bedroom, he chuckled as he found Casey in the same position he'd left him.

"I'm going to clean you."

He received a minute nod, so he wiped away the evidence of Casey's pleasure. Glancing around, he saw a washing basket and dropped the cloth in before crawling back onto the bed. Casey's arms half-heartedly lifted, and Luke assumed it meant Casey wanted him closer, so he laid next to him, resting his head on Casey's shoulder, his arm over his waist. When Casey's arms enclosed him, he sighed. It wasn't often he was in this position. Usually, he was the one holding the other person. He liked it, and a sense of rightness settled inside him.

Shadows were creeping into the room as the sun dipped below the horizon, and Luke didn't want to move, but Casey hadn't invited him to stay, so he needed to get himself up. As he moved, Casey tightened his grip.

"Stay, Marcus."

Luke flinched, then pulled away.

"Shit! Luke! I meant Luke! God, I'm so sorry. I was half asleep, and it slipped out. Luke, I'm so sorry. I didn't mean it."

Luke ignored his words and continued to get dressed, looking around the room for his t-shirt before remembering it was downstairs. He couldn't believe he'd let himself get involved with someone who was clearly—although not to Luke—still in love with someone else. He gave a slow, disbelieving shake of his head, nausea roiling in his stomach and headed to the bedroom door.

Casey grabbed his arm, trying to stop him. "Luke, please."

Luke shrugged him off and left the room, swallowing hard against the thickness in his throat and jogging down the stairs to tug on his t-shirt when he found it. He was pulling on his trainers when Casey ran down the steps, stopping in front of him, having pulled on some joggers and a jumper.

"I really am sorry. I can only explain by saying I was half asleep, and I've been with Marcus for five months. My brain hadn't caught up. I'm so sorry."

Luke looked at Casey and shook his head again, his mouth opening but realising he had nothing to say. He lifted his coat from the peg, grabbed his keys from the floor and exited the house with Casey's pleading following him. He should've known better than to think someone was interested in him as a person. He thought Casey was different, but he obviously wanted someone to warm his bed. No one wanted someone who couldn't even get a decent job as his siblings had, Luke would be no good at anything else.

His car started the first time, which was a bonus, and he drove off without glancing at Casey's house. He swallowed hard against the threat of tears. Well, if nothing else, he got laid. It was more than he had done for a while. The other guy didn't count.

What the hell had he been thinking? Why would someone like Casey, who was a bloody paramedic, for god's sake, want anything to do with him for more than sex? Even Casey was higher up on the job ladder than Luke was.

He white-knuckled the steering wheel and blew out a breath. It didn't matter. He would go back to being the same old Luke everyone knew and forget about

Casey and their time together. He'd stay single and alone. That would be the best option. He didn't need the drama having a relationship brought with it. With that decided, he headed home.

Luke was on tenterhooks by Sunday—Casey's next appointment. After he was ready for his day ahead, Luke checked his schedule, seeing a full day again, but not seeing Casey's name.

"Portia? Is this right? I had Casey booked in this afternoon, didn't I?"

Portia checked her computer and nodded. "Yes, you did, but he called yesterday to cancel. Said he'd been called into work."

Luke gave a bitter smile. "Thanks." He took the paper and headed down the corridor, the clank of the weights usually soothing, but today, grating. Yesterday, he'd made himself busy. On purpose. He went to his parents' house for the day and helped them out doing odd jobs, which had needed to be done for a while. It's amazing what he achieved when he needed the distraction. His parents were over the moon with the new lighting fixture he had put in. He'd stayed for dinner, too, which was a bonus as he hadn't been food shopping like he was supposed to, and his mum sent him home with leftovers. Win, win.

Entering his training room, he checked who his first client was and went about setting the room up. By lunchtime, Luke was hot, bothered and ready to go home and slide into bed for the next few days. Unfortunately, he had three more clients to see after lunch.

Traipsing to the staffroom, Luke tried to decide what to do that night. His parents had a rare night out at the theatre that Samuel had treated them to for Dad's retirement, and he had no idea what his siblings were doing. He rarely socialised with them anyway. Well, except Trent when they went to Crush, but that wouldn't be happening any time soon.

He grabbed his phone from his locker and his food from the fridge before sagging into a chair by the window and studying the raindrops on the glass. The weather mirrored how Luke felt, and it had since Saturday morning.

Shaking his head, Luke checked his phone, seeing five messages. Three were from Casey, which he ignored; one was from his brother Carter, asking if he was free on Wednesday to which he replied yes; and the final one was from Theo, asking what cakes Luke wanted him to bring that afternoon. That brightened his mood. Theo always brought cakes in for the staff when he had sessions with him, which was twice a week. The staff had never been so taken care of until Theo let it slip that he worked at a bakery. Portia's eyes had grown round, and Theo had joked about it being a sin having sweet food around health nuts, but Portia soon put the idea to rest.

Since then, Theo brought something each time he came.

"You can bring anything or nothing; it wouldn't matter to these people," Luke muttered, slowly shaking his head. Theo replied he would bring something, and could he also bring Jasper to watch? Usually, Luke wanted the sessions to be one-on-one because the client needed to focus on what was being taught, but Luke knew having Jasper there would not distract Theo from what he needed to learn, so he agreed.

Messages taken care of, he rested his phone on the table and dug into his egg salad. He supposed he should read the ones Casey sent, but he didn't think anything Casey said would change Luke's mind, so what was the point? There were over twenty messages and voicemails waiting on his phone, and his mind kept coming back around to the fact he had told Casey he could call him anytime day or night, especially if he was in trouble, and he'd hate it if Casey got hurt because Luke hadn't been answering.

Suitably chastened by his own conscience, Luke grimaced but picked up his phone again. Going to the messages first, he scrolled through them, seeing nothing but apologies and the same excuse he'd used when he'd contacted reception to cancel their appointment today. Checking the voicemails, he listened to the last one, which had been left around two hours ago.

"Luke, I know you don't want to hear from me, but I want to apologise. No excuse in the world can explain why I said Marcus instead of your name. Yes, I was tired. Yes, I was half-asleep, but it shouldn't have happened, and I'm so sorry. I truly am. I'm also sorry I couldn't get to our session today. I was called into work yesterday due to the number of accidents that happened this weekend. I'm working again today, and then my usual shifts for the next four days. I would like to talk to you if you'll let me. Well, I better get back to work. I'm sorry, Luke. Please don't let this be the end of us."

Luke's throat had closed up at the first sound of Casey's voice, but he couldn't stop the memory from repeating in his head. Casey saying another man's name when Luke was in his bed. He deleted all the voicemails and placed his phone on the table, staring outside while he fed his body what it needed to get through the remainder of the day.

At least he had Theo and Jasper, who, when they arrived, carried a dozen small cake boxes. Portia squealed as if she was a five-year-old and had never seen a cake before, even though they were brought in each time. Luke shook his head and grinned.

"If you spoil her too much, you'll never be able to leave," he said to Theo.

Theo flushed. "I don't mind."

Jasper chuckled. "Trust me. This is the best job in the world for him. Baking cakes all day long is how he relaxes."

Luke snickered when Theo elbowed Jasper, the latter fake-groaning as if Theo had punched him. Once the cakes were safely delivered to the staffroom, they carried on to the training room, Theo telling Luke about what had happened at the bakery that day. One good thing that had come about from Theo and Jasper's stalking incident—if anyone could say there was a good thing—was Theo learning to take some extra time away from Sweet Tooth. Even though he loved it there, Jasper had been worried he was working too much. Since Theo had come to Luke, he had reduced his hours to allow for the sessions. It wasn't much, but it was better than twenty-four-seven.

"Come on. Let's get started."

Luke took Theo through his warm-up routine and started by testing his reflexes. Several times, Theo ended up on the floor, and Luke could see Jasper wince from the corner of his eye, but Theo laughed and got right back up again. While they had a five-minute break, Jasper wrapped his arms around Theo with no regard for how sweaty he was. Luke transferred his gaze to the window, clenching his jaw, his mood lowering again. Unfortunately, Theo noticed the change in his demeanour when they started up again.

"What's the matter?" Theo stopped and tilted his head at Luke. "Something's happened."

Luke shook his head, ready to deny everything, but Jasper said, "Yeah, I noticed it, too."

Rubbing the back of his neck, he sighed and placed his hands on his hips. "Guy trouble. I'm fine."

"No, you're not. Tell me." Theo dropped to the mat with a groan and folded his legs. Jasper walked over with their drinks and sat behind Theo, who rested back against him with a smile.

Luke stared at the floor for a moment before sighing again and sitting down, thanking Jasper for his drink.

Resting his arms on his bent legs, he played with the lid of his bottle. He wasn't sure where to start.

"Amanda always tells me it's better to start at the beginning," Theo prompted.

Luke cleared his throat. "Some of it I can't tell you because of confidentiality, but I started having feelings for one of my clients." Theo's eyebrows rose, but he didn't interrupt. "The feelings appeared to be reciprocated, but he was already in a relationship. When their relationship ended, we slowly worked up to getting together. On Friday, we went out for dinner. And then…" He waved his hand to give them the idea they knew what had happened.

"And?"

"After, he asked me to stay, except he said the other guy's name, his ex's."

"Oh my god! What did you do?" Theo asked.

"I left. What else could I do?" Luke scoffed. "Way to make me feel like I meant something," he muttered.

Theo left Jasper's arms and came over to Luke, resting his hand on Luke's arm. "Sometimes, things happen the way they're supposed to. Occasionally, you'll get hurt because of it. I'd have a break for a bit, then sit down with him and talk it over. If you like him that much, it would be worth having a conversation if nothing else."

"Communication is everything. And part of communication is listening. Both sides need to listen, and both sides need to talk." Jasper's words hit a chord in Luke, and his breath hitched.

"You're right. It hurts."

"If he means anything at all to you, it will hurt."

"Thanks, guys."

Theo was Luke's last session as Casey had cancelled, so he hit the showers and directed the car towards home.

After he'd fixed his dinner, he braced his elbows on the table, staring at his phone before typing a message.

I've received your messages. Give me some time. I'll be in touch.

He'd had a long conversation with Otto about it once he'd plucked up the courage to explain what an idiot he was. To which Otto slapped him upside the head—over the phone, naturally—and told him not to be stupid. Casey was in the wrong. It didn't make it any easier to swallow.

Three days later, he had not received any more messages or voicemails from Casey, and although it was what he had asked for, he found he didn't like not having them to look at. Even when he wasn't looking at them.

He sat at the dinner table at his parents' house as Carter had requested, but there was no obvious reason for the summons. Either that or everyone thought he already knew, which was possible. Internally, he rolled his eyes. It was the usual case with his family. He was always the last to know something. He listened to the words of those around him but barely contributed to the conversation; he didn't have the energy.

After dinner, they had apple pie and custard, but before it was eaten, Carter gained everyone's attention.

"Thank you for coming." He looked at Lia and smiled, and Luke knew what was coming. "We have some news. We are expecting a baby."

The room exploded into shouts, squeals, conversation and the scraping of chairs as everyone went to congratulate the parents-to-be.

Luke sighed and slumped in his chair as he waited his turn. Yet another thing he would never be able to do... give his parents' grandchildren. He plastered on his smile when he approached Carter and Lia.

"Congratulations," he said through the thickness in his throat, hugging them both.

"Thank you," Carter replied. "Did you hear any more about your friend?"

Luke frowned and realised he'd never even spoken to Casey about what his brothers had said. "I've not been able to speak to him yet. But I will."

"Definitely speak to him. It sounds like he needs all the help he can get." Carter squeezed his biceps.

Thoroughly chastened yet again, even though he knew Carter didn't mean it that way, Luke bid good-night not long after. It was past nine o'clock by the time he got home, and once he'd settled himself on the sofa with a movie, he picked up his phone, debating whether to text or call. He decided to call as he knew Casey was working that night if Luke had got the shift pattern right.

When the call went to voicemail, he cleared his throat. "Hey, it's me. Um… I spoke to my brothers, you know, the lawyers, about what's happening to you. I didn't name names or anything," he said quickly. "They have some ideas about what you could do to help prove what's going on. I'm not sure if you're interested or not. Call me back. Bye."

He shut off the phone and rested his head on the back of the sofa. "Idiot." He hated leaving messages; he always sounded stupid. Staring at the TV, he watched the action, only half paying attention while his thoughts batted back and forth.

His phone ringing woke him, and he cursed when he moved his neck and pain streaked through him from how he had slept on the sofa. Fumbling around for his phone, he finally located it and squinted at the screen to answer it.

"Hello?" he mumbled.

"Luke?"

Cascy's voice had him blearily opening his eyes. "Hold on." Luke put the phone down and rubbed at his face, trying to wake up before he had this conversation. "Okay, I'm back." He grabbed his glass of water and gulped the disgusting room temperature liquid.

"I'm sorry I woke you. I thought you might be up."

"What time is it?"

"Eleven."

Luke cleared his throat. "Usually, I would be. I fell asleep on the sofa."

"Sorry. Do you want me to call back tomorrow?"

"No!" Luke pulled back the enthusiasm, taking shallow breaths to calm his heart rate. "No, it's okay. I'm awake now."

He heard Casey sigh on the other end. "I am sorry, Luke. I know it's unforgivable, what I did, but I am sorry."

Luke's heart broke at the weariness he heard in Casey's voice. It also pricked his instincts. "What's happened, Casey?"

"Nothing. I'm all right. I was returning your call."

"Casey."

"I'm fine."

He didn't sound fine, not one bit, but if Casey wasn't willing to tell him, what could Luke do? Mentally slapping himself in the head, he realised he could explain about his brothers. "Yes, my brothers. Sorry, my brain is a little foggy." He wet his lips, trying to circumvent his dry mouth.

Casey gave a half-hearted chuckle. "It's okay."

Luke reiterated what his brothers had told him about getting evidence of their interactions. Casey wasn't sure whether he would be able to because of the confidentiality policies of the hospital, but he agreed he might be able to catch some voice recordings if they were in the locker room or something.

He hesitated. "Are you going to tell me what's wrong?" Luke asked. He knew something had happened because Casey was not his usual bubbly self, and it can't just be because of their last encounter. "What did the asshole do?" His chest tightened, and his hands trembled with the thought that something had happened to him.

"I'm fine. Don't worry about me."

"Of course, I'm going to worry about you. I care about—" he faltered, having not wanted to expose his true feelings. "I care about what happens to you."

There was a pause. "I care about you, too. Bye, Luke."

The phone went dead, and Luke cursed. Not because Casey had figured out what he'd tried to hide, but because Casey was hiding something. Was it his job to find out what? Or should he leave it because Casey obviously didn't want him involved in his life? He wasn't sure.

CHAPTER THIRTEEN

CASEY

As he hung up the phone, Casey withheld a sob behind his hand. He would've broken down if he'd stayed on the phone any longer. Luke needed to be kept as far away from this debacle as he could.

The information Luke had given him from his brothers had been good advice, but he wasn't sure how helpful it would be if he wasn't at the hospital. Since the incident earlier that day—he shuddered at the thought—he wasn't sure if he *could* return. He and Chloe were on a break, parked in a layby while they ate, or at least, while he *tried* to eat. He climbed back into the cab after he hung up, smiling over at Chloe, though avoiding eye contact.

"All sorted?" she asked.

"Yeah," he replied. He could feel her eyes burning into him, but there was nothing he could do to alleviate her concerns when he had to keep his emotions locked down. It was the only way he would get through the night.

He ate on autopilot, finishing his drink before putting everything away, fatigue pulling at him. A hand landing on his arm had him flinching and Chloe pulling back sharply.

"Shit, sorry." She frowned and narrowed her gaze. "What's happened to make you so jumpy?"

"Nothing." He cleared his face of emotion and smiled.

"Bullshit."

"I'm fine."

"Says the man who jumped ten feet in the air at an action that usually would've calmed him."

Casey couldn't deny her words, but he also couldn't tell her what had happened. No one in the hospital could know. He turned to gaze out of the window and into the darkness, even though he couldn't see a damn thing. Closing his eyes, he clenched his jaw against the memory.

Acker's cock sprang from his open trousers, and he rubbed it against Casey's stomach, thankfully covered by his uniform.

"Come on, Casey. You have wanted this for months. We finally have time." Acker's voice whispered into his ear, making him shiver. "Fuck, you have me so hard."

The doctor's hips thrust against Casey's stomach, leaving a wet mark on his shirt.

Casey struggled against Acker's double-handed hold on his wrists even as the doctor's thrusts increased.

"That's it. Move against me."

Casey opened his eyes and breathed in deeply, letting the air escape slowly and quietly. He was saved from more questions by a call coming in. He was glad he was able to focus on the people he was helping, but if his ability to do his job began to diminish, he would call someone else in. He refused to put other people's lives in danger because of what was happening to him.

It had all started with the multi-car crash on the motorway on Saturday. It was supposed to have been his day off, but he'd been called in when there were more patients than staff could handle. Although he was a paramedic, he offered to help in A&E if needed. He and Alex had worked side by side several times throughout the afternoon and night until everyone had been dealt with. Sunday was a write-off because he'd been working for around seventeen hours, so he'd spent the day sleeping. Then, he'd had the start of his shifts as normal on Monday.

Through it all, he had managed to avoid Acker for the most part. He'd made the occasional comment about how working out was doing Casey a heap of favours because he looked amazing, and other small things. He'd even copped a feel of Casey's ass when they'd been working on the same patient once. But things like that, Casey could deal with.

Unfortunately, things had become worse that evening. Their first call had been a pregnant lady in dire need of a hospital. Once they had rushed her in, Casey had told Chloe he was going to grab his phone, which he'd left in his locker.

He would never forget his phone again.

"Casey!" Casey glanced over at Chloe. "Any updates?"

He checked the responder unit. "No, nothing else. We're almost there."

Casey concentrated on his job, forgetting about everything else apart from what his patients needed from him. As the night wore on, he found himself relaxing more and becoming calmer.

"You know, if you ever need an ear, Casey, I'm here. All right?"

Casey stared at his hands, knowing she knew something wasn't right, but unable to share his turmoil. "I know. Thank you."

She sighed and took them back to the hospital. The last place he wanted to be, but the only place he *could* be at the moment.

The nearer they drew, the more rigid his muscles became, all the calmness from earlier gone.

"Let me hear you moan, Casey. I'd love the sound in my ear." Acker huffed as he thrust against Casey.

Casey refused to let any noise exit his mouth. He couldn't make anyone else aware of what was happening because he knew the doctor would turn it back on him, and Casey would lose his job. He was pissed he couldn't get out of the hold the doctor had on him. His wrists were crossed at his back, and Acker held his opposite wrists, giving Casey no leverage to fight. All his work with Luke was for nothing.

"Fuck, you feel so good." Acker groaned against the skin of Casey's neck, and Casey's skin pebbled with goosebumps. The

doctor's tongue lapped at the skin of his neck as his thrusts increased. "Come on, Casey. Come on, baby."

Casey squeezed his eyes shut and turned his thoughts to his family, trying to dispel the negative thoughts. He was excited to see everyone again on Sunday after missing the previous week. It happened more than he wanted, but he revelled in the closeness they had when they were able to get together.

Chloe parked the ambulance in the bay, and they grabbed their belongings before heading into the hospital. They signed off their shift after passing the takeover information onto their replacements. Both chatted as they went to the locker room, and although Casey could feel a trembling in his muscles as he walked in, he breathed easier when he realised there were only two other people in there, and neither was Acker.

He hurried through his routine, swapping out stuff from his locker and trying not to look at the corner where the locker room turned into the shower room. His pulse and breathing increased, and he felt sweat dripping down his back. Of their own accord, his gaze flicked to the corner before quickly moving away again.

"Fuck, yes! Oh, baby, you make me feel so good. Fuck!" Acker tightened his grip on Casey's wrist, pressing closer together as the doctor's come saturated Casey's shirt. Acker's grip loosened but not enough for Casey to escape. He lifted his head and smiled at Casey. "Thank you, sweetheart." He moved in for a kiss, but Casey turned his head away. Acker chuckled. "Don't be like that." He thrust his hips once more before letting go of Casey completely.

Casey didn't move. There was nowhere he wanted to go except in the shower, and there was no way he was doing it right now.

"You need to clean yourself up, darling." Acker swiped a finger through the mess, smearing it further before tucking himself away and heading to his locker. Casey watched as he removed his shirt, retrieved a new one and replaced it before donning his white jacket again. "See you soon."

When Acker left the locker room, Casey shuddered and removed the shirt as quickly as he could, throwing it into the shower area. He slid down the wall to the floor, burying his head in his arms.

He refused to cry because he had to spend the next ten hours with Chloe, who would know something was up, but he needed a minute. Just a minute.

He slammed his locker shut and waved goodbye to the staff, exiting and running to his car. When he had locked himself in, he took some deep breaths before driving home. As soon as he was inside his house, he locked the door, slid to the floor and sobbed.

Three weeks had passed since the incident with Acker, and Casey had managed to avoid him for the majority. Every time Casey saw him walking down a corridor, he remembered somewhere he had to be, or he ducked into a room to get away from him. He was not averse to hiding if necessary, but it meant he hadn't managed to get any recordings.

It also meant it had also been four weeks since he'd last seen Luke. Casey tried hard not to think about him, but it wasn't easy. The night they'd spent together—well, the few hours—had been overwhelming and had made Casey feel less alone in the world. But he'd messed it up. He sighed.

He hadn't returned to the gym either. What was the point? Casey had several weeks of training under his belt, and although he wasn't an expert, he knew how to get out of holds. How he'd managed to get caught so easily by Acker was anyone's guess. It proved to him there wasn't much point to his training, and it was another excuse to stay away from Luke.

Lying on his bed, staring at the TV as pictures danced across it was not helping him, so he moved to get up and do something. He had to work again tomorrow; therefore, he didn't want to get too energetic. It was then his phone rang.

"Hey, Alex. What's up?"

"Hey. I need your help today, please?" Alex sounded grim.

"What's wrong?"

"Craig called me." Casey lifted his eyebrows at the news. "His court case is today, and he wants me to be there. I have no idea what to do. He called me out of the blue and asked me for help."

Casey could imagine Alex standing there, raking his fingers through his hair in panic. "Firstly, calm down. You'll be no use to him if you worry. Secondly, be there for him. Be whatever he needs. If he needs a shoulder to cry on, be it. If he needs to vent, listen. If he needs to sit quietly, sit with him and hold his hand. Just be there."

"I was thinking of getting some of the guys together and seeing if they wanted to come and support him, too."

"I don't know, Alex. He might not want them there." Casey shivered at the idea of anyone hearing what had happened to him.

"They don't have to go into the courtroom itself, but I thought if I turned up with some extra people for support, he might feel better about it. I don't know, Casey!"

"Alex, calm down. He asked for you. So be there. If you want to call some of the guys in, do it. I'm sure Craig is strong enough to tell you if he doesn't want them in the actual room."

"All right. Will you come?"

Casey swallowed hard. It wouldn't be his first choice, not because he didn't want to support Craig, but because it hit a bit too close to home. "Of course, I will. When?" he asked, channelling his inner calm.

After getting the details, Casey hung up and swapped out his joggers and t-shirt for jeans and a polo shirt. He had no time to do anything else, so he left and drove to the courthouse. He met Alex and several other guys on the steps around fifteen minutes later.

"Hi. Thanks for coming." Alex hugged Casey, and he could tell Alex was worried sick. Casey cupped his neck.

"You'll be fine." He locked gazes with him until Alex took a breath and nodded.

Alex turned when a car pulled up and jogged down the steps. Casey watched as Alex enfolded Craig in his arms, and Craig reciprocated. The pair had a tumultuous relationship—Alex wanted more but was willing to wait for Craig to be ready, even if he never would be—but you could tell from their embrace, it was a two-way street. He smiled softly, knowing Craig was healing, and Alex would be there, regardless. He saw Alex pull back and touch Craig's face, speaking to him, then threaded their fingers together and turned towards the rest of them.

"What are you guys doing here?" Craig said as he looked at them.

"We support our friends when they need it. End of," remarked Sean, receiving nods and agreements all around.

"And I support you, but I'm here in an official capacity, too. And, unfortunately, it's time to go in," Logan said.

The eight of them marched up the steps and into the allocated courtroom. Casey saw Johnson standing at the front, another guy sat at the table behind him, but the rest of the room was empty, except for one security guard. Sean nudged Casey's elbow, and he glanced at him. Sean indicated the public gallery. Casey pivoted and shuffled into the seating area with Sean, Zak, Trent and Max. Casey saw Alex talking to Craig before he sat next to him.

Casey could see the tension running through Alex, so rested his hand on Alex's knee in comfort. Alex briefly glanced at him, gave a small smile and returned his attention to Craig, who sat next to Johnson, talking.

Apart from when the usher requested they rise when the judge entered, they all sat in silence, listening to the horrors Craig had been through at the hands of his ex-boyfriend. Casey had been the paramedic who attended to Craig when his asshole of an ex had nearly killed him. Glancing across at the guy, Darren, Casey could see no remorse in his eyes, only anger.

The hearing wasn't particularly long, but Casey was physically and mentally exhausted by the time the judge left to deliberate. Casey tried to calm Alex during that time, talking to him about what his plans were after this was over. Alex had smiled and said, "Whatever Craig wants to do, I'll be with him."

Nodding in understanding, Casey smiled and wished he had that.

The judge came back and found Darren guilty and sentenced him to eight years in prison. Craig was such a strong guy to be able to go through everything he had and still fight at the end. Fuck. Casey knew their circumstances were different, but he wished he had the strength to get rid of Acker. He knew it was an impossible wish.

Craig returned to them, receiving hugs from them all, including Casey.

"We should go and celebrate," Max said.

"Um, thanks, guys, but I think I'm going to see…

someone," Craig replied, hesitated and added, "I'm going to see my psychologist. I need to get my head on straight again after that."

"Okay, no problem. Do you fancy meeting up afterwards?" Max asked.

"Sure. I'll call if I don't feel up to it, but I should be all right."

Craig and Alex waved goodbye. Casey couldn't decide whether to go with the guys to Crush or to head home and wallow. Deciding he needed some sort of distraction, he chose Crush. It would give him some time to relax, hopefully.

"How are things, Casey?" Trent asked as they sat in the bar, waiting for the drinks Analise was bringing over.

Casey glanced at Trent, seeing the similarities between him and Luke. Since he'd spent so much time staring at Trent's brother, it had become more obvious what the differences were too. He cleared his throat.

"All right, thanks. How's school?" Casey smiled when Trent grimaced and gave a full-body shiver.

"It involves kids. Enough said." He laughed.

"He loves kids, really," Max interrupted, laying his hand on Trent's arm.

Casey noticed he was wearing a ring. "Hey, are you guys engaged?"

Max beamed. "Yes! I thought we'd told everyone. Sorry."

Waving him off, Casey said, "It's okay. I've been out of the loop for a little while. When did this happen?"

"Well, Trent had his own court case last week, and when it was over, he proposed, right on the steps of the courthouse." Max stared at his fiancé with his head in his palm. "So sweet."

"Ah, it makes more sense now why you were smiling and giggling like kids at the end." Casey chuckled. "Congratulations, guys."

"Thanks."

The conversation carried on around him, Casey adding his opinions when asked, but he mostly sat drinking the time away. Strangely, his thoughts turned to dogs. He'd always loved them and would've loved to have one that he could cuddle up to and take care of, but his shifts prevented that companionship. One day, maybe. In the meantime, he might need to make a trip to the shelter to get his fill of the energetic animals. Or borrow Mrs Masters little dog from next door. Felix was a cheeky little guy.

After a couple of hours, Craig and Alex turned up to the cheering of the table, and they added some more chairs. Casey was content to stay silent, basking in the camaraderie surrounding him.

As he studied the people around their table, he felt a range of emotions. Trent and Max were exceedingly happy in their lovey-dovey stage; Sean, who was talking animatedly to Zak, was happy in a relationship with Asher; Zak, Casey knew, was going through a tough time, although he didn't know what was going on, he knew Zak had a young son; and Alex and Craig seemed to be getting on a lot better, sitting holding hands as they talked with the rest of the table.

Despite all the happiness around him, Casey didn't feel it himself. He *had* felt it… when he was with Luke, but he'd made a mess of it. No going back from it now.

All he could feel now was a deep-seated fear and absolute exhaustion tugging at him every minute of the day. He had no idea how to change that.

CHAPTER FOURTEEN

LUKE

Luke had not heard from Casey at all since they'd spoken about what his brothers had suggested, and he was concerned. He was also a bit angry. And hurt. He thought their budding relationship had meant something, but apparently, Casey was able to brush it under the carpet. He obviously didn't give a damn about Luke despite what he'd said numerous times.

The past few weeks had been torturous because Luke wanted to know what Casey was doing and *how* he was doing, since he wasn't attending the sessions anymore. The last time they'd spoken, he'd not sounded good, but Luke hadn't been able to bring himself to contact Casey again. He didn't want to push things when he didn't know what the outcome would be, but it was getting to the point where he *had* to know.

Luke's mood swayed from one side of the spectrum

to the other, although he was always upbeat and professional during his sessions. He kept hearing Jasper's words, *"Communication is key,"* on repeat in his head, so he decided to swallow his pride and call Casey after work.

Four weeks is a long time to wait to call someone, especially when you're not sure they want to hear from you, but Luke did it anyway.

As the phone rang, he considered hanging up but knew he needed to go through with it, even if to just get closure.

"Hey."

Casey's voice was soft, and Luke could tell he was uneasy.

"Hi." He wasn't sure what he wanted to say. "I... Are you all right?" he went with instead of what he wanted to say.

"Yeah, I'm good." That was bullshit if ever Luke heard it.

"I didn't... know if you wanted to hear from me since you've not returned to the gym."

"I got busy, and the sessions weren't helping me. I didn't see the point in continuing."

The quiet words sent shivers up Luke's spine. "But you were progressing well. Why do you think they weren't helping?" Casey stayed quiet, and a sense of foreboding rushed through Luke. "What happened, Casey? Tell me, *please?*"

"I'm fine."

"Casey, I'm imagining all these different things that

could've happened to you, and I'm worried sick. Please? Tell me what happened." Luke could barely get the words out.

"Nothing. I'm good. Thanks for calling, Luke."

The phone went dead.

"No fucking way, Casey!" he shouted to the empty room, heat burning through Luke. White-hot anger he had not felt in a long time. He signed out from work, the people around him giving him a wide berth, no doubt from the expression on his face. He stormed to his car, throwing his belongings in the back seat before screeching out of the car park towards Casey's house. He had no idea if Casey was even there, but it would be the first place he tried. And if Casey wasn't, he'd ring around to find him.

Throwing his car door open and slamming it behind him, he stormed up the path to Casey's house before taking a deep breath and knocking on the door. He knocked again after a minute of no response, and the door finally opened to show a meeker version of the man Luke had previously known.

When Casey saw who it was, his shoulders relaxed, and he let out a breath before opening the door. "Should've known you wouldn't listen," he grumbled as he shut—and locked—the door behind them.

"Well, despite what people say, I don't always follow the rules," Luke replied with a smile, wanting some reaction from Casey, and Luke was ecstatic when he chuckled, weak as it was.

"Do you want a drink?"

"Sure. Anything hot."

Casey trailed to the kitchen, and Luke followed at a slower pace, studying Casey's movements. He was less tense than he had been when he'd answered the door, but he was not the carefree, fun guy Luke had been introduced to. Something had happened to scare Casey, and Luke wanted to know what it was.

Once their tea was made and in their hands, Casey headed for the living room sofa, curling his knees underneath him as he cradled his cup. The epitome of withdrawn. Luke sat himself at the opposite end of the sofa with his knee up on the cushion so he could face Casey but give him breathing space. He clenched his jaw, nausea rolling through him at the possible reasons behind Casey's demeanour.

They sat in silence for a short time before Luke whispered, "Did he get to you?" He feared the answer.

Casey stared vacantly off into the room, and Luke watched as a single tear tracked its way down his cheek. It was answer enough.

"When?"

Casey swallowed. "The night I last spoke to you."

"Fuck, Casey. What did he do?" He gentled his hold on the mug, not wanting to break it.

Watching as Casey closed his eyes and shuddered, Luke trembled with the volume and intensity of the emotions going through him.

When Casey didn't answer, Luke prodded, "Did he rape you?"

Casey shook his head slowly. "He took away my

security.”

For a moment, Luke was confused before he realised Casey meant the asshole had stolen his sense of safety. Moving slowly, so he didn't scare Casey, Luke put his tea on the coffee table, reached for Casey's and did the same with that, then held his arms out to Casey. He refused to grab or pull at him; it had to be Casey's choice.

After a second of hesitation, Casey threw himself into Luke's arms, burrowing himself into Luke's chest and straddling his lap. Luke held Casey tight as he felt warm wetness soak into his t-shirt. He stroked a hand up and down his back repeatedly, whispering soothing words, trying to hold himself together, to be strong for him as Casey broke into pieces. Knowing Casey as he did, Luke would bet a year's salary, he had not told anyone else about what happened.

He had no idea how long they stayed that way, but Casey eventually moved to the side, snuggling into Luke.

“Do you have any plans on what to do about it?” Luke asked hesitantly.

Casey shook his head against Luke's chest. “I have no proof. If I go to my boss now, it's my word against his.”

“What if you could find other people he was doing this to or had done it to?”

Casey lifted his head, a crease between his brows. “What do you mean?”

“You might not be the only one going through this,

Casey," Luke said. "If other people are or have previously been through it, you might be able to get a case against him."

"But… I thought…" Casey didn't seem able to get his thoughts in order.

"You were the only one?" At Casey's nod, Luke said, "You might be. But you also might not be." Luke remembered something Casey had said before. "How long has he been at the hospital? Didn't you say he was fairly new?"

"He's been there just over a year now. He moved from York with his wife."

At the news about a wife, Luke raised his eyebrows. "Seriously?"

Casey shrugged. "He's made no secret of the fact he has a wife at home who does everything for him. It seems to be a point he makes regularly as if it gives him status."

Luke shook his head. "Asshole."

There weren't many options available to Casey if he didn't want to involve anyone else. It would be much easier if he was willing to talk to his brother Logan, but he knew Casey wouldn't.

"How have you been managing at work?" Luke asked.

Casey pulled away, and Luke immediately felt the loss. "I hide if I see him." He huffed. "Like a fucking scaredy-cat."

Luke cupped both his cheeks. "You are not. But I'm telling you right now, you do whatever it takes to make sure you're safe. If that means hiding, you fucking hide, you got me? Whatever it takes. Promise me." His jaw ached from how hard he was clenching it.

They stared at each other for a long moment before Casey nodded imperceptibly. Luke closed the gap slowly, giving Casey time to pull away if he wanted, and gently laid his lips on Casey's, wanting to give him something nice to take away the horrible memory. He did nothing more than rest them together and pull away, but it was one of the most meaningful kisses he'd ever had.

"Do you fancy pizza?"

Casey's words shocked him at first, but he laughed when he realised Casey was trying to break the seriousness of the situation. "Pizza's good," he said as he pulled his hands away.

Casey grabbed his hands before they left completely and held them to his cheeks again, staring at Luke. "Thank you." He leaned forward and pressed a kiss to Luke's lips and withdrew. As he stood, he reached for their cups. "I'll make another brew."

Luke watched him walk away and again thought how unbelievably strong the guy was. After what he'd been through, Casey was ploughing ahead with his life —in most ways, anyway. He wondered whether he could persuade Casey to speak to Carter, although he wasn't sure how much it would help. Especially as Carter said, there was nothing that could be done unless there was proof.

He leaned forward, elbows on his knees and

threaded his fingers through his hair, tugging at the strands to try and expel some of the frustration he felt at being so hopeless. Luke tried to think of different ways Casey could get the proof he needed, but all of the things he came up with involved Casey having to get up close and personal with the asshole. And that was in *no way* acceptable.

"What do you have on your pizza?" Casey called from the kitchen.

"Anything but pineapple!" he shouted back.

"Traitor. Pineapple is the best!"

Luke chuckled.

The scent of coffee came ahead of Casey's entry into the room. "Pizza will be around forty minutes, they said, and I thought coffee would be a better bet this time." He passed Luke's mug to him before sitting in his original seat.

Luke missed the heat and comfort of having him settled beside him, but it was better this way. "I was thinking. What if you could start a rumour about the doctor?"

Tilting his head, Casey said, "What kind of rumour?"

"Well, something like, have you heard what's being said about... whatever his name is?"

"And when they ask what I've heard?"

"Tell them anything. Maybe he got transferred because of something that happened in his old hospital. Or someone had asked you if he's been doing his job and worked well with everyone, then hint at why someone would ask you that. You thought the doctor was a good one, although a little creepy at times."

Casey was quiet, and Luke could see him concentrating. "It could work, although I'd need to be careful I didn't have the finger pointed at me."

"Definitely. Find a scapegoat nobody likes." Luke laughed.

Casey smiled. "If I mention it a few times to different people on different days, it might work. The hospital is bad for gossip, which will help. Thanks, Luke."

"Always here to lend a hand." Luke winked, glad Casey appeared to be cheering up. "Now, is there a programme we can watch that could give us ideas about different rumours we could tell?" Luke raised his eyebrows.

Casey laughed, which was music to his ears. "I don't think so, but I'm sure it won't be too hard to think of something." He reached for the remote and flicked through some channels. "How about this?"

When they came across *Tom & Jerry*, they settled in to watch, having found a common love of cartoons, until the pizza arrived. Switching it over to a movie when they had the food, they chatted and ate as if they had always been friends and never been apart; it reminded him of being with Otto. It was nice.

Luke knew it would end when he went home. He didn't care about the 'Marcus' thing now, but he knew they were a long way from being anything except friends. There was too much in between.

Jasper's voice rang through his head again: *"Communication is key."*

He sighed and placed his empty plate on the coffee table. Not looking at Casey, he rubbed the back of his neck and started to talk, "I don't care about the Marcus thing anymore. Yes, it hurt when you automatically said his name, but I understand and accept your explanation for it."

"You are such a good man, Luke. People don't say it enough, and you don't believe it even when they do. I've seen you around your family." The sofa dipped as Casey moved closer, cupping Luke's jaw and turning his face towards him. The sound of the movie disappeared into the background. "You are worth more than you give yourself credit for. You have given me so much more confidence to believe I can do things."

"It didn't help you." Luke's heart shattered. He hadn't helped by doing the one thing he considered himself good at—training others to escape from harm.

"But it would've in a different situation. If it had happened later when we'd done more training, I would've known how to get out of it. That's on him, Luke. Not you. Not me. I have to believe I can do this; otherwise, I won't be able to walk out that door every day. You," he pressed a finger to Luke's chest, "give me the confidence every time I feel like I can't go on. You," he tapped the side of Luke's head, "tell me what I need to remember to get out of situations I don't want to be in. You," he cupped Luke's chin, "lend me your strength when you're not even there."

Casey's voice cracked at the end, and Luke couldn't listen to anymore. He closed the gap between them, fusing their lips as Casey crawled closer and wrapped his arms around Luke's neck. Luke gripped the back of Casey's t-shirt, holding him close.

Several minutes later, air became a necessity, and Casey dragged his mouth away. "Make love to me, Luke. I know it's you. I promise."

Luke rested a finger over Casey's mouth. "I know you do." He gripped the back of Casey's thighs and stood, Casey locking his ankles behind his back as Luke walked to the stairs. He knew this might not be the answer to either of their issues, but he needed Casey. A friends-with-benefits thing might not be so bad, but he wanted more. Their lips joined as he reached the top of the stairs and turned towards Casey's bedroom, keeping his eyes open so he didn't trip over anything and hurt Casey. Turning sideways, Casey reached down and twisted the handle to open the door, and Luke strode to the bed, dropping Casey on the mattress with a bounce.

Chuckling, Casey yanked his own t-shirt over his head, and Luke did the same. They swiftly worked to undress until both were naked. Luke placed his hands on the bed, dipped his head to kiss Casey's knee, and followed the path all the way up his body to his mouth. Casey grabbed his head and sucked on his tongue as he thrust his hips up against Luke.

Luke pulled away with a grin and slid down Casey's body again. Widening Casey's legs, he pushed them back until Casey's ass was on show, and despite the whimper coming from above, Luke settled on his knees at the end of the bed and kissed each ass cheek before focusing on his puckered entrance. He licked at the small bud several times, pressing his tongue against the entrance and sucking against the skin, the sounds ramping his need higher. Casey moaned, and Luke pushed harder against the hole, entering Casey in small increments with his tongue. He pulled back and sucked against Casey's taint, earning him a sob.

Luke's hands squeezed his ass as he dived back to his bud, stretching him with his tongue again and enjoying every minute of it. Rimming was second to sex for Luke; he loved it. Giving and receiving. Casey's hips jerked as Luke licked and lapped and bit at his ass.

Moving his ministrations higher, he drew one of Casey's balls into his mouth, tonguing the sac before moving onto the other one. Withdrawing from them, Luke laved and tasted his way up Casey's body before taking his mouth once more.

Their tongues duelled as Luke explored Casey's mouth. He slid a hand to Casey's hole, using one finger to press against the tight circle until Casey bore down and allowed him to breach. Casey's breath caught, and his mouth fell open while Luke fingered him slowly, being careful because no lube had been used yet. Removing his finger, he lifted it to Casey's mouth and encouraged him to wet it before returning it to his hole.

"Fuck, Luke!"

"Move up the bed."

Luke refused to remove his finger, so Casey whined as he shifted himself up to the pillows, allowing Luke to reach the bedside table. He removed the lube and a condom and put them on the bed, joining their mouths in another heated kiss as he fingered Casey's ass in short movements.

Pulling away, gasping, Luke moved down Casey's body again until he was level with his ass. Unable to resist, he licked at the hole, flicking his tongue over the pucker and spearing his tongue inside.

"Oh, fuck," Casey keened.

Pulling away after several glorious minutes, Luke flipped Casey to his stomach but lifted him to his knees, putting him on display again. Luke lubed his fingers and pressed against Casey's hole as he kissed Casey's spine, preparing him properly but quickly.

Rolling a condom onto his cock, then slicking up, Luke was at Casey's entrance.

"You ready?"

"Fuck, yes!"

Luke chuckled and grunted as his cock sank into Casey's hot channel. He made small thrusts until he was balls deep, then withdrew and plunged back in, receiving an answering gasp from Casey.

"Jesus, Casey. Your ass is tight."

Luke gripped Casey's hips and powered into him over and over. Casey dropped his chest to the bed and smothered his shouts in the sheets. Luke was already too close to coming, so he slowed down, making smaller thrusts until he had no choice but to speed up again. Their hips slapped together, their mutual groans filling the room.

Pausing in his movements, Luke pulled Casey up to his hands and knees and slid an arm around Casey's chest, moulding his chest to Casey's spine. He rotated his hips, the motions slow and small as he kissed Casey's neck and under his ear.

Rearing up again, Luke held Casey's hips and increased his speed, leading Casey to drop to his chest again. Watching where they were joined, Casey's pucker stretched and welcomed Luke's cock as he thrust hard and fast.

"Fuck, fuck! Luke, please!"

Luke kept up a steady rhythm, knowing he didn't have much left in him. He was too close. Shifting positions slightly, Casey choked, and Luke hoped he'd hit the right place. Continuing his thrusts, Luke gripped Casey's ass cheeks, watching as he slid into the hole.

He slowed slightly, feeling the tell-tale tingling along his spine, but he was too far gone. He sped up again, cursing when he couldn't stop the orgasm from claiming him. His rhythm faltered as he released into the condom, holding Casey's hips tight against his own.

"Fuck, Casey. I'm sorry. Sorry. Fuck," he breathed, leaning down to cover his back with apologetic kisses as he thrust a few more times.

When he stopped, he breathed heavily then withdrew, tying the condom off and throwing it on the floor. He'd deal with it later. He had to finish Casey now.

His mouth returned to Casey's hole, his tongue

spearing inside as he reached under and wrapped his hands around Casey's cock. Precome smoothed his way, and Luke pumped and stroked in time with his tongue's thrusting. Incoherent noises came from Casey as Luke gave him everything he had.

Luke pushed two fingers in alongside his tongue, searching for Casey's prostate. Casey's cries increased as did his hips.

"Fuck, Luke! I'm coming!"

Warm fluid covered his hand as Casey came, his cries muffled by the mattress. Luke kept up his movements until Casey pulled away.

Lifting his hand to his mouth, Luke licked off Casey's come and laid down beside him.

"Jesus fucking Christ, Luke."

Casey moved until his head was resting on Luke's shoulder. They laid there as their breathing returned to normal.

Luke wasn't sure what Casey wanted him to do—a reminder of what happened last time flashed through his head, and he tensed.

"What's wrong, Luke?" Casey lifted his head to look at him and gave a small pained smile. "I know who you are, Luke. And I'd like it if you would stay."

Luke's mouth twitched, and he nodded. "All right. I'll have to be up early so I can head home to change before work."

Casey grinned. "No problem."

CHAPTER FIFTEEN

CASEY

As he walked towards the locker room, he was filled with equal parts dread and determination about what he was about to do. He had no idea if it would work or if he would get the finger pointed at him and lose his job, but he needed to do something. When he believed it was just himself who was the recipient, he was happy to let it go, but Luke had highlighted a good point when he said others might be receiving the same treatment. Casey wouldn't stand for it, and when things couldn't be taken to the higher-ups for help, people took things into their own hands.

He entered the room, hearing conversation before he was even fully inside. Two nurses were talking near Casey's locker. They were the perfect people, especially Clarissa. Unlocking it, he swapped out what he needed to before closing it again in case he had to make a quick exit.

"Come on, Casey. I know you want me," Acker whispered in his ear.

Casey shivered, shaking the memory off and making him even more determined to do this. "Hey, Clarissa?" He stepped over to the nurses. He lowered his voice, "You know what's happening around here. What's this I hear about Dr Acker?"

Clarissa frowned and shook her head. "What? I've not heard anything."

"Oh. Never mind." He turned to walk away until Clarissa's words brought him back.

"What have you heard?"

Inwardly, Casey both smiled and grimaced. "I heard he got transferred because of a sexual harassment case," he whispered, leaning close. "They said the hospital washed their hands of him because there were too many cases to hide."

"Oh my god! I've not heard about it. It wouldn't surprise me if it's true. Dr Acker gives me the creeps."

"Has he done anything to you?" Casey asked.

Clarissa shook her head. "I'm not shocked. What about you, Emma?"

"I've not heard anything, but Clarissa is right. There's something weird about that doctor."

"Hmm," Casey answered noncommittally. "Let me know if you hear anything, okay? I have to get to work."

"Will do. See you, Casey."

He left the locker room, trying to keep his pace steady and fighting the urge to run for the safety of the ambulance. When he got there, Chloe was already checking over the equipment, so he jumped in to help, distracting himself from the snowball he'd potentially just set in motion.

As the day wore on, he found his thoughts continually shifting to Luke. More than once, Chloe asked why he was smiling, and he shook his head at her. He had woken a couple of times the night Luke stayed to the feeling of Luke wrapped around him in some way or another, legs entangled, spooned, arms circling him. It was a fantastic feeling to have someone unconsciously need to be that close to him. Marcus had never been like that; whenever Casey woke, he was always at the other side of the bed, not touching him at all.

An alarm beeped into the darkness, and Casey groaned, lifting his hand to the bedside table to turn off his phone, but it wasn't there. There was movement beside him, and the noise stopped. A warm body returned to his back, making him sigh in contentment, especially when it was followed by a kiss to his nape.

"Sorry. I have to go," Luke mumbled.

More movement and the heat retreated. Casey blinked open his eyes several times, his eyes rolling back in his head because they wanted to close again. He rubbed a hand across his face and flipped onto his back, watching as Luke donned the clothes he'd worn the previous night.

"What time is it?" he croaked.

Luke glanced at him with a smile. "Six. Go back to sleep."

"What is this ungodly hour of the morning?"

Chuckling, Luke crawled next to Casey. "Don't you have to get up at this time of the morning when you work?"

"Yes, but on my days off, there is no such time. The day starts around nine."

Luke pressed a kiss to Casey's mouth and pulled away. "Lucky for you. I'll call you later. Get some more sleep."

Casey turned over, resting his head on the pillow Luke used, inhaling his scent as he heard Luke bustle around the room and close the bedroom door behind him. He could get used to this.

It was all he remembered until he woke up several hours later, but there had been a message waiting for him on his phone, wishing him a good day.

The thought that Casey should've been more reluctant to be intimate with someone after what happened with Acker crossed his mind, but he brushed it off. He knew the difference between Luke and Acker. There was no comparison at all.

As he entered the hospital at the end of his shift, Casey set his phone to record at the push of a button as he had decided to do and placed it in his pocket, holding it ready. Luke's brothers had told him to get evidence, so he would try. He had to be careful he didn't get any confidential information; otherwise, he'd be in a world of trouble with the hospital and most likely lose his job.

Casey stopped by one of the nurses' stations to speak with Gloria, who he'd not seen for a while. He'd been there a few minutes when he felt a touch to his lower back, much lower than was acceptable for a greeting. He twisted to the side, making the hand fall away, and faced Acker while sliding his hand into his pocket to start the recorder.

"Good evening, Casey, Gloria," Acker said in his usual easy-going manner.

"Good evening, Dr Acker," Gloria replied with a smile. "I see you're working alongside me and mine tonight."

Acker nodded. "Indeed. Is there anything I need to attend to at the moment?"

Gloria shook her head. "Dr Simons is finishing off his final walk-around, and he'll come to talk to you about any cases when he's done."

"Perfect. Thank you, Gloria." Acker turned to him, his gaze running down Casey's body as he rested his elbow on the counter and linked his fingers across his chest. "You're looking well, Casey. Did you enjoy your time off?"

"Yes, thank you." Casey refused to divulge too much about what he did.

"I heard things haven't worked out between you and your boy toy, but I see you've found someone else. Didn't take you long."

Casey would have loved to know who was giving Acker all the information about him. He chanced a glance at Gloria, who was over the other side of the counter, dealing with some paperwork. "Maybe not. But I'm happy. What more can I ask?" he said, trying not to let the anger rise to the surface. He smiled tightly, fisting his hands in his pockets. "Goodnight, Gloria."

"Night, Casey."

He pushed away from the desk he'd been resting on and pivoted to walk away, his heart pounding and a headache beginning in his temples. Turning the corner, he leaned back against the wall and closed his eyes, stiffening when a body came in contact with him. Blinking open frantically, he met Acker's gaze as Acker rested his hands on either side of Casey's head.

"You are so sexy in that uniform," Acker said, his breath coasting across Casey's skin. "I bet you'd look even better without it." He drew closer, brushing his nose against Casey's cheek.

Casey narrowed his eyes, slid his hands up Acker's chest as if he wanted what Acker was insinuating, making Acker groan and press closer until Casey pushed as hard as he could, sending Acker stumbling back.

Gritting his teeth, Casey said, "Thank you for the compliment, but I'm not interested and never will be."

"That's not what you said before." Acker smiled, his gaze burning into Casey's. Casey diverted his gaze over Acker's shoulder, not wanting to see his face.

"I never said anything before, and you know it."

Acker took a step forward, and Casey clenched his fists, his stomach rebelling. "You mean when you let me come all over you," he whispered.

Casey glanced around them, seeing no other people around. He wasn't sure if that was a good thing or not. "I didn't *let* you," he gritted out.

"Hmm. If you say so. I bet you've kept your shirt as a souvenir, haven't you?" Acker drew his bottom lip between his teeth and pressed a hand against his groin.

"Goodnight, Dr Acker," Casey spat, and he spun

before increasing to a jog towards the locker room. He needed to grab his stuff and leave. Quickly.

When he finally sat in his car, he took some deep breaths and held out his hands, which were shaking badly. He linked his fingers together and pressed them to his mouth, hoping to stifle the tears he felt coming. He wanted to get home. No, he wanted to see Luke. He pulled out his phone to call him.

And realised his phone was still recording.

Holy shit. He'd captured everything. Casey ended the recording, making sure to save the audio file, and dialled Luke.

"Hey. How was your shift?"

"It was good until the end. Can I come over?" He wasn't usually so forthright, but he needed to see Luke.

"Of course. I'm here." Luke rattled off his address, they said goodbye, and Casey pointed the car towards Luke's house. He needed a shower, which he hoped Luke wouldn't mind, and sleep, in that order. Maybe some food, too.

When he pulled up, Luke was waiting in the doorway.

"You didn't have to wait outside. It's not warm out here," Casey said as he approached.

"I don't mind. It's nice and toasty in here, so let's get you warmed up." Luke grabbed Casey's hand and dragged him over the threshold and into the heat.

Dropping his bag near the coats, Casey removed his and hung it up. He'd never been to Luke's, but it was exactly what he'd expected. A small house with what he could see was a small kitchen diner and a living room. The house probably had two bedrooms and a bathroom upstairs. It was decorated in what Casey described as autumn colours, so browns, beiges, deep reds and dark oranges.

"Very nice," Casey commented with a smile, instantly feeling at home.

"Thanks." Luke dropped his gaze to the floor and fidgeted. Interpreting the body language, Casey decided he should compliment Luke more often. He needed to get used to it. He was such a great guy but lacked confidence.

Casey strode over to him, stopping when they were toe to toe, and he had to look up at Luke. "Kiss me?"

Luke grinned. "No question about it." He leaned down and captured Casey's lips, walking him backwards until Casey's back hit the wall.

Casey tore his mouth away from Luke's. "Wait." He breathed deeply, closing his eyes but remaining in place. The same position he had been in with Acker not long before. He felt Luke pull away, but Casey opened his eyes and grabbed for him. "No, stay."

"But you're trembling, Casey. I've obviously scared you."

Casey shook his head vehemently. "No, you haven't. *He* has. But I'm not going to let him win."

Luke frowned but stepped forward again, caging Casey against the wall. Casey rested his shaking hands against Luke's chest, sliding them up and down the fabric of his t-shirt.

"What did he do?"

"Mainly talk. But he caught me off guard and caged me like we are now."

Luke swore and went to move away again.

"No! If I pull away from this, he'll win. Give me a moment." Casey yanked Luke forward until their bodies were aligned completely. He moved Luke's hands to brace either side of his head and gripped Luke's shirt. Lifting his gaze to roam Luke's pinched features, he smiled. "I know it's you, Luke," he whispered as his heart rate decreased, and he calmed.

"It's me." Luke brushed his mouth against Casey's gently.

Casey smoothed his hands up Luke's body to grip his hair, deepening the kiss while Luke wrapped his arms around his back, holding him tight. His lips parted at Luke's insistence, and Luke's tongue explored his mouth, Casey sucking on it in anticipation of what was to come.

The doorbell rang, making them jump, and Luke chuckled.

"Sorry. I ordered Chinese."

Casey rolled his eyes, heaving an exhale, and released Luke so he could answer the door, moving into the living room to explore the pictures around the room. There was a lot of his family like there was a lot of Casey's family at his own house. Family meant a huge amount to them both, which Casey had always thought was a great indication of a good man. Studying the photos, he saw the resemblance between the siblings and parents, although Luke looked more like Trent than any of the others. Chuckling at one with Luke holding a football with a frown on his face, Casey stood.

"I hated football with a passion," Luke commented from behind him. Casey, surprisingly, didn't jump, even though he hadn't known Luke was there.

"I can see."

"Mum made me try it out for several weeks before giving up any chance I would enjoy it."

"Why did they want you to play football?"

Luke rested the bag of food on the coffee table and stood tall again. He huffed a laugh, staring at the photo. "They didn't force me to start. I'd begged and begged them to let play, and they finally gave in. When I turned around and said I hated it, they made me continue to make sure. I didn't like football, but I learned a valuable lesson."

"What was it?" Casey sat on the sofa, crossing his legs underneath him.

"Not to whinge too much." Luke chuckled.

Casey laughed. "Yeah, I understand. There was a whole lot of whinging and whining in my house growing up. We were a wild bunch."

"I thought it was bad enough with five, but there were six of you. I have no idea how our parents coped." Luke opened the bag and emptied to contents. "I'll grab some plates. I bought a variety so you can pick and choose if you like."

Casey studied the foil boxes, seeing five different

dishes, chips and two bags of prawn crackers. "Are you feeding an army I didn't know about?" he called.

"Nah. Any leftovers will get eaten, don't worry. If not by me, then by my meddling, intrusive siblings if they visit." Luke's voice steadily came closer as he returned to the room.

"I'm so glad I'm not the only one."

"What? Who has annoying siblings?" Luke snorted. "I think we both have dibs on that category."

They opened the containers, and each took some food before settling back into the cushions. They continued telling each other about their antics as children until their food had gone, and Luke made them a cup of tea.

Casey leaned his head back against the sofa and closed his eyes.

"Are you ready to talk about it?"

Blowing out a breath, Casey lifted his head and pulled out his phone. "No need. I managed to get a recording."

"Seriously? That's great." Luke grimaced. "Sorry. Not great that it happened."

Casey waved him away. "I know what you meant." He pressed play, and they listened through the conversation with Acker and Gloria. As it progressed, Casey tensed. Luke moved over to sit next to him and enclosed him in his arms. Casey could feel himself shaking again, but not from fear this time. From anger.

"Fuck. He's an asshole. I am so proud of you, Casey."

Casey snorted. "Why?"

"Because you're determined not to let him ruin your life."

"I don't want to give him the power, but it's getting harder each time something happens." Casey pulled away from Luke and switched off his phone. He rested his feet on the floor and leaned onto his knees, head lowered.

A hand rubbed his back in soothing circles.

"How did he know you were with me? Have you told anyone? Not that I mind!" Luke's questions were quiet, though his declaration wasn't.

"I know you don't." Casey sighed. "I honestly don't know. Unless he saw us at the gym one day?" He shrugged. "No telling where the information came from. Oh, which reminds me, I spoke to one of the gossips in the hospital and asked her if she'd heard about Acker's previous job. It's one thing done. Tomorrow, I will speak to someone else and set up another rumour. I have no idea if it will work, but it certainly won't hurt."

"Just be careful, Casey. I know it was my idea, but it's your job on the line."

Casey didn't reply because Luke was right. "Could I borrow your shower? Unless you want me to go home, which I can."

Luke smiled. "Go right ahead. Or you could have some company if you want to?"

"As much as I would love that, I need a shower and some sleep. Sorry."

Grinning, Luke said, "Don't be daft. It's fine. You look like you're about to keel over any minute, anyway. I was offering to stop you from falling."

"Ah, so you were offering to be my chair, were you?" Casey stood, smirking.

"Yes, kind of." Luke paused. "That imagery has sexual connotations I never even thought of until now." He raised his eyebrows.

Laughing, Casey strode to his bag and picked it up, heading towards the stairs after Luke gave him directions.

"I'll be up to tuck you in once I've cleared up."

"Oh, fuck. Let me help. I completely forgot." Casey dropped his bag on a step and turned.

"No! Go get your shower. I'm fine. Go on."

"You sure?"

Luke nodded. "Definitely. I'll be there soon."

Casey climbed the stairs slowly, looking forward to a bed.

CHAPTER SIXTEEN

LUKE

A week later, Luke was still vibrating with anger at the situation Casey was in. He'd spent more and more of his time beating his rage out of himself through the pounding of his feet on the pavement. He had not seen Casey since the night Casey had asked to visit Luke due to his shifts, and Luke had become inundated at work. His schedule had filled up excessively, and although he wasn't going to complain, he was knackered.

The rhythm of his footsteps proved he wasn't tired enough to sleep, though.

He had enjoyed the morning he'd woken next to Casey—in fact, both mornings. This time, they had risen at the same time to get ready for work. Casey had to hurry because he didn't have a spare set of his uniform with him, so he needed to drop by his house to get one before heading on to work. They'd managed to enjoy a long, unhurried kiss and fondle before he left, which had set Luke up for the day. Shame it couldn't happen every night.

Basement Jaxx played in his ears as he tried to concentrate on where he was going, but his thoughts kept getting pulled back to Casey. With every breath he heaved, with every drop of sweat he made, it reminded him of what they'd shared.

He entered a park and set himself up to run a circuit around the treeline. The winter sun streamed through the branches as he ran. Around the halfway mark, he grinned, and pulling the earbuds from his ears and hooking them around his neck, he slowed to a walk to watch the father and son duo.

Luke hadn't had a lot of interactions with Zak, but he'd had some and knew him through Trent and Max. He'd never met his son, but the two-year-old was unwaveringly Zak's. There was no denying it.

"Hey," he said as he approached the pair, who were near the edge of the shimmering pond, watching the ducks.

Zak glanced up and smiled when he saw Luke. He grabbed Dane's hand and pulled him away from the water, walking over. "Hi. I didn't know you lived around here?"

"I don't. I run. Apparently, extremely far." Luke chuckled.

Zak nodded knowingly. "Our issues always find a way of chasing after us, don't they?"

"You got that right."

Zak wiggled the hand holding Dane's, gaining the little boy's attention. "Hey, bud. This is Luke. Say hi."

Dane stared up at Luke, mouth open, then looked down and scooted closer to his father. They both laughed.

"How are things with you?" Luke asked.

Zak grimaced and massaged the back of his neck. "Not great, to be honest, but we're getting there."

Luke tilted his head. "I know we don't know each other very well, but I'm happy to help if you need anything. Even if it's just an ear."

"Thank you." He sighed. "Your brother is helping me with a legal issue, but sometimes, I would love to…" he looked off into the distance, "let it all go for a few hours. Do you know?"

Luke nodded. "Yeah, I know what you mean." He paused. "Maybe you should come to the gym sometime, let off some steam. I'd be happy to spot you."

"That would be great. I'll speak to Emily to see if she can help out and let you know."

"Emily?"

"Ethan's sister. She usually babysits for me if I need her to."

"Ah." Luke smiled. "Well, I better leave you to your day." He crouched down, making himself smaller. "Bye, Dane."

Dane looked at him with wide eyes.

"I'm far too tall for kids," Luke joked.

"Nah, he's been a lot more clingy lately," Zak explained as he lifted Dane into his arms. "Understandable given the circumstances." Zak gave a small smile.

"It was good to see you, Zak. Make sure to contact the gym or me to sort out something."

"I will."

Luke waved and began to jog again, slowly because his muscles had cooled while he'd been talking. He didn't want to hurt himself. Placing the earbuds back in, he zoned back into his rhythm, hoping his journey home was less fraught with anger than it had been on the way there.

The next evening, he received a knock at the door just as he started his movie. Frowning, he checked the time, seeing it was just after eight-thirty. He hadn't been expecting any visitors.

A smile spread across his face as he saw Casey standing on his doorstep. "Hello. Fancy seeing you here." Luke opened the door wider so Casey could enter.

"I thought you'd like some company. I'm working nights tomorrow, so can't go to sleep yet; otherwise, I will be awake early and knackered when my shift starts."

"You know you're welcome any time. I was sitting down to watch a movie." Luke leaned forward and pressed a brief kiss to Casey's lips, not wanting to start anything too heavy straight away. He wanted Casey to be able to relax first. He led the way into the living room, where the movie was paused.

"What have you chosen?"

"*The Bone Collector.*"

"Good choice."

Luke went and fetched some drinks and snacks and brought them all into the living room to see Casey tucked into the corner of the sofa. He grinned as he placed the tray on the table.

"Help yourself to whatever you want. Or I could order takeaway if you're hungry." Luke sat on the opposite side of the sofa.

"No, this is great. Thanks. Coffee is my liiiiiiiiife!" Casey sang and picked up the mug.

Chuckling, Luke said, "You only say that because you need to stay awake. If you needed to sleep, you'd say it was the bane of your existence."

Casey glanced at him through narrowed eyes. "How do you know me so well?"

They laughed, and Luke switched on the film. Time went fast with their joint efforts of trying to remember the plot and ending up in fits of laughter several times. It was a wonderful, relaxing evening, and something Luke had not realised he'd needed.

As the film came to an end, Luke asked, "Are you staying over?"

Casey chewed his bottom lip. "No. I better let you get some sleep. I'll be up for another few hours."

He stood. "It's fine. Stay up if you want and come to

bed when you're ready. I would stay up, but it's a school night," he deadpanned.

Casey snorted. "Yeah, all right. If you're sure that I won't disturb you."

Luke trailed over to him, resting one hand on the back of the sofa, the other hand on the arm and leaning down to kiss his lips. "You won't disturb me. And if you do, it will be in the best way possible."

Smiling, Casey cupped his face and pulled him closer. Luke pressed a knee into the cushion next to Casey's hips and leaned in. Their kiss didn't last long, but it was sweet and meaningful.

"Night, Casey. See you soon." Luke pulled away.

"Night."

He trudged up the stairs and got ready for bed before turning the light off and settling down. On the verge of sleep, he shot awake when he heard a crash and a bellow. Luke jumped out of bed and ran downstairs, stopping when Casey shouted for him to stay where he was at the bottom of the stairs.

"There's glass everywhere. I don't want you to get it in your feet."

"What the fuck happened?" Luke asked, heart rate decreasing. Looking around the living room, he saw shards of glass sprinkled across the wooden floor and rug and a brick sitting proudly in the centre. He glanced at the window and saw the damage.

"Someone threw it through the window."

Luke could see Casey was shaken by what had happened; it wasn't just audible in his wavering voice, it was visible in his body. He needed to reach him. Watching where he was going, he skirted the mess and wrapped his arms around Casey.

"Did you get anything on you?" he asked as he stroked Casey's back.

"No, I'd got up to turn the light back on so I could see what I was doing when it happened."

The cold breeze had goosebumps rising on Luke's bare chest. "Right, call the police. I need to get this window boarded up as soon as possible. I'm going to get dressed." Luke held Casey's face up, his gaze roaming Casey's face to check for injuries.

"I'm fine. Honestly. Just a little shocked."

"All right. I'll be back in a minute."

He manoeuvred his way back to the hallway and ran up the stairs to get dressed and grab some shoes. When he was ready, he jogged back down and saw Casey with the phone in his hand.

"Have you called them?" Casey shook his head. "What's wrong?" he asked as he brought Casey his shoes.

Casey cleared his throat. "It might have been Acker. If I call the police, I'll have to tell them about him."

Luke enfolded Casey in his arms again, allowing him to bury his head in Luke's neck. "I'm assuming Acker is the asshole; therefore, you will, yes. But it might give you a stronger case with the hospital if you have police records to back you up." He held Casey tightly until he felt him pull away.

"You're right." He sighed and picked up his phone,

dialling on speakerphone. Luke took in the mess as the call connected. "Logan, I need your help."

Casey briefly explained what had happened, but not his suspicions, and Logan said he'd be there as soon as he could. In the meantime, he was sending Kade and Joey to them. Casey explained to Luke that Kade Stirling and Joey Kirkland were police officer friends of Logan's and happened to be on duty that night. It didn't take them long to arrive.

"Casey, how are you?" one of the officers said. He was about the same height as Luke was, defined muscles and had short black hair and bright blue eyes.

"I'm all right, Kade. Thanks." Casey stood next to Luke, who rested an arm around him. "This is Luke Walker."

Kade held out his hand. "Nice to meet you, Luke, though, I would've preferred it to be under different circumstances."

While they'd been talking, the other officer, Joey, had been looking around. "There doesn't seem to be anything on the brick, Kade. Just a plain nasty brick."

"Any ideas who it could be?" Kade asked them.

Luke glanced at Casey, letting him decide where he wanted to go with the answer.

Casey nodded slowly. "If it's all right with you, Kade, can I answer the questions when Logan gets here? I don't want to have to go through it twice."

Kade narrowed his gaze, and veins bulged in his forehead. "Answer me one thing, Casey. Do you feel safe with Luke?"

"Yes! God, yes." Casey turned and burrowed himself back into Luke's chest, and Luke wrapped his arms around him. "It's not him, Kade. It's..." Casey trailed off.

"All right. Joey, let's get whatever evidence we can find and clean up. We need to get the window boarded as soon as possible."

"I'll call someone to fix the window," Luke said, pulling out his phone.

"Tell them to come to the front door and not the window when they first get here. We need to make sure no outdoor evidence gets trampled," Kade said.

"Sure."

Luke guided Casey into the kitchen and sat him at the small wooden table. He flicked the kettle on and grabbed six mugs from the cupboard while he spoke with someone about boarding up the window. He made all of them coffee, leaving two mugs without water until Logan and, undoubtedly, Ava arrived. He blew out a breath. This would be good. Luke's family would be up in arms once they knew about what had happened, just as much as Casey's family would be.

He turned and put one mug in front of Casey and keeping one for himself. "Ava is going to murder me for not ringing her first." He snorted.

"Oh god, I didn't think, Luke. I forget she's your sister. Sorry."

"It's fine. Saves me having to tell my family." He chuckled, then sobered, listening to the subdued murmurs of the men in his living room. "How are you?"

There was a long exhale before Casey answered. "Tired now."

"The shock will be wearing off. The exhaustion will be settling in. As soon as this is sorted, we'll get you to bed." Luke rested his hand over Casey's wrist, who then turned his hand and threaded their fingers together.

"You do realise, don't you, we are uniting two large families with our relationship?" Luke said blandly, trying to distract him.

Casey's brow furrowed, then cleared as he groaned. "Oh, no! With your four siblings and my five, it will be chaos!" He dropped his head to the table, barely missing his mug.

Luke snickered. "Thought you'd like the idea."

"CASEY!"

Casey jumped, knocking his mug. "Logan, you ass! I've spilled coffee all over me."

Logan came barrelling through the kitchen door and crouched next to his brother. "Are you all right?"

"Yes, Logan. I'm fine." Casey sounded exasperated, and Logan had only just arrived. Luke held in a chuckle, his gaze meeting his sister's and saw the worry in her eyes.

Logan glanced at Luke, nodded, then lingered on their joined hands before returning to Casey. "What happened?"

"Does Kade need to hear this as well?" Casey asked.

"Yes."

"Can you get him in here? I'm not doing this more than once unless I have to."

Logan narrowed his gaze but called for Kade as he rose and sat at the table. When everyone was in his small kitchen with their coffee, Luke sat next to Casey again, who promptly grabbed his hand and held on for dear life.

"What's going on, Casey?" Logan asked. Luke could see the tension in Logan's body, the whiteness of his knuckles as he gripped his notepad, the clenching of his jaw.

Casey stared at Luke, who nodded and squeezed his hand before leaning forward and whispering in his ear, "You're fine, Casey. We'll sort this out. Together." He pulled back and cupped Casey's cheek. "I'm here, and I'm not going anywhere." He joined their lips for a brief moment.

Watching Casey swallow and turn his flushed gaze to his brother, Luke inwardly smiled. Casey was so cute when he was embarrassed.

"It's possible the person who did this is a doctor at the hospital."

"Why do you think that?"

Casey inhaled. "He's been harassing me."

Luke watched the anger flow across Logan's face and knew it was only going to get worse, especially with what else Casey had to tell them. Maybe talking to his brother was not the best choice for Casey.

"What's he been doing?" Kade asked when Logan didn't seem able to speak.

"Innuendos, brushing up against me, touching me inappropriately." Casey swallowed hard and glanced at Luke, who nodded in encouragement. "And…" Casey stopped. The blood was long gone in Luke's hand with how hard Casey was holding it, but he refused to pull away. He could help with this.

"The guy cornered him and masturbated over him at work," Luke finished with the information Casey had eventually given him a few days earlier. The thought that his training had not helped Casey was a sore point with Luke.

Casey's gaze was on the table. Luke's gaze was on Logan, who was staring at his brother, anger clear in his expression.

"How long has it been going on?" Kade asked.

"It started getting worse around four months ago," Casey admitted quietly.

"FOUR MONTHS!" Logan burst out of his chair, knocking it over, and stalked out of the kitchen.

Ava righted the chair and took a seat. She leaned forward to Casey. "He's not angry at you, Casey. He's angry at the situation. You should've told us."

Watching a puddle of tears gather on the table beneath Casey's face had Luke pulling him into his arms, Casey straddling his lap. Casey tucked his head between Luke's shoulder and neck and cried. While he tried to calm him, Luke watched the officers leave the room, including his sister. No doubt he would be getting a roasting after this was all done, too.

When Casey's breathing levelled out, Luke quieted his nonsensical murmurings and let the silence reign. He didn't want to push Casey too hard and send him back to tears. Pressing a kiss to Casey's forehead, Luke knew they needed to go through the rest of it with the police, but he was as reluctant to do so as Casey appeared to be.

"Come on, sweetheart. Let's get it over with, and you can start feeling better." Luke pushed Casey's face up and used his thumbs to wipe the tear tracks. It devastated him to see Casey so beat down. "You can do this, Casey. You're strong and brave and selfless."

He leaned forward and kissed Casey, alternating between nibbling at his bottom lip and sipping from his upper. As Casey relaxed into him, he gentled the kiss and pulled back.

"Deep breath, now." He waited as Casey followed his instructions. "Come on."

Luke helped Casey to stand, linked their fingers together and led him to the living room. Logan and Ava stood by the TV, gesturing wildly, seemingly arguing. Luke raised his eyebrows. It's not often he saw his sister take a stand. Kade and Joey were near the window, sweeping up and pointing at things as they conversed. The brick was no longer in the middle of the floor.

Ava spotted them first and came over. "Are you okay, Casey?"

Casey nodded, pressing closer to Luke, who squeezed his hand. "I'm good," he croaked.

"There is more to the story," Luke said.

"Fucking hell!" Logan muttered, hands on hips.

Luke glared at him and continued, "Casey managed to get evidence."

"Why the fuck did you not lead with that information," Logan growled.

"Logan! Calm the fuck down," Ava shouted.

Raising his eyebrows again, Luke turned his gaze to his sister. Her mouth curled, then turned sombre again. "What evidence did you get, Casey?"

"A conversation between the two of us. I don't know if it's useable because it happened in the hospital and confidentiality and all that, but I have it."

"Where is it?" Ava asked.

"On my phone."

"Can I listen?"

Casey glanced at Logan and back. "I'd prefer it if Kade or Joey did."

Ava nodded and smiled, understanding what Casey had not said about the potential reaction of Logan. "Kade?" She walked over to the officer with Casey's phone and spoke with him before he took it and indicated for Joey to follow him out of the house. Ava returned to them. "We will need to go through this in a lot more detail, Casey. I know you don't want to, but we need every bit of information we can get to nail this bastard down."

Casey's shoulders slumped, but he nodded.

"The guy should be here to secure the window soon. He said he wouldn't long," Luke said.

"Good. I'd feel better if you could sleep somewhere else tonight," Ava declared.

Luke peered at Casey. "We'll head to Mum's." Casey shook his head, but Luke silenced him. "If it is the doctor, he's less likely to know where Mum's house is than if you go to any house you usually go to. You'll be safer there." He glanced at Logan, who nodded after a minute staring contest.

Casey was done. He was exhausted. After Kade and Joey had returned, saying they had transferred a copy of the voice file to Kade's phone, the officers had agreed Luke and Casey could leave. They both hiked the stairs to Luke's room, and Luke sat Casey on the bed as he moved around him, filling a bag. Casey could do nothing more than watch. He guessed he was still in shock, but he was slowly coming out of it.

"I don't want to drag you any further into this, Luke."

Luke smiled at him. "I'm not going anywhere, Casey. Forget it."

"But what about your job?"

"It will be there. We're not emigrating; we're going to Mum's for a day or two."

"What about my job?" Casey argued.

"Well, in the morning..." Luke checked his watch

and grimaced. "*Later* this morning, we will ring the hospital and ask for a couple of days off, explaining a simplified version of what happened. They should give it to you."

"Depends how swamped they are," Casey muttered.

Luke crouched in front of him, resting his hands by Casey's hips, holding Casey's gaze. "We will sort it out either way. Let's get to Mum's, get some sleep and figure it out after."

Casey didn't reply; he focused on his hands, wringing in his lap. He'd already dragged Luke into this stupid thing; he didn't want to bring Luke's parents into it as well. He swallowed hard and pressed his lips together, wishing there was another way. As they headed down the stairs, Logan met them in the hallway.

"I'm sorry, Casey. I shouldn't have yelled. It's…" He cleared his throat and looked away, biting the side of his cheek, a clear sign he was troubled. "Stay safe, okay? I'll call you later." Logan pulled him into a bone-crushing hug, and Casey refrained from crying, but only just.

The drive to Luke's parents didn't take long, but the pair of them were silent, lost in their thoughts. At least, Casey was. He stared into the night sky while he tried to figure out the best way to sort it all out without other people getting caught in the crossfire. So unaware of his surroundings, he hadn't realised they'd arrived until Luke turned off the engine, the ticking of it cooling the only sound around them.

"They're awake if you're worried about disturbing them," Luke confided. "I rang them to let them know."

"I don't want anyone to get hurt because of me." He felt guilty for bringing other people into this when it was his problem.

"I know you don't." Luke clasped Casey's hand in his. "It won't come to that. This is a place to regroup and rest, nothing else. I've been checking as I drove, and we haven't been followed. We're safe here."

Casey studied the man before him. Being taller and more muscular than Casey, Luke could be seen as a deterrent, but he didn't want Luke to have to be with him all the time. It wasn't fair on Luke. "I want to start training again," he said slowly.

Luke nodded. "All right. We can start as soon as you're ready." His gaze moved to something outside the car, and Casey tensed. "It's okay. It's Dad. Let's go inside and get some sleep."

Casey hesitated but, eventually, agreed.

"Luke, Casey. Glad to have you here." Luke's dad was an older version of Luke, without a doubt, with a lot of grey in his hair and crinkles around his welcoming face. It gave Casey an idea of what Luke would look like when he aged.

"Casey, this is my dad, Charles."

"Nice to meet you, Mr Walker." Casey side-eyed Luke, mentally chastising him for believing he would call his dad by his first name.

Luke grinned and dragged him inside the house, dropping their bags in the hallway while they removed their coats and shoes.

"Luke!" An older lady, yet again with features that

could never deny the relationship between them, came bustling forward and wrapped Luke in her arms.

"This is my wife, Catherine." Mr Walker smiled as he introduced her to Casey.

"Nice to meet you, Mrs Walker. Sorry for the interruption, especially in the middle of the night."

"Pfft." She waved him away, dragging him close to her and surrounding him in motherly affection. His eyes pricked again, but he refused to break down. As she pulled away, she cupped his cheek as his own mother usually did. "You are not interrupting. Anyone who is in need is welcome here with open arms. Especially if they mean a lot to one of my children." She smiled across at Luke and let Casey go. "Luke, I changed the sheets on the bed in your room. You know where everything is. Go get some rest, the both of you."

Luke kissed his mother's cheek, grabbed the bags and threaded his fingers through Casey's once more. "Night." He dragged him towards the stairs.

Mortification swept through Casey that Luke's parents knew they would be sleeping in the same bed. "Are you not bothered about me sleeping in the same bed as you under your parents' roof?" he whispered.

Luke grinned. "Nope."

"Why? I would be."

"Never done it before. And besides, we're on the other side of the house from where they will be." He winked suggestively.

"Luke!" Casey's voice came out strangled.

Luke laughed and tugged him up the stairs and

towards the back of the house. The house rivalled his own parents', and he knew instinctively there would be more than enough room for them. Dragging Casey away from the pictures lining the hallway, Luke stopped in front of a door.

"This is me." He rubbed the back of his neck, seeming a little unsure now that they stood there. "It's not changed a huge amount since I was younger, but at least there are no weird posters or pictures anymore." He chuckled.

"It'll be great however it looks," Casey reassured.

Luke pushed open the door and pulled Casey in behind him, closing them in after.

Casey let go of Luke's hand and wandered around the space. There was a double bed in the centre of one wall with bedside tables either side; a large, over-stuffed armchair sat by the window and a bookcase, which was full to the brim with books; a wardrobe and chest of drawers covered with aged stickers completed the furniture. Casey could tell it had been a teenager's room at one point, and he grinned.

"Nice choice." He indicated some stickers from the nineties of pop and rock bands.

"Shut up," Luke admonished, good-naturedly. "I really need to get them sanded off and repaint the furniture." He rested the bags on the bed. "I know you haven't got much with you, so I brought some extra clothes in case you need them. Plus, there are some of my old clothes in the drawers and wardrobe, no doubt. They might fit you better."

"This is more than enough, Luke. Thank you." The tightness in his chest felt overwhelming, and it was all he could do to keep it inside rather than bursting into tears like he had done already that night.

Luke stepped closer and wrapped his arms around Casey. "Thank you for letting me help."

They stayed in their bubble for a short time, then Luke pulled back. "Let's get to bed."

Circling each other as they got ready lit a desire in Casey. The ease of the silence between them was reassuring and went a long way to calm him. It was how he had always envisaged a relationship being. He refused to get too caught up in it. It was only temporary, and after everything that had happened, he was certain Luke wouldn't want anything to do with him once it was over.

"Casey?"

"Yes?"

"Everything okay? You've been studying that t-shirt for a few minutes now."

Casey looked at the fabric in his hands, shook his head and pulled the t-shirt over his head. "Sorry, a little distracted."

Luke held out his arms from where he sat on the bed, covers already turned down. "Come here."

Casey sank onto the mattress, grateful to realise the bed didn't creak. Not that he thought they would be doing anything, but just the idea that they might would make him unable to meet Luke's parents' eyes the next morning. Luke folded Casey close before pulling the duvet over them. The light dusting of hair on Luke's bare chest abraded Casey's cheek, and he rubbed against it with a smile. He rested his hand on Luke's stomach and pressed himself tight against his side.

Luke kissed the top of his head. "Try and get some sleep. Wake me if you need anything."

Casey nodded and closed his eyes. Try as he might, he couldn't sleep. Visions of Acker, Luke, Logan, work colleagues and others flashed through his mind, and he fidgeted. Knowing he was disturbing Luke, he rolled away to his other side. Seconds later, Luke spooned behind him.

"Can't you sleep?"

Casey shook his head. "Sorry. I don't mean to keep you up. I'll get up."

"No." Luke rolled him onto his back. "I'll help you sleep."

"How?"

Luke pressed their lips together, sliding his tongue into Casey's mouth as soon as Casey gasped. He took Casey's lips hard and demanding, and Casey felt his cock responding to the stimulus. Casey rocked his hips, gaining limited friction from the boxers and duvet over him. Luke bit at Casey's bottom lip before pulling back, though Casey followed.

Chuckling, Luke lifted Casey's t-shirt and kissed his stomach, painting his abs with his tongue while his hands freed Casey's growing erection from the now too tight boxers.

"This will be hard and fast." Luke smirked.

"Fuck," Casey breathed as Luke sank onto Casey's shaft, swallowing most of his length.

Luke's tongue smoothed along the underside of Casey's cock as Luke lifted his head and licked around, getting it wet. Encircling the base, Luke winked at Casey and sucked at the head before swallowing him down once more.

"Oh, fu—" Casey's words were stopped by the feel of Luke's throat convulsing around his cock. Luke was right about it being hard and fast. Casey wouldn't last long.

Luke bobbed his head, setting a rhythm designed to make him come. Up and down, swirling his tongue on the underside with every lift and swallowing with every downwards stroke with a wet sound. When Luke pressed a finger against Casey's hole, Casey's arousal spiked, and he gripped the sheets beneath him.

"Fuck, Luke. I'm not going to last." Casey gasped with each breath he took. Light-headedness became his new friend.

Luke tightened his lips and increased his speed, using his hand to bring more friction. Tingling began to speed down Casey's spine, and he called out a whispered warning. Luke's finger breached his hole, and Casey exploded into Luke's mouth with an open-mouthed, silent shout.

He came back to himself when the sensitivity of his cock being licked clean was too much for him to bear.

"Jesus, Luke."

Luke wiped the corners of his mouth with his

fingers, pulled Casey's boxers back over his spent cock and shuffled back up the bed. Dragging Casey's lethargic body over his once more, Luke kissed his forehead.

"Sleep."

The next day was a whirlwind of making a statement with Kade and Joey about the events of the previous night, but also the harassment. Casey had been pulled aside by Luke's mother that morning.

"Now, I am in no way saying you have to do this, Casey, but I would like you to think about what I'm about to say," she began. Casey nodded, and she continued, *"If what is happening to you was happening to Claire or Alice, what would you suggest they do?"*

That morning, they had explained everything to Luke's parents and understanding dawned in his head. "I would've fought tooth and nail for them to tell someone," he said quietly.

Mrs Walker nodded. "So, why won't you give yourself the same treatment? You deserve it as much as they do." She waved him away when he opened his mouth to answer. "I know your job is slightly different to some, but if you told someone, regardless of whether it is brushed under the carpet or not, someone knows. Someone will be keeping an eye on that guy, even if they say they aren't. They will not give him much leeway before they wash their hands of him. It's not worth the hassle to the hospital to have to keep covering things up."

Casey sat and stared at her. He'd never thought of it that way before.

"They will also not be allowed to fire or demote you. It would be seen as an injustice, and the hospital will be put under fire for it, especially with the evidence you have. They cannot risk it." She grasped his hands. "The way I see it, it's a win-win situation, except for maybe your reputation. Some people won't believe you—that's a given—but you need to think of the greater good. Think of who you can help by acknowledging what's happening. Think of how you can help yourself."

Casey sat there long after Mrs Walker had left him to his thoughts. Luke finally pulled him in for a hug and brought him back to himself. As soon as he had, Casey knew what he had to do.

Since he'd called Logan, everything had begun happening. He'd made the statement with the police, he'd provided the evidence he had, and he had called the hospital requesting a meeting with his boss, which was set for that afternoon. Logan was coming with him for the discussion, although Casey was going to try and persuade him to stay outside while he spoke with Dr Rogerson.

He'd also spoken to Alex, who went ballistic at him for not telling him before. Even when Casey had argued that he'd been busy with Craig, Alex had yelled that Casey was his best friend and shouldn't have been doing it on his own. Thoroughly chastened, Casey had agreed to keep Alex in the loop from then on. They'd also had a brief discussion about Luke, where Alex had teased him mercilessly.

A plate of food was placed before him, and he jumped, having been lost in his thoughts yet again.

"I thought you might be hungry as you'd not eaten much breakfast," Luke said.

Casey smiled at him. "Thanks, but I don't know if I can."

Luke rested his arm around Casey's shoulders and pulled him until his head was on Luke's shoulder. "Everything will be fine." He rubbed a hand up and down Casey's arm.

"And if I lose my job?" He spoke his worst fear.

"You won't." Luke paused. "But if you do, you'll find another one."

Casey chuckled. "So simple."

"Hey! I am not simple!"

Casey lifted his head, laughing as he pushed against Luke's chest. "Not you, you idiot."

"Oh, so now I'm an idiot, too. So full of compliments today." Luke grinned. "That's better."

Resting his hand on Luke's jaw, he whispered, "Thank you, Luke."

"You don't need to thank me. You need to thank yourself."

"Why?"

"For being brave enough and strong enough to do what you know is right."

"Time to go, Casey." Logan's soft words made him close his eyes and wilt.

Luke cupped his jaw. "You are strong. Remember what you told me before?" He waited until Casey shook his head. "Take my confidence in you, take the training I've given you and take whatever extra strength from me you need to be able to do this."

Casey kissed him. He had no choice. Whoever made Luke believe he wasn't as important or successful or loved as the rest of his siblings should rot in hell. This man before him was everything. Breaking the kiss, he rested their foreheads together. "I know it's too soon, but I love you, Luke." He had no choice in it either.

Luke stared at him, mouth open, eyes wide. "Really?"

Casey smiled and nodded.

Luke dragged him into a hug and whispered in Casey's ear, "I love you, too."

They kissed again until Logan cleared his throat and reminded them Casey needed to leave.

Feeling lighter and heavier at the same time was a new experience for Casey. He was usually so upbeat and happy, but he hadn't realised how quiet and reserved he'd become until he felt that joy again.

"You doing okay over there?" Logan asked as he parked the car.

Casey peered over at him and gave a small smile. "I am as good as can be expected."

"Even with the declarations of love?" His brother smirked.

"Shut up! You shouldn't have been eavesdropping. Remember what Mum always said about that." Casey smiled more genuinely and felt the damn tell-tale heat infusing his cheeks.

Logan grinned, then sobered. "You're doing the right thing."

"I know. It's hard because I don't know what the outcome will be."

"True."

They wandered along the corridors of the hospital, using lifts where necessary until they reached Rogerson's door. Casey stood in front of it, breathing deeply to try and calm his nerves.

"Can you stay out here?" he asked Logan.

"Not on your life," Logan murmured from beside him.

Casey rolled his eyes, knowing it had been a long shot.

"Ready?"

"Nope."

Logan knocked on the door. The fucker.

"Come in."

Logan opened the door and indicated for Casey to enter first.

"Casey, nice to see you." Rogerson's gaze flicked to Logan. "I didn't realise you were bringing a friend."

Logan stepped forward, holding out his hand. "Detective Sergeant Logan Taylor and Casey's brother. Nice to meet you."

Rogerson's eyes narrowed as he flicked his gaze between them both. "Do I need a lawyer?" He chuckled, although Casey could tell he was only half-joking.

"Not at all," Logan replied. "Unless *you* think you need one."

Rogerson narrowed his eyes at them, then turned his focus to Casey. "What can I do for you, Casey? You said the matter was urgent."

Casey cleared his throat and sat in the visitor chair, Logan sitting beside him. "Yes. I would like to make a complaint against Dr Acker."

"For what?"

Though his boss asked the question, Casey could see the man's shoulders lower slightly. "Sexual harassment."

Rogerson inhaled and leaned forward, linking his fingers as he rested them on the desk. "That is quite a bold claim, Casey. Do you have any evidence?"

"He does," Logan answered for him.

"May I see the evidence?"

Logan indicated for Casey to play the voice file. When it finished, Rogerson said, "It was taken within the hospital walls, which is against policy."

"Actually, it's not."

Rogerson and Logan glanced at Casey when he spoke. Logan nodded, though his gaze was narrowed. Casey had not given him this information because he'd only just figured it out.

"Policy states that confidentiality must be upheld at all times. There were no people around when the recording was taken."

"But there could have been." Rogerson had a point.

"But there wasn't. If there had been, and they were heard discussing patients, I'm sure it would be inadmissible in court."

Silence reigned for a moment as Rogerson stared at Casey. "You're taking things that far?"

Casey shrugged. "I don't want to."

"Unfortunately, due to an incident that happened last night, Casey has had to make a formal statement regarding the harassment. This does not mean the case has to go to court, but it does mean the police will be contacting various people for statements regarding Dr Acker's professional and personal behaviour. There is no option to stop that from happening. However, your co-operation will be greatly appreciated if you wish to keep this quiet."

Rogerson rubbed his hands over his face, sat back in his creaky chair and sighed. "Fine. Tell me what you need."

"I have a list of the people we need to speak to. I would also recommend Dr Acker is put on paid absence while the investigation is continuing."

"All right. How quickly can we get this done?"

"How quickly can we get the people from that list here?" Logan countered.

Casey watched as his brother worked his magic with his boss. Logan called in Kade and Joey to take over the interviews as Logan couldn't do them, and Rogerson contacted the staff members.

"Why do you need to speak with this person? It says they were a patient."

Logan nodded. "Yes, they were on 14 September. There were in the room where Casey had an altercation with Dr Acker. Although the patient appeared to be asleep, I want to confirm this."

"I cannot give out their information."

"Then you can call them and get permission before the police are in the room."

When everything was set up, Casey and Logan followed Rogerson to a conference room where Kade and Joey were already waiting.

"All the people you asked for are on their way or can be called from the hospital floor when you need them."

"Thank you, Dr Rogerson. We'll be in touch later today," Logan said.

Rogerson stared at Casey with pursed lips and walked away. Casey deflated and sat on a chair, exhaling heavily.

"Are you okay?" Logan asked.

"I've no idea." He rubbed his sweaty palms against his jeans and tried to swallow against the lump in his throat.

"Luke is on his way to pick you up."

"Why can't I stay?"

"Because we don't want you unintentionally putting pressure on the staff." He held up his hand. "I know you wouldn't mean to, but it's better if we do this clean, then we will be able to defend our actions if needed."

"All right."

CHAPTER EIGHTEEN

LUKE

Waiting for Logan to call with more information was a lesson in patience for sure. Casey paced Luke's parents' house from front to back and top to bottom. He couldn't eat, he couldn't sleep, he couldn't sit still. The only time he could settle was when Luke had his arms around him. They received the occasional text from Casey's brother, but they were not helpful ones, only telling them that he was still waiting for more information, at which Casey rambled and cursed.

It was the following evening before there was a knock at the door and Logan finally appeared.

"What happened?"

Logan smiled. "The doctor won't be a problem any longer."

Casey gasped, a hand covering his mouth. "Why?" Luke put his arm around Casey's waist.

"Sit down. I have a lot to tell you."

His mother bustled in with a tray of coffees for everyone, as always, seeming to know when something was needed without having to be asked, then left Luke, Casey and Logan to it.

"For god's sake, Logan, tell me."

"Acker has been fired, but he's been released on bail."

"Seriously?" Casey moved his gaze to Luke, his eyes and mouth wide.

It was more than they had expected. They never, even for a moment, believed Acker would lose his job, especially with how high up in the chain he was and how many recommendations he received.

"There was too much evidence against him."

"Were there others in the same situation?" Luke asked, knowing it was something Casey had worried endlessly about.

"Not that have come up so far. That's not to say there aren't." Logan gulped some coffee, replacing it on the table and picking up his notebook. "Okay. We spoke to the patient, who willingly admitted she heard the conversation between you and Acker in her room that day. Although she says you seemed unwilling, she didn't want to say anything because she wasn't sure if it was," Logan smirked, "'your kind of kink' were her words."

Luke chuckled. "Fair enough." Casey slapped his shoulder with the back of his hand, though a smile graced his lips.

"She was able to remember enough to show it *was*

unwilling. Chloe explained your change in behaviour and her growing concerns about your mental health. You may want to give her a call after this. She's extremely worried about you."

"I will." Casey sighed and lowered his gaze to his lap, his shoulders slumping. "I should've told her."

"Hindsight and all. Don't worry, she'll be okay with it. You're safe. That's all that matters." Luke rested his hand on the back of Casey's neck.

"What about Kinton. I don't expect you got much from him," Casey said, leaning into Luke.

Logan's mouth curled up. "Actually, you owe Kinton a great debt."

Casey frowned and sat upright again. "What?"

"What did you do with your shirt?" Logan asked, ignoring Casey's question.

"What shirt? Oh, I threw it into the shower area, then..." Casey hesitated, studying the floor with a furrowed brow. "I've no idea. Fuck, it would've been good evidence. Shit. I never even thought of that." Casey slumped back on the sofa and sighed again.

"That is why you owe Kinton," Logan stated. "Kinton entered the locker room as Acker was leaving the day of the incident. I'm assuming it's why you didn't hear the door open a second time. Kinton said he saw Acker's grin, then saw you on the floor and put two and two together. Kinton knew you didn't like him, so he thought you wouldn't accept his help or like him seeing you like that and stayed behind the lockers until you left. He picked up the shirt, realised what was on it and put it in a bag in his locker."

"Why?"

"So you'd have the evidence if you ever needed it," Luke surmised to which Logan nodded.

"Yes. It's because of him and the additional CCTV footage we managed to get hold of from the day in the corridor, which was the final nail in Acker's coffin."

"Do you know if he's done it before at the other hospital?"

"Don't know at the minute. Kade and Joey are looking into some leads, and Acker wasn't confirming anything."

"What happens now?" Luke asked.

"Well, we need to investigate last night. Acker is adamant it wasn't him, which means there is someone else with a grudge against one of you."

Luke frowned. He had no idea of anyone who might feel that way about him. As he was about to say so, the front door slammed.

"Luke! Where are you?" Carter's shout headed their way, and Luke rose as he entered the room. "Oh, sorry." He glanced at Logan. "Hey, Logan. What are you doing here?"

Logan stood and shook hands with Carter. "Something with Casey."

Carter gazed at Luke, then Casey, then Luke again.

"Casey, is it okay to tell him? He might be able to help more?" Luke crouched in front of Casey, taking his hands.

"He knows, anyway, just not that it was me." Casey smiled. "It's fine."

"Casey is the guy I was asking you about."

Carter swore. "Fuck, Logan. If I'd known…"

Logan waved him away. "They're good at keeping secrets." Logan glared at Luke and Casey, who snickered.

They filled Carter in on everything that had happened so far. By that point, Luke could see Casey was flagging, and he gripped his hand and led him up the stairs after saying goodnight to everyone. Trailing into the en-suite, Luke removed Casey's clothes before taking off his own and wrapped Casey in his arms under the warm spray. Neither moved for a while, and Luke knew the water would stay hot—with a family of seven in total, his parents made sure to have a decent boiler. Luke managed to get Casey to stand for the time it took to wash his hair and body and his own before drying them both off and trudging to the bed.

Luke pulled back the covers and tucked Casey in, crawling across him to get on the other side to the music of Casey's laughter. Enclosing Casey in his arms once more, they kissed leisurely and settled down. It was only as he drifted off to sleep, he realised Carter had not explained why he'd been looking for Luke.

Luke supported the weights as Zak laid them to rest in the stand. Zak sat up and blew out a breath. "Bloody hell. I'm going to be aching tomorrow."

Grinning, Luke said, "Probably not tomorrow, but the day after, definitely."

"You're a taskmaster when it comes to this." Zak gulped his water, finishing half the bottle in one go.

"Only when the client wants me to be. It's your own fault."

Zak laughed. "I'm surprised you had room to fit me in. When I spoke to the receptionist, she said you worked more with clients in need of evasive training."

"Yeah, the number of people wanting the training has increased lately. I'm not sure why, but it keeps me busy."

"Have you thought about doing it as a business?" Zak asked, wiping his face with his towel.

"What do you mean?"

"Well, here, surely, you only get your wages, and the company takes most of the profit."

"Yeah." Luke frowned, not sure where Zak was going.

"Why not open your own business instead. You'd get a say in where the profits go. And once you make enough, you could donate some to a charity of your choice if you felt bad about reaping all the rewards."

"It sounds like a lot of hassle." Luke had enough drama for a lifetime with everything that had happened over the last week.

"I run my own business, and it's not too bad. I know

it's not in the same field, but the general business side of things will be the same. I'm happy to go through it with you if you're interested."

Luke had never contemplated running his own business before; he didn't know if he was capable of doing it. He was nothing like his siblings in that respect. He had some savings he could put into it, but would people be interested in it when it was already being provided at the gym?

When he asked Zak that question, he replied, "I bet you'd find a lot of the people are here because *you* train them, not because of where the training is being held."

"I'll have to think about it. Thanks."

"You're welcome. Remember to give me a ring if you need to know anything."

It had certainly piqued his interest, and when he saw Casey that evening, he explained what Zak had said about the business venture.

"That's a fantastic idea. Are you going to do it?" Casey asked, straddling Luke and lifting his t-shirt over his head. They'd not seen each other for three days because of Casey's night shifts, and both were eager to be as close as they could get.

"I don't know. I've never thought about it before. I don't know what's involved." Luke kissed Casey, exploring his mouth with his tongue.

"So, take Zak up on his offer and talk it through with him. See if it's something you might like to do. If not, no harm, no foul," Casey said as he pulled away, gasping.

By that point, they were both so hard, talking was limited to moans and groans until Luke stilled when he was balls deep inside Casey.

"I love you."

"You're not supposed to say that when you're having sex. It makes me feel like you only want me for my body," Casey pouted, pretending to cry, then whimpered when Luke tickled him and slid a little deeper.

"Fuck, you feel so good. And I'm not having sex with you." Luke leaned down and stopped before their lips touched. "I'm making love to you."

"I love you," Casey said, lifting the final space to seal their lips.

Luke sat across from Zak at a table in Sweet Tooth. Theo had brought their coffees and cakes, and they sat chatting about Dane and their weekend plans. After their conversation a couple of days before, and the discussion with Casey, Luke called Zak to ask to meet and talk about the potential business. Zak had been more than happy to and suggested getting together at a café so Zak could get Dane out of the house for a little while.

Hence, the reason they were watching as Dane wore more than ate the cake, but as Zak said, he was happy and not throwing a tantrum, so in Zak's book, it was a good thing.

Zak had pulled out a pad of paper and turned the

conversation onto the subject at hand. "So, one of the first things you need to think about is what you want to provide. Do you just want to give evasive training? Do you want to do weight training, too? Do you want to provide pro-bono classes? There are so many options. Once you have decided, you can start looking for a place that will fit your needs."

"I prefer the evasive training to weight training, that's for sure. I love the idea of free classes, although I wouldn't be able to do too many if I wanted to keep the business afloat, surely?" Luke frowned.

"That's true. But you can figure out those details when you create a business plan. For now, you need ideas of what you'd prefer to do and find somewhere you would be able to do it."

"All right. Evasive training classes and I'd like to do something with places that provide shelter for abused people." Luke knew there was a women's shelter that helped those in abusive relationships, but he wanted to provide it to *all* people, not just women. "It needs to be all-inclusive."

Zak nodded. "Agreed. You need to decide the different details about each area you want to provide. So, like evasive training… is it one on one or in classes or pairs? Think about how it would work and see if there are any other options you might not have thought of."

"Basically, I have to think of all the intricate details about each area before I can do anything else." Luke grinned, though the overwhelming amount of information was just that… overwhelming. He rubbed the back of his neck.

"Yeah." Zak laughed. "Start as you mean to go on. Don't make something available if you are not one hundred percent sure you want to provide it. I made that mistake." Zak rooted in the changing bag next to him and pulled out some wipes.

"Why?"

Zak leaned forward to wipe Dane's hands and pushed a cup closer to the young boy. "When I first started, I didn't have a huge catalogue for people to look through. When someone asked me if I could do something, I said yes, even if I didn't like making them. I ended up spending an entire year making these fancy ornate chests of drawers, and I hated every minute of it." Zak shook his head as he sat back with a smile. "I fulfilled the orders I'd already agreed to but refused any new ones. Don't get me wrong, the money was good, but I have never made one since."

Luke chuckled. "Sounds fair. It's a long process if you don't enjoy it."

"Definitely."

They spoke some more about the various aspects of starting a business before Zak and Dane left for home. Once he was alone, Luke ordered another coffee and sat staring out the window as he thought about the information Zak had provided. There was a lot to think about and discuss with other people. He suddenly remembered Carter and dialled his brother.

"Hey," he said when Carter answered his phone.

"What's up, little brother?"

Luke could hear rustling on the other end of the line. "Are you busy? I can call back later."

"Nah, I'm good. Just reshuffling some papers."

"Oh, so that's what you do when you're at work. You move paper from one side of the desk to the other," Luke teased. He didn't do it often, but he was feeling content if a little unsure.

Carter hesitated, then replied, "Yep, it's all I do. You found me out."

Luke was pleased to hear Carter return the banter. "I'm ringing because I remembered you never told me why you were coming to see me the other day."

"Oh. To be honest, it was to give you some more information about helping your friend—Casey. After you told me what happened, it wasn't relevant anymore."

"That's okay. Well, I'll let you go. I know you are busy despite what you say."

"I always have time for you, Luke. Always will. Is everything all right with you?"

Luke returned his gaze to the bustling streets outside the window and smiled, nodding slowly. "Yeah. Things are going great."

"I'm glad to hear it. You deserve to be happy. You do so much for others; it's finally time to do something for yourself."

"What do you mean?" Luke squirmed in his seat. Carter had never said anything like that before.

Carter sighed. "You're so quiet, withdrawn even. I

hate seeing you like that. When you're around Casey or talk about your job, you light up. Helping people as you do, it's a similar thing to what I do here. I want to help people be safe, happy, get what they deserve. You do the same with your training. You provide people with the chance to reclaim what they've lost or become confident in their abilities."

Luke was speechless. His job was not as significant as Carter's and to hear him talk the way he was confused him. "My job is not important, Carter. I—"

"You save people's lives, Luke."

"No, I don't. I train them. I'm not a doctor or anything."

Carter blew out a breath and muttered something Luke couldn't hear. "Luke, you train people to get away from attackers. You train people and give them confidence in themselves. Trust me when I say you have saved someone's life without realising it."

Luke stared at the top of the table, unable to process what Carter was saying. He needed to know what had happened to his clients before he could help them, but the actual details had not even registered with him.

"I hadn't realised how inferior you felt. Fuck, Luke. I'm sorry. You must hate us."

"No!" he shouted, then after looking around with a grimace and an apology, he quieted. "No, I don't hate any of you. You all do such amazing jobs, I guess... I didn't understand how my job measured up."

"You're probably the best of us all, Luke." Carter chuckled.

"No way. Maybe… we all help in our own way," he said with raised eyebrows. He had never thought his job was as important as the rest of his siblings, but maybe it was. Other than for creating a training programme for each client, he had never considered what happened when the clients weren't at his sessions. It made his conversation with Zak earlier even more profound and gave him ideas for his business.

He was going ahead with it for sure. It might take a while to get it up and running, but he wanted something that could help a variety of people. Luke explained his idea to Carter, who offered to speak to one of his colleagues about business law stuff Luke had no idea about. Carter even offered to be a silent partner if Luke needed the extra financial backing. It was more than he had ever expected, but he was grateful for the help.

They spoke for a long while before Carter had to head off to a meeting. As Luke sat nursing his empty mug, he realised he *was* happy. Things were looking up for him, and he felt lighter.

The following day, he spoke to his dad about the business idea. His dad, and the siblings who eavesdropped, thought it was a fantastic idea, and they spent the afternoon bouncing ideas around about the different areas he could offer classes and training in. Luke had never felt as much a part of the family as he did at that moment.

CHAPTER NINETEEN

CASEY

Casey had worried about going back to work after everything that had happened with Acker, but he'd not realised how many people hadn't liked the former doctor. Casey had been approached by several members of staff—wanting to gossip, naturally—who asked how he was and if he needed anything. It got to be a little annoying after a while, but he'd prefer it to what he had been through, and most of the people meant well.

After a long conversation with Chloe, they were back on good terms. She had been so upset that she hadn't known what he was going through, and he had to spend several days trying to explain it wasn't her fault he had been an ass and kept secrets. Eventually, her sadness had moved to anger at him, briefly, and he'd had to apologise profoundly with chocolate and flowers. If anyone had been on the outside looking in, they would have thought he was wooing her. She had come around when he'd dropped to his knees and begged her to forgive him.

Kinton was another matter. He was nowhere to be found, although Casey knew he worked because he'd asked Gloria whether she'd seen him around, which she confirmed she had. Trying to find him so Casey could have a conversation with him was proving difficult, though. If he didn't find him soon, he'd have to stake out his house.

Luckily for him, Casey caught sight of Kinton in the restaurant that day. He crept up behind him and dropped into the seat next to him, making Kinton spill his coffee on the table.

"Fuck! Casey, you asshole." Kinton grabbed a few napkins and mopped up the spill.

"I'll get you another one after we've talked." Casey twisted on his seat, so he was facing him and rested one arm on the back of the seat and one elbow on the table. "Why are you avoiding me?"

Kinton sighed and sipped at his remaining drink. "I didn't think you'd want to talk to me."

"Bullshit. You have to know I've been trying to talk to you."

"I don't want you to pretend to be my friend because I helped you out. I don't need pity friends, Casey." Kinton went to stand, but Casey grabbed his arm.

"Wait. I'm not doing this out of pity. Yes, I want to thank you. What you did was… fuck, it was everything.

I liked you beforehand. I just found you a little… blinkered."

"Blinkered? What's that supposed to mean?"

Casey sighed. "Sometimes, your comments seemed a little shallow." Casey grimaced. "Sorry."

Kinton lowered his head, staring into his cup. "I don't do well at socialising. Sometimes, when I try to be funny, it comes out wrong. I'm not a horrible person, Casey."

"I know you're not, but just try to be you. Don't try to be someone you're not."

"Sorry."

"Look. You have nothing to be sorry for. After everything you've done for me, the slate is clean." Casey stuck his hand forward. "Hi, I'm Casey. Nice to meet you."

Kinton gaped at him as if he were deranged, but his mouth quirked up, and he shook Casey's hand. "Kinton. You, too."

They stared at each other for a moment before cracking up. Casey stood. "Don't go running out on me while I get your drink now. No more hiding. You hear?"

Grinning, Kinton flipped him off.

Casey snickered as he strode to the coffee machine. Maybe Kinton wasn't so bad, after all.

Casey pulled into the car park at the hospital, pointing his car into a space before killing the engine. Luke had treated him to a bubble bath before he had to leave for work, and it had turned into a veritable splash park when they'd been unable to keep their hands to themselves. He grinned—he'd left Luke mopping the bathroom floor.

Ducking his head into the backseat, he grabbed his backpack and stepped back into something hard. He flinched away, putting a hand on his chest. "Fuck!" He turned his head to look over his shoulder, but an arm came around his throat, and he dropped his bag to grip at it. The pressure was choking him, and he could see black spots begin to float in front of his eyes. He tried to elbow the person behind him, but it did nothing. He tried to remember what Luke had taught him and went lax in the hold, but the person went to the floor with him. Casey's feet slid along the loose chippings of the car park surface as he tried to gain purchase to push up and away from the pressure.

Feeling himself getting weaker by the minute, he closed his eyes and tried everything he could think of to get away. As darkness rolled over him, his last thought was of Luke.

His eyes blinked blearily, the ache in his jaw disturbing his peace. He couldn't remember what had happened for it to hurt so much. Trying to swallow against his dry mouth, he realised he couldn't, and suddenly, it all came crashing back.

Casey's eyes flew open, his arms and legs jerked, pulling against the restraints that were keeping his arms above his head and his legs spread-eagled, and he took in his surroundings. He immediately saw a nice-looking bedroom, which had the feel of a hotel from the leaflets and such that he could see, but there was no one else in the room.

Heart settling a little, his focus went to the pressure in his jaw again, and he realised it was some sort of ball gag or similar because there was a strap going around his head, and a smooth spherical shape in his mouth.

Taking note of his body, he knew his wrists and ankles were tied up with rope and had little to no give in them. He was naked but covered with a white duvet, which had his heart hammering against his chest. Someone had stripped him off while he had been unconscious. His nostrils flared as he tried to calm himself, knowing his brain would not work when he was panicking.

Stretching his neck, he tried to see any clues about where he was but couldn't see anything of note. The leaflets were too far away to read. His eyes scanned for anything that he might be able to use, but nothing was in reach.

He had no idea who had kidnapped him or how long had passed since he'd been taken.

A door clicked, then slammed shut, and Casey wavered between pretending to be unconscious still or glaring at whoever came around the corner. He chose to glare, although it lost some of the heat behind it when Acker came into view.

"Ah, Casey! I see you've finally woken up. Glad you managed to get some rest."

Acker wore a thick, black coat that was unbuttoned, revealing trousers and a v-neck jumper over the top of a shirt—basically, what he wore at work minus the white coat. His hair was a little more scruffy than usual, and he had several days of scruff along his jaw.

"Like what you see?" Acker asked with a smirk.

There were so many things he could think of to say to the bastard, but all that came out was incoherent gargling.

"Maybe I can let you take that off later, and you can tell me how much you're enjoying my cock."

Fear raced down his spine, and his limbs trembled, his skin clammy, though cold. He'd been so stupid to think he was out of danger just because Acker had been fired; it had never occurred to him that Acker might try to get retribution. To top it all, Casey had been putting off the training sessions with Luke until after Christmas; that decision came back to bite him.

Casey watched Acker remove his coat and hang it across the back of the desk chair before running a hand through his hair. The man lifted an armchair and pulled it closer to the bed. Instinctively, Casey tried to move away, but the restraints stopped him.

"Now, now. No hurting yourself." He sat, crossing his legs and clasping his hands. "If you had just let yourself feel what you obviously do, I wouldn't have needed to go to these lengths. We could've had such fun, just you and me. Now, though, I have to use these," he indicated the ropes, "to make sure you're safe." He shook his head like Casey was an errant child.

Casey closed his eyes, trying to withhold the tears and sobs he could feel building up inside him. He refused to let the guy know how close to breaking he was.

A touch to his bare arm had him flinching and his eyes flying open again. Acker smoothed a hand along his biceps to his shoulder and under the duvet. Casey's trembling increased along with his breathing, and he clenched his fists.

"Such smooth skin. I had such a nice time undressing you. You were so co-operative and willing; it was all I could do to stop myself from taking you there and then." He licked his lips.

Acker slid the duvet down Casey's body, revealing him inch by inch, but stopping short of his hips, which although Casey appreciated, he didn't understand until Acker said, "I can't go any further yet. I need to wait a little while before I get my reward, and if I see you naked now, I won't hesitate to make you mine. But I can…"

Casey pulled against the ropes as Acker climbed onto the bed and kneeled beside him, watching with subdued fear as the man undid his trousers and removed his dick. The groan that accompanied the stroking sent goosebumps across Casey's skin.

Acker had one hand on his cock and his other he

slid across Casey's abdomen, the touch soft and at odds with his behaviour. He squeezed his eyes shut again when Acker's fingers flicked over his nipples, then opened them quickly when he realised he'd prefer to see what the man was doing than be surprised.

Apart from Acker's deep breathing and whispered words, Casey couldn't hear anything around them, not even through the small window. It was very unnerving to be at the mercy of a man he had gotten fired.

"Oh, baby! Yes, that's it. You're going to be mine soon. I'm going to take your ass and make you realise who it belongs to."

Casey watched, dread flowing through him, as Acker stroked his way to his orgasm, spraying his release over Casey's torso. Despite the shudders of revulsion going through him, he was glad it hadn't been his face.

"Fuck, yes. That felt good. It'll be even better soon." Acker rubbed his come into Casey's skin, making Casey's nostrils flare in annoyance.

Acker stood, tucking his spent dick away and making himself presentable again. "Well, as much as I'd love to keep you company, I have someplace to be. I will be back in a few hours to stake my claim." He leered and pulled the duvet back over Casey's chest. "I'll let you keep that one on you. You can learn what I smell like."

He leaned down, pressing a kiss to Casey's cheek and whispering, "I can't wait to kiss you, too. Hmm." Acker nuzzled his nose against Casey's skin to his neck before sucking hard on the skin, marking him if Casey wasn't mistaken. The fucker.

When Casey was alone again, he tried to move his jaw a little to ease the strain. He couldn't figure out where the ropes were attached because it wasn't visible to him, though he assumed there was some sort of hook underneath the bed.

He wondered what time it was. Acker had left the lights on for him, which was a small gift, he supposed, but Casey should've been at work by now. Would anyone even have checked up on him if he hadn't turned up? If so, who would they have rung? Probably his parents. Or maybe Logan as he was Casey's second contact. Or maybe they haven't even tried contacting him except for on his own phone. Where was his phone? He lifted his head again and tried to see if his bag was anywhere, but he couldn't see it, nor could he see his clothes. He'd put his phone in his jeans pocket, and he had a spare phone in his bag, but neither was any good if he couldn't reach them.

Exhaling through his nose was less satisfactory than sighing, but it was all he could do. He couldn't see a way out of the fucked-up situation, and he had no idea if anyone would be able to find him, even if they knew he was missing instead of just absent.

Try as he might, he couldn't stop the tears from leaking out of the corners of his eyes as he thought about how helpless he was. There were no comforting thoughts of being saved, of seeing Luke or his family again. Undoubtedly, Acker would either move him or kill him once he'd raped him; there was no way he'd let Casey go.

Every time Casey felt himself slipping into a doze, he moved and pinched the skin of his arm to keep him awake. He refused to fall asleep when Acker could return at any moment.

There was still the same level of darkness creeping through the window when the door clicked, quieter than last time, and Casey began to hyperventilate, knowing what was coming and that he couldn't do anything to stop him.

When a face peered around the corner, his eyes widened, and tears overflowed at an alarming rate.

Logan mouthed, "Is he here?" and Casey shook his head vehemently.

Barrelling around the corner and onto the bed, Logan cupped his brother's face, wiping away the tears which were replaced by others straight away.

"Casey, are you all right? Has he…?" he whispered.

Casey shook his head, his vision blurred.

"I'm so sorry, Casey. I can't undo you just yet. We've had news that Acker's on his way. I'm sorry to leave you like this, but we need to catch him here."

The pained catch in Logan's voice was heartbreaking, not only because Casey couldn't leave straight away, but because he knew it killed Logan to leave him here as bait. If it ended up with Acker behind bars, he'd stay here as long as necessary.

He tried to communicate with his eyes that it was

fine and tilted his chin towards the entrance, indicating for Logan to leave.

"I don't want to leave you," Logan cried.

"O! O!" Casey tried to say, "Go!" and he must've made his point because Logan pressed a kiss to his forehead and stood. He gave one last glance at Casey before Casey heard the door click shut again.

Now that he knew someone was here, he could get through whatever Acker dealt out. He had no idea how they'd found him, but he would be forever grateful for it.

Time passed slowly, or it seemed to at least. He had no way of telling how long it had been before the door clicked open, and Acker strode into the room, carrying two takeaway coffee cups and a paper bag, which, by the scent, contained food.

"How are you, Casey? I've brought you some caffeine to keep you going. We have the rest of the night to enjoy ourselves now. I'm going to take a shower first, and then we can have some fu—"

"Police! Hands where I can see them!"

Kade, Joey, Logan and another officer entered the room, shouting their orders, and Acker scrambled back towards the window, holding his hands in front of him after dropping the cups and bag to the floor.

"Drop to your knees," Kade ordered, stepping closer slowly. "Now, on your stomach on the floor."

Casey couldn't see if Acker was following instructions, but he assumed the man was. Joey read Acker his rights and Kade dragged him to his feet, his hands locked behind his back in handcuffs.

"Logan, step back." Kade's voice was stern, and Casey flicked his gaze to his brother. Logan was standing with his gun still pointed at Acker, his finger caressing the trigger, visible even from where Casey lay. "Stand down," Kade ordered.

Logan inhaled deeply, clenched his jaw and lowered his gun, returning it to his holster. The atmosphere in the room relaxed a little. Kade passed Acker to two officers Casey hadn't seen, then turned to him.

"Casey, we can release you, but it would help the case if we could take some photos for evidence. Are you okay with that?" Casey closed his eyes, wanting nothing more than to get away from this, but he steeled himself and nodded. "We'll be as quick as we can."

Kade and Joey took photos of different angles, of the knots of rope, the disgusting leftover dried fluid on his chest, his face, everything they could think of that would help. Then, using gloves, they took a sample of the semen and, finally, sliced through the rope holding his arms and legs carefully and removed the ball gag.

The minute he was free of the gag, his jaw cramped, and he cried out in pain. Logan was there immediately, wrapping him in his arms while Casey worked his jaw to minimise the pain.

"Shower," he croaked.

"I'll help." Logan stood and, holding Casey under his arms, lifted him to his feet. Unfortunately, Casey's legs didn't want to work, and he fell into Logan's chest. Logan picked him up and carried him towards the exit.

"Shower!" Casey said, working against his dry mouth.

"We're going to the room across the hallway. We need to get evidence from this one, and we don't want you to wash it away."

Casey relaxed into Logan, closing his eyes until Logan stopped. Opening his eyes again, he noticed there was already a steaming bath waiting for him. Logan lowered him into the water, and Casey whimpered at the heat, but it soothed him seconds later. He submerged himself to his chin, then turned his gaze to Logan, whose face looked like he'd aged a decade since Casey had last seen him.

"I'm okay," Casey whispered.

Logan clenched his jaw, then stood, stepping towards the sink and running the tap. When he turned back, he was holding a glass of water, which he helped Casey to drink.

"How long?" Casey asked after he'd cleared his throat several times.

"Eleven hours," Logan hissed. "Eleven fucking hours."

"Thank you."

"For what? You just spent eleven hours with this lunatic. Why are you thanking me when we should've found you sooner?" Logan sank onto the closed toilet seat and rubbed at his closely shaved hair.

"Because you arrived just in time," Casey explained.

"The evidence on your chest proves that statement wrong," he growled.

Casey sighed. "He came back just now to finish what he started. If you had arrived slightly later..." He didn't finish the sentence, not wanting to think about what could've happened. "How's Luke?"

Logan gave a non-humorous laugh. "In pieces. He's with Ava."

"Can I talk to him?"

Logan nodded, pulling out his phone and dialled, putting it on speakerphone.

"Logan?" Ava's voice rang through.

"It's Casey."

"Oh, fuck. Thank god."

"Can I talk to Luke?"

"Sure. Luke!"

There was some fumbling on the other end before Luke said, "Casey?" so hesitantly, Casey burst into tears.

CHAPTER TWENTY

LUKE

SIX HOURS EARLIER

A phone ringing woke Luke from his sleep, and he fumbled around for the bedside table, dragging his phone to him and struggling to answer it.

"Hello?"

"Luke, it's Logan."

Luke was immediately awake. "Why are you ringing? Is Casey okay?"

"That's what I was going to ask you. Is he with you?"

"No. He left for work normal time, just after half six. Why?"

There was a pause before Logan said, "He didn't turn up for work."

"What! Where the fuck is he?" Luke swung his legs off the bed and strode to his wardrobe to grab some clothes. He put the phone on speaker as he fumbled into them.

"We don't know. No one has seen him, and his car isn't in the car park that we can see."

"So, where is he?" Luke asked again.

"I don't know, Luke," Logan growled.

"There's no way he could just disappear unless… Acker. I bet that asshole has him."

"Let's not jump to conclusions."

Luke took the phone back off speaker and held it to his ear. "Come on, Logan. He's going to be pissed that Casey's lost him his job."

"Can you think of anywhere else he could be?"

"No! If he was going anywhere, he would've told me. Or at least someone. For him to just disappear. You know as well as I do that's not him."

"Yeah." Logan sighed. "I didn't want to think about that, though."

"Where are you?"

"I'm at the station. I'm going to speak to Kade and Joey, see if I can get them to do a check for Casey's car without anyone picking up on it."

Luke sank onto the bottom step of the stairs, staring at the front door. "What can I do?"

"Keep trying to call him. See if you get through. Other than that, just hang tight."

"Okay," he said quietly. "If that asshole has him…"

"I know."

Logan hung up, and Luke was surrounded by silence, not even the ticking of the heating keeping him company. He pressed his hands to his cheeks, then slid them to his hair and tugged at the strands. Casey had to be found. If Acker had him, there was no telling what he'd do.

Unable to sit still any longer, he headed to the kitchen to make some coffee. No doubt Logan would find his way there before long.

It wasn't Logan who was the first to arrive, it was his sister.

"What are you doing here?" he asked Ava.

"Neither Logan nor I can work on Casey's disappearance, so I thought I'd come to keep you company."

Luke made another coffee and passed it to Ava, then sat down next to her. He blew out a breath and rubbed his arms. "I don't understand where he could be." He wrapped his fist in his other hand and rested both against his mouth, staring at nothing as thoughts whirled around his head, trying to connect the dots. "If I'd just trained him sooner…"

Ava's hand came to the back of his neck, the secure hold settling him slightly. "You could not have predicted this would happen, Luke. You're not psychic. There's a chance that even someone with superior training would still have been taken. *If* he has been taken."

"I'm telling you now, if he has just gone on a shopping spree, I'm going to kill him," Luke said, trying to lighten the mood.

"You and me both, but we'd probably only get the leftovers once Logan was finished with him."

They smiled at that, and Luke focused on his coffee, choking down every mouthful, watching the minutes pass by with no further information.

Two hours later, Logan turned up with Casey's parents—and Luke's—in tow. Luke busied around making drinks for everyone until Mrs Taylor shooed him out of the way and took over. Pacing through the rooms, to the living room where Logan was talking with Ava and their dads, to the kitchen where their mums were busy cooking up a storm, to the front door, to upstairs, to downstairs again. He couldn't sit still.

Nausea flared in his stomach as visions of Casey being with that asshole flew through his mind. He felt so hopeless, especially as it was partly his fault. He should've pushed Casey to start training again instead of agreeing to wait until after Christmas. If he had, Casey would've had more experience and might have been able to fight him off.

His phone rang, and he fumbled to get it from his pocket, shoulders slumping when he realised it was Carter.

"Hey," he mumbled.

"I just got the message Dad left. Is Casey back?"

Luke swallowed against the lump in his throat. "No."

"What's happening then?"

He couldn't answer, the tears too close to the surface. Heading to the living room, he passed the phone over to Logan, who checked the screen before putting it to his ear. Luke didn't listen to what was said, he climbed the stairs slowly, sinking to the step at the halfway mark, the memories of him and Casey together bombarding him.

Clasping his hands over his head and pulling his elbows in tight, he rested his head on his knees, breathing deeply to stop the flood of tears, but it didn't work.

He startled as a blanket was draped over his shoulders, and he lifted his head to see his mum beside him. "I should've helped him, Mum. We could've prevented this." His voice broke and his mum folded him into her arms as he sobbed.

Having no idea how long he stayed that way, it wasn't until Logan's raised voice that he blinked tiredly and sat upright.

"We think we've found him!" Logan called.

Luke scrambled up and took the steps down two at a time, slipping at the bottom and righting himself before entering the living room. Logan stood, holding the phone to his ear.

"I'm coming with you... No, Kade, I'm coming, that's final... You can arrest him by all means, but I'll be there for Casey... All right, I'll meet you there... Half an hour, right." He hung up and focused on Luke, relaying the information. "Casey's car has been found in a hotel car park, and Acker has been seen entering and exiting several times over the past few hours. I'm going to meet Kade and Joey there."

Logan headed past Luke, who stopped him with a hand on his arm. "Can I come?"

"No, Luke. You wait here. Casey will need you when we get him home."

Luke shrank back, understanding that Casey might not want anything to do with Luke depending on what had happened to him. And rightly so. He was the last person Casey should feel safe with. He headed up the stairs to the bedroom, not looking at the bed, and hunkered down next to the chest of drawers, resting his arms on his bent knees and lowering his head.

He heard the continued hustle and bustle from downstairs, but it was distanced as if he was dreaming it. What was his point on this earth if he couldn't help the one person who meant everything to him?

"Luke!"

Ava's voice penetrated his daze, and she burst into his room, a smile on her face. She held out the phone, which he took, still staring at Ava, who was nodding repeatedly. It wasn't until she mouthed, "Casey," that he realised.

"Casey?" he asked hesitantly, not knowing why he would want to talk to him of all people.

The moment he said Casey's name, huge wracking sobs were heard on the other end of the line, and Luke held the phone tighter to his ear, his tears dripping down his face.

"He can still hear you, Luke, he's just a little over-whelmed. He's all right, though. He'll be back soon."

Luke's throat was too tight to get any words out. Casey was okay. He blew out a breath.

"Don't you dare, Luke," Casey's scratchy, hoarse voice whipped through his ear. "I know you. This was *not* your fault. Do you hear me? This is on him, as always. Never on you."

Shaking his head, Luke lowered it to his hand, sighing. "Get better, Casey."

"Don't you fucking dare, Luke." His voice was growing stronger by the minute. "If you are not in that house when I return in less than an hour, I will find you and beat the shit out of you. Do you understand me?"

Luke tried to find some humour in the fact that Casey was being demanding all of a sudden, but he felt numb, empty. "I love you," he whispered and held out the phone to Ava.

When she took it, he heaved himself off the floor and towards the stairs. He didn't need whatever he would leave behind. Before he reached the front door, a hand swung him around.

"Don't." Casey's dad stared him down. "I know what you're thinking because I'm thinking it too but about me. Every one of us here tonight, and those that are not, could beat themselves up about what happened and blame themselves, and they probably will. But in here," William pressed a finger to Luke's chest, "you *know* who's to blame. You *know* where you belong. You *know* where Casey belongs. Now, tell me why I should let you walk out that door, and if the reason is good enough, I'll let you go without any hesitation."

Luke stared at William and that little crack in his walls crumbled like dust. William caught him before he hit the floor. By the time he came back, his throat and eyes were sore, and his limbs were aching.

"Come on. Let's get you up and settled before loverboy gets home." William's voice rumbled next to Luke's ear.

When he finally sat on the sofa with a coffee wrapped in his hands, he felt a little better. He was wrung out, though.

"Is he still here?"

The voice he hoped to hear every day for the rest of his life shouted his name, and Luke stood, the drink was taken from his hands. As Casey entered the room with a little assistance from Logan, Luke felt tears welling again, even though he'd thought he was all out.

"Don't you dare do that to me again, you asshole!" Casey croaked. "I thought you'd left me. I can't do this without you."

Casey fell into Luke's arms, and they both cried, holding each other so tight, he was sure neither could breathe. When Casey sagged against him, Luke helped him to the sofa, then Casey curled up against him as close as he could get.

"I'm so sorry. It brought back so many things you had helped me to get rid of. Or at least, I thought I'd thrown out. It just goes to show that healing takes time," Luke said.

"It definitely does."

Over the next few days, Luke and Casey talked about everything that they'd been through during those harrowing eleven hours—well, six for Luke. Casey had wanted everything to be out in the open; therefore, although it was extremely painful for both of them, Casey detailed exactly what had happened to him. Luke felt like his thoughts weren't worth what Casey had been through, but after an argument, where Casey told him exactly what he thought of that idea, Luke had relented and explained where his thoughts had gone. Then, he'd done one better and talked about his life and how inferior he always felt. He hadn't needed to explain that part because Casey had figured it out, but it was good to clear the air.

The hospital had given Casey some time off, but he had no choice but to go back over Christmas for his scheduled shifts because he was needed, and Casey refused to be a burden to anyone despite what he'd been through.

"Luke! Look who's come for a visit!" Casey called from the front of the house. Luke headed that way, smiling when he saw the little fluffy Bichon Frise dog in Casey's arms.

"Hey, Felix," Luke said, scratching the dog behind his ears. "To what do we owe this pleasure?" He glanced at Casey whose cheeks darkened.

"Well, Mrs Masters has sprained her ankle and can't take Felix for his usual walks, so I offered as I'm here for the next few days. Would you like to come with us?" Casey asked, snuggling his face into the dog's fluffy fur.

"Sure. Let me just put our coffees into the travel mugs, and we can take them with us."

As they walked along the streets, their fingers interlinked, Felix stopping and sniffing at every little thing, Luke felt completely content. The insecurities, which he knew he would struggle with from time to time, were nowhere to be seen as they put one step in front of the other.

"Penny for them?" Casey asked, wrapping his arm around Luke's waist instead.

Luke inhaled deeply, exhaling through his nose. "I'm happy. No, more than that. Content? Ecstatic? Elated? I've no idea what is the right word, but it all comes down to you." He stopped them and slid his other arm around Casey's waist, enclosing them in a circle of arms. "I love you. Thank you for putting up with me." He pressed a kiss to Casey's lips.

"You're welcome, but then I have to thank you for putting up with me. We're two peas in a pod, Luke, but we're learning, and that's all we can do." He lifted his head, but before their lips could touch, Casey was yanked to the side when Felix pulled on his lead.

They laughed and continued on.

When they had returned Felix to Mrs Masters and had confirmed they could walk him for the next few days, they got ready for their dinner out. They had arranged to go out for a meal with Alex, Craig, Theo and Jasper so each of their closest friends could get to know one another way from the chaos that was the Crush family as they were becoming known.

They had decided against Romano's this time because it was still too fresh for them all, although the restaurant was up and running as usual, so they were trying the new Indian place that had opened a couple of months ago.

He and Casey were the first to arrive. "I wonder who will be late," he joked.

"Probably Alex." Casey grinned.

"I don't know, it depends how much Jasper distracts Theo."

"I resent that remark," Theo said, appearing at the table with Jasper by his side.

They all laughed, and the newcomers sat. "I didn't distract him too much, by the way," Jasper said with a sparkle in his eye. He leaned forward and lowered his voice, "I made sure to start getting ready early so we could have some fun and not be late." He winked and sat back, a smug look on his face.

Theo's cheeks flushed a deep red and chuckles sounded around the table when he backhanded Jasper on the chest. "Shush, Jasper. They do not want to know about that."

"I'm sure they would be happy to hear about it, but it's just for us, sweetheart." Jasper kissed him. When he pulled back, he whispered, "And maybe for my books."

Theo dropped his face into his hands, and they all laughed again.

"Can anyone join in or is it reserved just for you?"

Luke twisted his head and saw Alex and Craig, hovering nearby.

Casey jumped up from his seat and threw his arms around them both, barely missing knocking into a waiter in his exuberance. "You made it!"

Alex chuckled. "Of course, we did, you silly goof." He wrapped his arms around Casey and held him tightly, whispering in his ear. When they pulled away, there were tears in both their eyes. "Come on. Introduce us properly to the new posse."

"Jesus, Alex. How old are you?" Casey asked.

"Old enough to tan your hide, but I'm refraining," Alex groused. "I've been told I need to behave."

"Thank you, Craig." Casey smirked.

"You're welcome," Craig said quietly.

Casey had told Luke that Craig and Alex's relationship was still in the first stages due to Craig's history, but Casey believed Alex would be good for him.

"Hey, Craig. How are you doing?" Luke said, standing to hug the man.

"Good, thanks. Busy, as always, but good."

"Glad to hear it. Well, sit down, you guys. You're making the place look untidy as Mum would say." Luke indicated the remaining seats, and everyone settled down.

"Okay," Casey started, pointing at each person as he said their name, "Jasper, Theo, Alex, Craig, Casey, Luke. I think we're sorted with names."

Luke huffed a laugh. "All right, joker. I think we know now. Let's see what the menu says."

Conversation flowed throughout the evening, and they spent a good three hours at the restaurant. It had been a long time since Luke had enjoyed something as simple as a meal with friends. Everyone seemed to get on with everyone else, which would help their 'worlds' merge. No one showed any sign of being uncomfortable or hesitant once the initial introductions were over. Alex and Casey told several stories about their work, Jasper spoke about his books, Theo about his baking, Craig about his designing, and Luke about his potential new business venture.

All in all, everyone had something to contribute, and no one seemed to feel left out. It was great.

Luke told Casey those thoughts when they were on their way home.

"Of course. They're our friends, and we have good taste." He winked.

After arriving at Casey's, they dropped by Mrs Masters to take Felix out for a quick walk, then entered the house. Luke realised he hadn't been home properly in a while, except to grab some clothes. He had wanted to be close to Casey, and Casey had seemed to need the same. It was something they needed to discuss, but he'd leave it for another day. They were riding a high that night, and their lovemaking showed it.

The following day, Luke returned from work to find Casey snuggled up on the sofa fast asleep with little Felix cuddled up next to his chest. The serene sight was the nudge he needed to bring up an idea that had been brewing in him for a few days.

He tiptoed into the kitchen and began making coffee for them both. Within seconds, Felix came bounding into the room, yipping at his heels.

"Hey, Felix. Have you been keeping Casey company for me?" Luke asked, crouching down to greet the little fella.

"He has. Mrs Masters had a hospital appointment, so I said I'd look after him."

"Sorry if I woke you." Luke stood, leaning forward to kiss him.

"No, it's okay. I didn't think I was tired, but I obviously was."

Luke brought their mugs to the table and sat adjacent to Casey. "Have you ever thought about getting a dog for yourself?"

Casey nodded, gulping down some of his drink before answering, "Yes. I've always wanted one, but my shifts aren't convenient for taking care of one. It's okay when I'm off, but then I spend four days hardly being here. I didn't think it was fair on a dog to have to put up with that."

"Maybe you should start a dog walking business around your shifts," Luke joked.

Casey tilted his head. "How awesome would that be!" He bounced in his seat. "I'd love that, but it would take some figuring out to make it work around my awkward shifts still."

"We'll sort something out for you one day, I'm sure." Luke cupped Casey's chin, bringing them closer together. "You are so considerate of others, Casey

Taylor." He kissed him. A slow, deep one that curled his toes and quickened his pulse.

Casey abruptly stood. "I'm going to take Felix back. He's already late. Then," he stared at Luke, "we're finishing what you started."

CHAPTER TWENTY-ONE

CASEY

Luke and Casey had decided to invite their friends and family over to Casey's house for a 'takeaway' birthday party. Luke had laughed when Casey had suggested it as their Christmas party as well, but the idea grew because Casey was working throughout the Christmas holiday, and there were only a few days until Christmas anyway.

Unfortunately, when they counted how many people had been invited and agreed to come, they changed the venue to Casey's parents' house instead. As nicely sized as Casey's house was, it wouldn't fit thirty people.

Both Casey's and Luke's parents had taken over the kitchen and, even though a takeaway was being ordered, they created some snacks and desserts to go with it, much to Casey's amusement and gratitude.

The idea behind the party was to get everyone introduced to everyone else. Although some of each family knew some of the other family, Casey wanted everyone to know everyone. Luke smiled when Casey practically stamped his foot with his determination to merge their families. It wasn't just blood families, they had invited their friends to join, too.

Casey stood on the back porch of his parents' house, taking a breather in the cold afternoon air, jumping slightly when hands slid around his waist. He didn't jump as easily now.

"Is it everything you hoped it would be?" Luke asked, pressing a kiss to the side of his neck.

Casey closed his eyes, smiled and rested his head back against Luke's shoulder. "Yes. Everyone is getting on well."

"Did you think they wouldn't?" Luke chuckled.

"I wasn't sure. People always struggle with big families, but we've both got large families, so it's probably another day in the life of," Casey said. "It was maybe a stupid idea."

"No, it's not. Everyone gets to feel comfortable with each other now, which is great. I will say, though, we may have a problem regarding Sunday lunches."

Casey glanced at Luke, seeing the crinkling around his eyes and the pursing of his lips. "Why's that?"

"We're being claimed by both families. We might have to start a schedule of which house we eat at each week."

Casey snorted. "God, I never thought of that." He sighed. "We should merge the lunches, too. One week have it at my parents', the next week at yours."

Luke was silent for a moment. "That's a good idea."

"I have my moments," Casey joked.

Casey hummed in delight as Luke sucked his earlobe into his mouth.

"God, I can't wait until we can go home," Luke groaned, his hips pressing Casey against the balustrade.

"Me either." Casey turned his head to capture Luke's mouth with his, lifting his hand to clutch the back of Luke's head and threading their fingers together on Casey's stomach. Luke's free hand pressed against Casey's cock, making him whimper into Luke's mouth.

A throat clearing had them breaking apart, though neither turned around, not wanting to give the guest a view of their rather prominent erections. "Sorry to interrupt. Your presence is requested by the heads of the houses." Samuel spoke with a hint of amusement.

Luke snorted and pulled away. Casey readjusted himself before turning to face the house. "We'll be there in a few minutes."

Samuel nodded and left with a grin.

Luke blew out a breath and pressed a hand to his groin. "Never start something that cannot be finished, Luke," he admonished himself while smiling and shaking his head.

"Yes, you naughty boy." Casey pushed at his shoulder in jest, then leaned forward and kissed Luke briefly. "Come on."

They entered the house, heading to where the conversation was loudest.

"Here they are!" Luke's mother called. Luke slipped his arm around Casey's waist, and they stood just inside the door. "We wanted to wish you a happy birthday and let you know we are here if you ever need us."

"Here, here!" said several voices.

"Thanks, everyone. I'm glad you could be here," Casey replied, trying to keep his emotions under control.

"We do have a gift for you both." Casey's dad took over the conversation, and his mum brought a box forward to them. Casey's birthday gifts were piled in one of the other rooms.

Casey grasped the palm-sized box, feeling the weight of it, and looked to Luke, who shrugged. He held the box with one hand and used his other to get purchase on the paper. Before he had the chance to rip it off, there was a commotion at the front of the house. Casey frowned at what sounded like shouting and singing.

A murmur rippled around the room, and Logan, Ava, Casey's dad and Luke's dad all exited, heading towards the noise. Casey wanted to know what was going on, so he placed the box down and stepped out, closely followed by Luke.

"I wanna see Case," a slurred voice said, and Casey raised his eyebrows. He pushed his way through to the front door to see Logan standing in front of Marcus, whose face lit up when he saw Casey and the rear lights of a taxi, pulling away. "Case! I'm sorry, Casey. Go to whatever gym you want." His words were slow and mumbled, but Casey got the idea.

"Go home, Marcus. Sleep it off," he called, crossing his arms over his chest.

"No! I want you. Can't sleep without you."

"Get some rest, Marcus. You don't want me at all." Luke stepped up beside him, sliding an arm around him.

"Yes, I do. I can give you more than *he* can." Marcus indicated Luke with a floppy wave of his arm. "You shouldn't have rushed into something with him. I can give you everything."

Marcus moved to step closer but was stopped by Logan.

"I think it's time you went home," Logan said.

"No! Casey is mine! No one can take him from me, not even you in your fancy little house." Marcus pointed at Luke.

Logan held up his hand as if knowing Casey wanted to speak, so he waited. "How did you know where Casey was?"

Marcus scrunched up his nose and waved his arms again. "Easy. I wanted to talk to him, but he went to *that* guy's house. It was supposed to be me!" Marcus rubbed at his head. "He was supposed to be in *my* bed, not his."

"Did it make you angry?" Logan continued, and Casey covered his mouth with his hand, having a feeling he knew where this conversation was going to end.

"Hell, yeah. Why choose *him*? What's wrong with me?"

Logan prodded, "What happened?"

"The lights went off, but Casey didn't come out to go home. It meant he was sleeping with him." Marcus grimaced.

"What happened?" Logan asked again.

"I proved I was better for him. That *he* couldn't keep him safe. But it was so loud." Marcus whispered the last sentence.

"I think that's all I need to know for now. Come on, Marcus, let me take you somewhere to help you sober up," Logan declared and guided the mumbling man to Logan's car. Ava followed. Once they'd got him situated in the back seat, Logan turned around. "We'll be back in a short while." And they left.

Casey stood, staring down the driveway long after the car had disappeared, his thoughts bouncing around in his head. How could he have been so wrong about Marcus? Was he just like this because Casey broke up with him, or would he have turned out that way no matter what Casey did?

Luke kissed the side of his head. "Are you okay?"

Casey shook his head and sighed. "He seemed like such a nice person when we first met. So considerate and caring. He's best friends with a vet who is a genuinely nice guy. How can people hide stuff like that?"

"I don't know. Maybe he just needs—"

"Casey! You need to open your gift!" Claire called from the doorway. His sister was impatient as always.

Luke chuckled. "Never mind. Come on. Let's lighten the mood some and see what they bought us. Though, if it's a puppy, you're looking after it."

Casey snickered, his chest loosening, and grabbed Luke's hand as they walked through the house. "I think the box is too small for a puppy to be in it."

"About time," Claire grumbled.

"Where were we?" Casey murmured as he picked up the box. At Luke's nod, he ripped the paper off and lifted the lid from the box, revealing two sets of keys. He took them out and held them up with a frown on his face.

"We want you to feel welcome in both houses, so those are keys to each of your parents' houses. One for Luke to open our house, and one for Casey to open Charles and Catherine's house. You will always be welcome," Casey's mum explained.

Casey gripped the keys, staring at them as tears dripped down his face. He was not normally so emotional, but lately… He moved the tags that were attached and saw the words 'Mum and Dad Taylor' on one and 'Mum and Dad Walker' on the other. He closed his eyes as his emotions overflowed like his tears, and he was engulfed in Luke's arms. Casey tucked his head in Luke's neck and wrapped his arms tightly around his waist, blocking everyone else out.

He heard Luke thank everyone, and then he was

being picked up and carried somewhere. He didn't care where.

When the voices were muffled behind a closed door, Casey lifted his head a little. "Sorry. It's…"

"I know, sweetheart. Don't worry. Everyone is having fun; let's leave them to it for a little while." Luke pressed a kiss to Casey's lips, still carrying him.

Casey felt something solid but uneven press against his back, and he blinked open his eyes to see they were in his dad's office. He dropped his head back against the shelves as Luke licked and nibbled the skin of his neck. Casey tunnelled his fingers through Luke's hair and flexed his hips against Luke's stomach.

"Let's have a little fun ourselves," Luke whispered, grazing Casey's mouth with his own but not kissing him.

The shelves pushed against his back as Luke pressed forward, Luke's hand coming between them and undoing Casey's trousers. Casey's cock went rock hard at the notion they were going to fuck in his dad's office, and his cheeks burned with mortification and arousal. He almost pushed Luke away but lost his train of thought.

"Hold onto the shelves above you for a minute," Luke ordered, and Casey reached up, his fingers gripping tightly.

Luke bared Casey's ass to the cool air, leaving his trousers and briefs around his upper thighs before Casey heard the clink of Luke's belt. His ass clenched in anticipation. A wrapper was placed at Luke's mouth before he tore it open with his teeth and threw the remains on the floor. He reached under Casey, no doubt rolling the condom on his cock, and lifted another packet to his teeth, repeating the same action, but this time squirting some lube on his fingers and smearing it in Casey's crack.

Repositioning Casey's legs over his forearms, despite the restrictions of his jeans, Luke wrapped one arm around Casey's waist, lifting his leg high, and the other hand began preparing Casey's hole.

"Luke! I don't know if I can hold myself up," he choked.

"Let go, Casey. I've got you."

Casey let one hand free, and he dropped slightly until Luke had his weight. The lower position had Luke's cock pressing against Casey's ass. Luke continued to prepare him with several fingers before Casey couldn't take anymore.

"Fuck me," he whispered against Luke's mouth.

"With pleasure."

Luke placed his hands on the shelves at Casey's lower back, lifting Casey's legs higher, and pressed his cock forward, breaching Casey's hole with a steady but slow thrust. Casey dropped his head back again, banging against the shelf, the pleasure of Luke's entry streaming through him.

When Luke was situated, Casey cupped Luke's face and kissed him with everything he had. Luke began to move, thrusting and withdrawing in increasingly larger increments until he was pounding Casey against Luke's hands on the shelves. Casey was going to be bruised tomorrow, but he didn't care.

The only sounds in the large office were their breathing, the thump, thump of their movements and the slickness of their coupling. It was an intoxicating mixture, which threw Casey closer to climax.

"Fuck, Casey. I'm there. Sorry, I can't hold on anymore."

Luke thrust a few more times through his climax before bringing one of his hands forward to wrap around Casey's cock.

"Shit, oh!" Casey had been close anyway, but the firm, fast stroking had him orgasming within seconds.

As Luke withdrew, and they came down from their mutual high, Casey giggled into the quiet room.

"Not what I would usually want to hear after an experience like that," Luke commented dryly.

The words made Casey laugh harder, stifling the sounds in Luke's neck. Luke helped Casey stand, cupping the back of his head when he'd found his feet. "What's so funny, Mr Taylor?"

"I'm never going to be able to look at my father's office in the same way again," he muttered through his laughter.

Luke snorted and pressed a kiss to his forehead. "It probably wasn't the best idea. Sorry."

"Let's remember to pick up the rubbish before we leave, okay?"

They stood in their embrace until their laughter subsided. Pulling back, Luke said, "Do you feel better?"

Casey nodded with a smile. "Much." He was so lucky to have a guy like Luke.

"Glad to be of service."

They righted their clothes, Casey lamenting that he was going to have to run up the stairs to change his jumper, and picked up the rubbish, Luke tucking it away in his pocket for disposal later. Barely withholding their smiles, they left the office holding hands and snuck down the hallway so Casey could run upstairs.

"You can reassure Luke you're not the only one who's done that."

Casey turned at Liam's voice, his cheeks darkening with embarrassment. "Sorry."

Liam chuckled. "Nothing to be sorry for. As I said, you're not the only ones." Liam smirked but hesitated. "Are you okay?"

Casey glanced towards the stairs, inhaled and nodded. "Yes, I am."

"I'm glad you've found him. He's a nice guy."

"That he is."

"I'll let you get changed. Remember to think of a plausible excuse as to why you've changed your clothes if that's what you were planning." Liam chuckled as he descended the stairs.

Casey shook his head and continued to his old bedroom, where he kept several changes of clothes. Thankfully.

"So, what's this I hear about a 'lake story' from Trent?" Casey asked when there were several of Luke's family members close by. A ripple of amusement ran through the crowd, while Luke groaned.

"Go on, Lulu. Tell the story." Carter grinned.

Casey had heard Luke being called Lulu several times, but no one had explained why yet. He made a mental note to ask Luke later.

"God, did you have to remember that small tidbit of information Trent let slip weeks ago?" Luke groaned, dropping his head back to stare at the sky.

"Yep. It sounded intriguing."

"It is," Trent said. "Would you like me to start, Luke?"

Luke huffed and waved his hand. "Go right ahead. You can't make it sound much worse than the truth."

Trent leaned his elbows on his knees, an eager expression on his face. "Well, the story begins when I was about sixteen, which made Luke ten. We were on holiday in the Lake District in a large cabin on the lake. It was the summer, so we spent many hours splashing in the water."

"Jesus, Trent. How long do you want us to be here?" Carter complained.

"I'm setting the scene!" Trent threw an empty water bottle in Carter's direction. "Anyway, before I was so rudely interrupted. None of us had any friends in the area, so it was just us, and you probably know what happens when you add siblings together for any length of time without sufficient distractions?" Trent raised his eyebrows at Casey, who nodded. "Well, tricks ran rampant throughout the week-long vacation."

"I'm getting old, Trent," Carter grumbled.

"I know you are. You don't need to tell us." Trent came back to the conversation. "Luke had a growth spurt just before we left for the holiday, so some of his clothes didn't fit him, and he had to borrow Carter's sometimes. There are four years between them, so you can imagine the difference." Chuckles followed the words. "Well, anyway, this particular day, Luke needed to borrow a pair of swim trunks because the only ones that had fit him had mysteriously disappeared, so he borrowed a pair from Carter."

Luke groaned and rubbed his face with his hands. Casey rested his hand on the back of his neck, minutely enjoying his discomfort.

"We spent a while in the lake until Dad called us for lunch. Within seconds, me and Carter had grabbed and stripped Luke, leaving him naked with only the water for cover."

"They stood on the edge of the lake, laughing and waving the trunks at me, like the assholes they are, then went inside for lunch. I had no idea what to do. There were people around who I was sure would see me if I streaked naked to the cabin."

"What happened?" Casey asked, trying to hold in a laugh.

"Mum asked us where Luke was. We told her he didn't want to get out of the water." Trent snickered. "After several minutes, we heard him shouting before he came rushing through the door with a handful of mud held across his dick.”

“The good news is that they got punished for it,” Luke said, smirking. “They were grounded for two weeks when we returned home.”

“The punishment didn’t fit the crime!” Carter complained.

“You should’ve received a lot more than that, you little weasel!” Luke said, standing up and advancing on his brother.

Carter held up his hand. “Stop! You’re bigger than me now! It’s an unfair advantage!”

Everyone laughed as they watched Luke wrestle with Carter on the grass. Once they’d fought it out of their system, Luke came back to sit with Casey, wrapping his arm around his shoulder, then pulling away. “I don’t know if I should be cuddling you when you made me remember that awful time of my life!” he mocked.

Casey giggled and pulled Luke close. “You’re big enough to deal with it.” He kissed him gently. “My hero.”

Fake vomiting noises came from around them, and Casey held up his middle finger as he kissed Luke again.

CHAPTER TWENTY-TWO

LUKE

The day before Christmas Eve, Luke and Casey went to Casey's parents' house for an early Christmas present opening. Although Casey had received presents two days earlier for his birthday, his parents had always made sure the two occasions were separate regarding presents to make up for Casey rarely receiving anything the rest of the year.

The whole household opened the presents on whichever day worked out best for their children's shift patterns. Christine, Casey's mum, had lamented the fact it had been two weeks early one year because both Logan's and Casey's shifts had clashed. Luke's parents had been lucky up to now and had been able to celebrate properly despite Ava's shifts, although Luke didn't know how that happened when Logan and Ava were partners.

Luke sat in an armchair furthest from the Christmas

tree with Casey sitting by his feet, resting his head on Luke's knee as they watched the grown-up children fight over who got to open the presents first. Casey sniggered when Alice nearly ended up *in* the tree instead of next to it.

"Children!" shouted his mum. "I've had better behaviour from three-year-olds," she admonished, then threw a wink in Luke's direction. "I think your dad should go first."

Groans and mumbles followed her pronouncement, but everyone sat while William reached for a gift from his small pile. "To Dad, Merry Christmas. Love, Liam." After he read the label, William tore open the paper and chuckled when he saw a universal remote control. He picked up a piece of paper that had been resting on top and read, "Think of the devilry you can cause now."

The kids started yelling at Liam about "unfair advantage" and "helping the enemy."

Obviously, seeing Luke's confusion, Casey said, "Whenever we come to visit, there is a 'discussion,'" Casey held up air quotes, "about who gets to choose what's on the TV. We usually flip a coin."

Luke laughed. "We have a rota at my parents' house."

William heard his remark. "We tried it, and the kids kept swapping their names around." He glared at Logan.

"It wasn't me!"

Several "Yes, it was!" got thrown in his direction before Christine called for James to open a gift.

And so, it went until it was time for Christine to finish off their Christmas dinner.

"We'll open the rest of them after lunch," Casey said as he climbed onto Luke's lap and rested his head on his shoulder. "Did you like your gift?"

Luke looked at the watch he'd been given by Casey's parents and smiled. "They didn't have to do that, but I love it. It's one of those silicone strap ones, too, so I might be able to wear it during the training sessions. But we'll see. I don't want to ruin it."

Casey cupped Luke's face and stared at him with a small smile. "I love you."

Luke's gaze roamed across Casey's face, and he lifted his chin for a kiss, which Casey happily provided. When they broke apart, Luke answered, "I love you."

"I keep expecting your family to buy you a dog!"

Laughing, Casey asked, "Why?"

"Because you love them so much."

"Casey! Don't think you're getting out of your duties because you brought a fella with you. Get in here!" Christine shouted.

Dropping his head to Luke's chest, Casey grumbled but pushed off Luke's lap and shuffled in the direction of the kitchen. Luke placed his present on the side table and wandered around the room, picking up the bits of wrapping paper that had been strewn across the floor. Christmas was not so different in Casey's house as it was in his own.

As he filled his arms with as much as he could, William came back into the room with a rubbish bag.

"You didn't have to but thank you." He held open the bag while Luke dropped the paper inside.

"It's the least I can do after you invited me here." Luke continued around the room until it had all been collected and disposed of.

"Sit with me." The tone was friendly and in no way an order, but Luke wouldn't deny Casey's father a conversation, even when nerves fluttered in his stomach, and his palms began to sweat. "I haven't had the chance to thank you for helping Casey with everything that's happened lately."

"You don't need to—"

William held up his hand. "I know I don't need to, but I want to. Casey has always been the lively, fun, energetic son out of them all, but it pains me to say, I thought his behaviour change was related to getting older and calming down more." William's eyebrows lowered as he stared at the floor between them. "I never once asked him if something else was going on, but that's my cross to bear. I'm so glad he had you. I don't know what would've happened if he hadn't."

Luke didn't want to think about it either, but he hadn't done much for Casey, and he told William that. "I hadn't taught him enough to help him."

"It's not just the physical teaching you helped him with. You helped him emotionally. You supported him when he was at his lowest, and none of us will ever forget that. Even if your relationship doesn't work out —but I believe it will—you will always be a part of our family now."

Luke swallowed against the lump in his throat, trying to keep the emotions inside. William must have realised because he smiled and changed the subject. "I hear you are thinking about opening your own business." Luke nodded, unable to talk. "If you need any help or support, you come to me, okay?"

"Thank you," he whispered.

William stood, and when Luke followed suit, he stepped forward and wrapped his arms around Luke, holding him tightly. "You are not alone in this. You have your family, and now, you have our family. We will all support you."

Tears overflowed, but Luke withheld the sob that wanted to escape. William pulled back, wiped at the tears from his cheeks, kissed his forehead and left. Luke sat in the armchair and covered his face with his hands, trying to calm down. To receive those compliments was overwhelming, and they meant as much as they had when coming from his own family.

Hands slid across his shoulder blades, and a body slid into the chair, squeezing in next to him, and Luke was cradled against Casey's chest. They stayed entwined for several minutes before Luke pulled back, sniffing.

"You'd do anything to get out of your chores, wouldn't you?" Luke teased, wetly.

"Yep." Casey grinned, then sobered. "Are you okay?"

"I'm great." Luke exhaled heavily. "Let's go help in the kitchen."

"Before you go," Logan said, entering the living room. "I need to talk to you about Marcus."

Casey dropped his head back against the chair with a loud sigh.

Luke chuckled. "What about him?" He rested his hand on Casey's knee.

"I'm assuming you want to press charges against him for breaking your window?" Logan sat adjacent to them.

Luke glanced at Casey, who rolled his head towards Luke and shrugged. "It's up to you."

Shaking his head, Luke said, "No, it's up to both of us." He peered at Logan. "Suggestions?"

Logan leaned his elbows on his knees and rubbed his palms together back and forth. "Officially, yes, you should. He needs to account for his behaviour." Logan paused. "Personally, I would see if you can reach an arrangement outside of police involvement. The reason I say this—and I will deny everything I'm saying if anyone asks—is because it's more hassle than it's worth going through with the arrest and everything else involved. If you can get him to pay for damages, make it clear Casey is not interested in him any longer, and he needs to stay away, it would be the better option."

Luke sighed, knowing Logan was right. He couldn't be bothered to go through the process of involving the police any more than they already had been. "I'm happy to do that. What do you think, Casey?"

Casey chewed on his bottom lip as he stared at the ceiling. "Yeah, let's do that."

"Okay. I'll contact him to arrange the initial conversation," Logan said.

"Thanks, Logan."

"Oi! Stop skiving and get in here, you losers!" James shouted.

They piled all the gifts into Luke's car and waved before heading towards Casey's house. Casey worked the following day, so they planned a cosy night in with a movie and an early night.

Luke laid on the sofa, stretching his legs along the length and reached for the remote, switching on the movie choices. He flicked through some until Casey came to rest on top of him, placing his head on Luke's chest.

"What're we watching?" Casey asked as he twined their legs together and got comfortable.

"Well, there are plenty of Christmas films to choose from, like *Die Hard, Love Actually, Home Alone, The Grinch*—"

"How about *Die Hard*?" Casey interrupted with a laugh. "You'll be here until New Year's listing them off.

Luke grinned and set the film to play. He tucked one hand behind his head, the other smoothing up and down Casey's back as the movie began. "Did you have a good day?"

Casey smiled up at him before refocusing on the TV.

"Yes, it was amazing. Even more so because you were there with me."

Luke leaned down and pressed a kiss to Casey's head. They watched as John McClane did his thing until Casey began to fidget. Positioned as he was, every little movement pressed Casey's stomach against Luke's rapidly hardening cock, but he tried to ignore it. At least until Casey's hand slid under his t-shirt and slowly lifted it, bunching it at Luke's underarms. Casey smoothed his cheek against Luke's chest and gently sliding his nose over Luke's nipples before capturing one with his lips.

Hips thrusting up, Luke hissed and pressed his head into the cushion behind him as Casey plucked at his free nub with his fingers. Luke reached down, grasping Casey's t-shirt in his fingers and drawing it up until he could pull it over Casey's head. Casey returned to his ministrations, and Luke raked his nails up and down Casey's spine.

After one particularly strong suck which had Luke gasping, he gripped Casey's ass and squeezed, dragging him close. Casey popped off his nub and yanked Luke's t-shirt off before joining their lips in a heated, nought to sixty kiss. Luke pulled Casey's hips to his, grinding and straining against each other as their denim-covered cocks pressed together. Using Casey's hips as leverage, Luke lifted and dropped his hips, sliding their groins faster.

Casey tore his lips away, gasping as he gripped the back of Luke's neck and threw his head back. "Fuck!"

Luke let go and fumbled with Casey's fastenings until his cock sprung free, then repeated the process with his own. When their dripping shafts met between them, they groaned in unison. Luke wrapped his hand around both cocks, smearing precome before stroking. His hand wasn't big enough to encircle them fully, but it was enough to make his eyes roll back in his head.

Casey swore and used one hand to push his jeans further down his legs until he was able to kick them off. Every movement had their dicks slipping and sliding in Luke's fist. When Casey was free of the fabric, he brought his mouth back to Luke's, bracing his hands beside Luke's head as his hips fucked Luke's hand.

Luke smoothed his free hand down Casey's back and over his ass, loving the feeling of him naked when Luke was partially clothed. He slid one finger down Casey's crack, making him buck forwards. He could stay there forever, but Luke wanted to spend time worshipping Casey's body as he deserved.

He let go of their cocks, much to Casey's disapproval. "Up," he said, smacking Casey's ass and causing him to hump against Luke again. Casey grumbled the whole time, watching as Luke stood and removed the rest of his clothes. "Bed."

Casey turned and headed towards the stairs, Luke following and watching the tight little ass sway in front of him. They got halfway up the stairs before Luke couldn't take anymore, and he grabbed Casey's arm and spun him face-first to the wall, pressing close and lining his cock with Casey's crack. His hips rolled, using

Casey's delectable ass as a valley for his pleasure. Casey pushed back, simpering when Luke encircled Casey's cock, allowing him to thrust forward into his fist and back against Luke's shaft.

Luke's mouth bit and licked across Casey's shoulder and up the column of his neck until he reached under his ear lobe, where he pressed his teeth a little harder, much to Casey's delight if his whimper was anything to go by.

Casey's hands were braced against the wall, keeping space for Luke to reach every part of him. Taking him up on the offer, Luke's free hand flicked and rubbed against Casey's nipples, making them hard. Dropping his head back against Luke's shoulder, Casey's breath heaved as their arousal flew higher.

It took everything he had in him, but Luke moved back, releasing Casey from his hold, although steadying him so he didn't fall. Luke grabbed Casey's hand and dragged him the rest of the way up the stairs and to the bedroom before spinning Casey around and attacking his mouth as he simultaneously kicked the door shut and walked towards the bed.

Casey's hands were in his hair, Luke's hands were all over whatever part of Casey he could reach as their tongues duelled, fought and retreated until they broke for air.

They reached the bed, and Luke indicated for Casey to get on. Casey crawled, swaying his ass invitingly, and dropped to his elbows as he looked over his shoulder at Luke with a smirk. Luke growled and smacked his ass before joining him. His mouth attached to Casey's hole without prior warning, causing Casey to startle and gasp. Luke's hands slid up and down Casey's spine, gripping his ass cheeks occasionally as he devoured Casey's ass.

He felt Casey shivering continually. So, with a final lick and thrust of his tongue at the place Luke would willingly stay for hours, he flipped Casey onto his back and covered him before sealing their lips once more.

Their cocks rubbed against each other as their hands roamed the exposed skin available to them. Luke broke the kiss, tasting his way along Casey's jaw, down his neck and to his nub. Casey gripped Luke's strands as he teased and plucked at each nipple in turn before kissing lower and lower.

When he licked a stripe up the underside of Casey's cock, Casey shouted and transferred his hold to the sheets below. His legs widened, giving Luke room to move. And move he did. He sucked Casey's dick, swiping his tongue across the head to collect the precome before swallowing down as far as he could and rising and swirling across his tip. Luke repeated the process several times, making Casey incoherent.

Pulling off a final time, he reached across to the bedside table, picking up a condom and the lube bottle. Luke rolled the condom on and squirted some lube onto his fingers. He sank onto Casey's cock once more as his fingers explored and prepared Casey's channel. Casey's hips bucked against his fingers, forcing his dick further into Luke's mouth, making him gag. Apologies rained from above him, but Luke did it again purposefully, showing Casey he was fine.

When Casey was fully prepared, Luke slicked his shaft and moved closer. He kneeled upright as he aimed his cock at Casey's entrance, pausing before sliding in to check with Casey. At Casey's keening cry, Luke pushed forward, breaching him and continuing until he was fully seated. There, he stopped, leaning down to capture Casey's mouth in a sweet, intoxicating kiss. Casey wrapped his arms and legs around Luke's back, giving himself up to the kiss.

As their tongues slid along each other's, Luke canted his hips to withdraw slightly before thrusting back in, small movements that pressed his cock against Casey's prostate repeatedly. When Casey couldn't continue with the kiss because his breathing was impaired, Luke sat up, changing their positions so he could pound Casey's ass. Casey's hand reached up to the headboard, holding on as Luke snapped his hips back and forth, the slap of their skin echoing around the room. He came closer to his orgasm, so he surrounded Casey's cock with his hand and stroked in time with his hips. Casey cried out at the extra stimulation, and Luke felt Casey's ass contract as he spilled over Luke's fist.

That added tightening sent Luke over the edge, and he bellowed as he climaxed. His hips slowed, thrusting gently until he became too sensitive, at which point, he withdrew. Resting his forehead on Casey's stomach while holding on to the condom, he regained his breath before removing and throwing away the condom in the bin next to the bed.

Pressing a kiss to Casey's softening cock, he stood on wobbly legs and stumbled to the bathroom for a cloth.

Once they were both cleaned, Luke manoeuvred Casey under the covers and wrapped him in his arms.

"That was…" Casey tried.

"Amazing."

"Remarkable. Incredible. Mind-blowing. Staggering."

"If you can think of all those words, I've not done my job well enough. Your brain should be numb like mine is." Luke chuckled.

They were silent for a few moments before Casey said, "It's a good job we know how *Die Hard* ends."

They both laughed until their sides hurt, and Luke remembered the TV was still on, the muffled sounds drifting up the stairs now he concentrated on them.

"Don't worry about it. It will turn itself off in a few hours. I'm too comfy to move," Casey mumbled, snuggling deeper into Luke's embrace.

Luke lay awake for a while after Casey's breathing had evened out in sleep. He almost didn't want to sleep; he was afraid this was all a dream.

Everything he had ever wanted was right before his eyes.

CASEY

"We both want one, so why not go and have a look? There might not even be one we bond with," Luke said.

"But would it be fair on the dog to be transferred between houses? Sometimes at your house, sometimes at mine. Wouldn't it be confusing for the dog?" Casey wrung his hands together as he tried to calm himself. He wasn't sure how to go about asking what he wanted to ask. "It would be better if they only had one house to worry about, especially if it's a puppy."

Luke narrowed his gaze at Casey, then raised his eyebrows and wrapped an arm around him. Using his finger to tilt Casey's head back, Luke smirked. "Is this your way of asking me to move in, Casey?"

Casey's eyes widened, and his mouth gaped. How the hell had he figured it out? "Yes," he squeaked, sliding his chin off Luke's finger, hiding his face in his chest and feeling the rumble of Luke's laughter.

"Well, your house is closer to your job and the gym and also where my business will be run from, so…" he paused, and Casey held his breath. "I'd love to, especially as the main draw is because it's where you are," he whispered.

Casey lifted his head and smiled, biting his bottom lip. "Can we go have a look today?"

Luke laughed again. "Sure. We can nip by Sweet Tooth for a coffee to go." His phone rang, and he pulled it from his pocket. "Hey, Otto." He was silent as he listened, then a grin crossed his face. "Yeah, sure. We're heading to the animal shelter to look at dogs." He gazed at Casey as he spoke. "Meet us there. I'll grab you a coffee on the way."

After picking up their drinks from Theo, they aimed the car towards All Seasons Animal Shelter, on the outskirts of Cambridge. As they pulled into the car park, they saw Otto leaning against his car, on his phone. He lifted his head and waved, pocketing his phone. Casey had gotten on well with Otto the minute they had met, and when the guy had moved back from London three months ago, they'd helped him get settled. He was settled enough to want a dog from what Luke had told him on the drive over there.

"Hey, guys. Sorry to crash your trip," Otto said, appearing not at all sorry.

"Oh, look, I have two drinks, Luke. Thanks so much," Casey teased.

Otto narrowed his gaze, and Casey laughed, handing one over. "I've not had my coffee yet this morning, so cut it out," Otto groused.

They chatted while they drank their drinks, disposed of the cups in the bin and entered through a large door. They came across a gate and were about to open it when scurrying feet came bounding through the area beyond.

"Dexter! Get back here. You're going the wrong way if you want food, dog," a voice grumbled as it came closer.

Casey gasped as a guy came around the corner and grabbed hold of the playful terrier. The guy lifted his head and smiled. "Welcome to…" he paused when he caught sight of Casey.

Face to face with Marcus's best friend, Casey wasn't sure what to do. He grabbed hold of Luke's hand and moved closer to him, swallowing hard. The guy noticed the movement, and his gaze softened.

"He's an asshole, and I've not spoken to him for months. You have nothing to worry about from me. I promise." The guy stayed still and allowed the words to sink in.

Luke glanced from Casey to the guy, frowning. "Who are you?"

"I'm Heath. I *was* friends with Marcus."

Luke squeezed Casey's hand until Casey glanced up at him. "Do you want to stay?"

Casey swallowed again, hesitating, but studied Heath again and nodded.

Heath's shoulders relaxed a fraction, and his smile warmed more. "Come on through. Please lock the gate behind you. I'm going to grab Rory."

They entered the foyer and waited. Casey smoothed a hand down the front of his clothes.

"Are you sure you're okay with this?"

Casey nodded. "He seems like he's honest, and I never got the feeling he would lie." Casey's voice was strained, and he shrugged. "But I didn't with Marcus either."

Otto moved closer. "We'll be here, regardless."

"Thanks." Casey threw a small smile in Otto's direction.

"Hi. Welcome to All Seasons Animal Shelter. I'm the manager, Rory. What pet can I get you today? Oh, sorry, I forgot, we only have dogs!"

They laughed, which broke the tension a little.

"I think we'd like to look at some dogs, please," Luke joked.

"Come right this way. Any preferences? How many are you looking for? Anything I can point you in the right direction towards?" Rory asked as they walked through a maze of corridors until they exited into a large open space of kennels, grass and storage sheds.

"We're not sure what we want, but we're hoping we'll know it when we see it." Luke thumbed over his shoulder towards Otto. "And he wants something small."

"Okay. How about we wander down the kennels,

and you can have a look at them all, and we can narrow down the search if we need to."

They did just that, greeting small and large dogs of every breed they could imagine and more. Casey fell in love with two larger dogs, whereas Luke found a smaller one he liked.

"All right. Let's get one out at a time, and you can take a walk around the area with each of them."

Rory entered the kennel of a German Shepherd and led him out. The gorgeous, caramel-coloured dog came to Casey's waist, but his temperament oozed calm. They all fussed over him, and Rory transferred the lead to Casey, indicating a route they could take. Otto stayed behind to have a look at the one he liked.

As they walked, Luke and Casey discussed their plans for moving in, which would happen as soon as Casey could persuade Luke to do it. The German Shepherd, named Tiger, strolled nicely next to them, never pulling on his lead. By the time they got back to his kennel, Tiger was a firm favourite already.

They swapped over to Nessie, a lovely Border-Collie, who was a bit more excitable and had them running with her around the area. Once they returned, they took Samson out, a small but yappy Shih Tzu.

When they had seen all the dogs, they needed to make a decision.

"You don't have to decide right now if you don't want to. It's completely up to you," Rory said.

Casey glanced at Luke with his bottom lip between

his teeth. Luke shook his head and smiled. "Which one have you fallen in love with?"

"I can't decide. I like them all. Which did you like?"

Luke closed his eyes and shook his head again. Turning to Rory, he said, "How would Nessie and Samson fare together? Would there be issues, do you think?"

Casey gaped. Luke couldn't be serious. His stomach fluttered with the idea of having two dogs around him.

"I think Nessie would encourage Samson, whereas Samson would calm Nessie. They have often been on walks together, and we've had no issues. No guarantees, unfortunately." Rory had a sparkle in his eye as he answered.

"We'll take the two, please."

"Seriously?" Casey bounced on his toes, clapping his hands together and pressing them to his mouth.

"Perfect. What we need to do now is arrange for us to visit your house to make sure you have enough space for the two of them, and if all goes well, you can come back and pick them up a couple of days afterwards."

They filled out the relevant paperwork and arranged for a visit the following Monday. When they returned to their cars, Casey asked, "Did you not find what you were looking for, Otto?"

Otto smirked. "Dunstan is coming home with me in a few days if my visit goes okay."

Casey grinned and threw his arms around Otto. "That's great news. That little terrier will be good for you."

They said their goodbyes to Otto, after some teasing towards Luke for being a softie, and turned to Luke's car.

"Casey!" Heath's voice called across the car park. He came to a stop several feet in front of them.

Luke came to stand next to Casey with his arm around his shoulders, a silent show of support.

"I *am* sorry about Marcus. I never believed he was like that. I've known him for over five years, and he's never shown any kind of behaviour that concerned me." He sighed. "As soon as I heard about it, I spoke to Marcus. He confirmed everything and didn't seem particularly repentant, so I told him to stay away from me. I've not seen him since."

Casey inhaled shakily. "I'm sorry you lost your friend."

"Thanks. I'm sorry he hurt you."

Casey swallowed hard, indicating their car. "We have to go."

Heath nodded and retreated. Casey stumbled around the car to the passenger side and sat heavily, leaning his head back.

"Are you okay?"

"Yeah," he whispered. "It was just a bit of a surprise is all."

Luke closed Casey's door, and Casey shut his eyes as he waited for Luke to get in the driver's seat.

Tuesday morning, they woke bright and early. Today was the day Casey had been so excited about. The previous day, they had been confirmed as a suitable placement for the dogs they wanted, and today, they were picking them up.

After they received the go-ahead, they had raced to the pet store to buy all the things they would need for the dogs. It had never occurred to them at the time, but both dogs ate different food and needed different things, but they managed with the help of the staff.

When they got home, everything was unloaded and placed where they thought was best. Casey wanted to give them one of the upstairs bedrooms as a room for the two of them, and Luke agreed, more than happy to let him have his way. They'd bought two beds for each dog: one for downstairs, one for upstairs. Casey thought they might have gone a bit overboard, but he didn't care.

He paced the house until it was time to leave and bounced in his seat the whole journey to the shelter. It was probably one of the reasons Luke said he'd drive.

Rory met them at the door, taking them straight back to the kennels when he saw how excited Casey was.

"Here they are. We've had them together in the kennels since first thing this morning to get them used to being together, and I have to say, they are doing amazingly well," Rory said as he led them through the door and out to the outdoor area where the dogs were waiting.

"Hey," Casey said, crouching down. Both dogs came up and sniffed, licked and trampled all over him, much to Casey's delight and laughter.

Luke snorted but walked over to join in. "Hey, Nessie." The Border Collie nudged his hand with her nose, and he stroked her head. Not to be outdone, Samson clambered up to Luke and yapped at him, trying to climb him. "Hey, Samson." Luke chuckled.

"Looks like you won't have any problems with these two. I'm glad they're going to a good home," Rory said with a smile.

Luke glanced at Casey. "Let's take them home."

Casey smiled as he nodded and nuzzled into Nessie's fur.

Several hours later, Casey ran and played in the back garden with the dogs. He didn't think he had smiled this much in a long time. The dogs tumbled Casey to the ground, then covered him, and his laughter echoing into the sky. He was content in a way he hadn't been in… ever.

He wondered if things would have been different if he hadn't gone to Luke for training. Would they have met at Luke's party? Or would they have met somewhere else? Or not met at all? It didn't bear thinking about because Luke meant the world to him, and Casey would do everything in his power to never let anything hurt him.

He grinned. His training continued tomorrow, and he was in no doubt that he would hate Luke by the end of it. But he knew what Luke could do to make things up to Casey, and it would start with a kiss.

Would you like to read more about Crush? Book 7, Covert Strength is coming April 8. If you've not read it already, why not try First Kiss?

Would you like to see where the Crush series began? Sign up to my newsletter to get the prequel short story, Love Conquers.

COVERT STRENGTH

CRUSH SERIES BOOK 7

A single father receives more than he bargained for in the shape of an ex-military man in this emotional, low angst MM romance.

Can one night change their entire future?

Zak's son means more to him than anything or anyone else. He refuses to allow another person to be a part of their lives who might not stick around. One night stands are all he can afford. When one night turns into more than he bargained for, he is blindsided in more ways than one.

Kenzo was honorably discharged from the military when he was in an accident. Adrift, he focuses on what he can do to help those in a similar situation. But hiding his roommate's condition is taking its toll. One night with Zak turns his world upside down, and he finds he can't go back to the way things were before.

What happens when secrets unfold and trust is tested to its limit?

ABOUT ELOUISE EAST

I am a bestselling author of contemporary MM romance. I write a variety of themes: sweet and fluffy to high angst to taboo, but there is a huge nod in the direction of friendships being integral to each character's experience. I write books that are emotionally realistic, even if liberties are taken with other aspects of my stories.

Reading and writing have always been a part of my life, although my debut book wasn't published until July 2019, when I was 36 years old. My experience has come from reading thousands of books over the years and being a perfectionist when it comes to trying to make things right. I live in the centre of the UK with my two children, who make life worth living, keep me (in)sane and make me laugh.

STALK ME HERE... ;-)
WEBSITE: https://elouiseeast.com/
NEWSLETTER: https://elouiseeast.com/newsletter
LINKTREE: https://linktr.ee/elouiseeastauthor

BOOKS BY ELOUISE EAST

<u>CRUSH</u>

First Kiss

Instant Desire

Primary Seduction

Deep Down

A Crush for Christmas

Life Support

Covert Strength

Love Scene

Lawful Attraction

<u>JUST A LITTLE CRUSH</u>

Star-Crossed

He's Behind You

A Special Love (newsletter story)

<u>DADDY</u>

Love Me, Daddy

Soothe Me, Daddy

Spoil Me, Daddy

DARK & DIVERGENT

A Biker Make Three

Forbidden Temptation

Too Many Secrets

CHARMED

Treehouse Whispers